# Endorsements

"*People of the Book* humbled me as I was remin̲[...]̲ ity as a Christian to preach Christ more boldly. The smells, sights, and sounds of life in Saudi Arabia came alive again as Kathi Macias transported me back to the world I once knew, one in which I spent so many years of my life. Not only does Kathi do an extraordinary job in bringing the characters to life, but *People of the Book* shows the touch of a loving Savior to a lost world and illustrates the true meaning of what it means to pick up your cross and follow Christ. A must-read for every serious Christian."—**Dolly Dahdal**, a former Saudi citizen

"A strong and moving story! All choices have consequences, some more life-affecting than others. *People of the Book* examines the cost of life-altering choices, both good and bad."—**Gayle Roper**, author of *A Rose Revealed* and *Shadows on the Sand*

"*People of the Book* will rock your world. Macias demonstrates the reality of Christian persecution present in the Muslim world with an action-packed story and real-world characters. You'll find yourself praying for the safety of the heroines (former Muslims who accept Jesus Christ) as their Lord and Savior. Buy a copy for you, your church library, and your missions-minded friends."—**Jan Coates**, author of *Set Free* and *Attitude-inize*

"Through this 'Extreme Devotion' series, Kathi has shown her extraordinary gift of telling a compelling story that comes alive in the hearts and minds of the readers. I also felt compassion for the extreme situations these characters found themselves in. In *People of the Book*, Kathi shows God's word is alive and well. It has the power to transform lives in incredible ways. The reader sees that God can do far more than we can ever imagine! Thank you, Kathi, for reminding me to pray for a culture and a people I don't often think about. I felt concern for the young women in this novel as they struggled with their faith, hope, and fear as they could be killed for taking a stand for Christ. Kathi Macias once again has skillfully penned a thought-provoking, believable, captivating missions-minded novel. One I can't stop thinking about and highly recommend!"—**Nora St. Laurent**, ACFW Book Club coordinator, the Book Club Network

"I finished this book days ago and can't get the characters out of my head or heart. Kathi has done an amazing job bringing this subject to life with sensitivity and grace. Reading this story will change you."—**Laurie Alice Eakes**, award-winning author of *Lady in the Mist*

"Certain stories need to be told. This is one of them. *People of the Book* by Kathi Macias is an intricately plotted narrative of a young Muslim woman's insatiable hunger for a touch from Allah during Ramadan. The touch comes, but not in the manner she expects. The experience radically changes her life and her newfound Christian faith marks her as a traitor of Islam. Through Kathi's extraordinary writing, we see God reaching the human heart. The author's writing is savvy and places the reader into the heroine's mind, emotions, and skin. I forgot I was holding a book, as the pages melted away, transporting me into the story, where I remained to the last word on the last page.—**Robin Jansen Shope**, author of the book and movie, *The Christmas Edition: Journey to Paradise*

"Be forewarned. Somewhere between the first word and the last, you may forget to breathe. But you will always remember this story, appropriate for our time. I promise."—**Eva Marie Everson**, author of *Chasing Sunsets*

"Young women developing a friendship through an online chat room shouldn't be trouble—unless one or more of them is from Saudi Arabia and the topic of discussion is Isa Masih—Jesus Christ. *People of the Book* is a tale of searching and finding, of love, courage, and sacrifice. And if the inevitable clash of a young girl's faith and Muslim family honor is painted with deadly and heartwrenching realism, interwoven throughout is the comforting reminder that cradling the smallest falling sparrow are the everlasting arms of a loving heavenly Father. A story that will challenge hearts and minds."—**Jeanette Windle**, author of *Veiled Freedom* and *Freedom's Stand*

# People of
## *the Book*

Book 4 in
the "Extreme Devotion" series

# Kathi Macias

NEW HOPE
PUBLISHERS
Birmingham, Alabama

New Hope® Publishers
P. O. Box 12065
Birmingham, AL 35202-2065
www.newhopepublishers.com

New Hope Publishers is a division of WMU®.

Library of Congress Cataloging-in-Publication Data

Macias, Kathi, 1948-
  People of the book / Kathi Macias.
    p. cm.
  ISBN 978-1-59669-282-4 (pbk.)
  1.  Teenage girls--Saudi Arabia--Fiction. 2.  Christian converts from Islam--Fiction. 3.  Persecution--Fiction. 4.  Saudi Arabia--Fiction.  I. Title.
  PS3563.I42319P46 2011
  813'.54--dc22

                                            2010039577


ISBN-10: 1-59669-282-0
ISBN-13: 978-1-59669-282-4

N114128 • 0411 • 5M1

# Dedication

To the "people of the Book": May we never forget the privilege and responsibility of being identified as such;

To those who have not yet joined us as "people of the Book": We humbly invite you to do so.

To the One whose heart for all mankind is revealed in the Book: Thank You for Your priceless gift.

To my husband, Al, and our children/grandchildren: May we be joined through all eternity as grateful "people of the Book"— whatever the cost.

ॐॐॐ ॐॐॐ ॐॐॐ

# Prologue

FARAH MOHAMMED AL OTAIBI LAY BRUISED AND BLOODY ON THE floor beside her bed. The image of her soft mattress floated in and out of her consciousness, as did the rank smells of urine and feces and blood. But she had no strength to drag herself from her current position. Even the slightest movement brought stabs of excruciating pain, so she tried to remember to keep her breathing shallow and her body still.

How long had she been here? Hours, certainly. Days? She couldn't be sure. Her father and brother had covered the windows with heavy, dark cloth, blocking out any light that might help her keep track of time.

Hunger wasn't an issue, for who could think of food when the pain was so intense? But thirst? Oh, how she longed for just a sip of cool water! Surely her mother would sneak in soon and bring her some. She had always taken care of her before—

*Before...*

The memory was back, though she tried desperately to block it out. Impossible. She could never forget that moment in time, for it was the dividing line between the before and after of her life. Before the tragedy that led to her brother's discovery. Before her father had flown into a rage over what he considered his daughter's betrayal and treachery. Before they had threatened to kill her in order to preserve the family's honor. Before her mother had tried to intervene.

Hot tears pricked the back of Farah's eyelids, as the vision of her mother's face before—and after—swam in front of her eyes. The pain in her heart at that moment far exceeded anything she felt in her body. Then suddenly, inexplicably, the meaning of her name—Farah, joy and cheerfulness—burst into her consciousness. Despite her agony and sorrow, Farah was unable to hold back the brief burst of laughter that exploded from her aching chest. How absurd that her parents had given her a name that implied happiness, and yet she now wondered if she had ever truly understood or experienced any of it in her not quite nineteen years of life.

But then she had met Isa, and everything—both good and bad—had changed forever.

Unlike the other two females in the household, she did not worship him or hang on his every word.

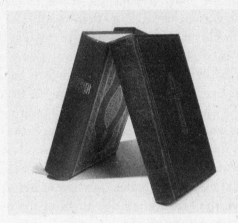

## Chapter 1

THE DIVIDING LINE BETWEEN THE BEFORE AND AFTER OF FARAH'S life had actually been drawn earlier than she realized, during Ramadan, the eighteenth such observance of the holy month during Farah's brief lifetime.

For as long as Farah Mohammed Al Otaibi could remember, she had been fascinated with this most revered of Muslim holy days. Though women in the Saudi Kingdom didn't observe Ramadan in quite the same way or to the extent that the men did, Farah took every opportunity during that time to fast and pray, to read the Quran, to perform acts of charity and kindness to others, and to draw closer to Allah and to the one true faith, Islam—even if she had to do most of it in the privacy of her room, rather than at the mosque with her father and brother. At the same time, she had to admit that her father had shown great deference to her in allowing her to practice her faith beyond the point of most Muslim women. Farah suspected that her pursuit of religion was the only reason her parents hadn't insisted on arranging a marriage for her by this time.

Kathi Macias

Each year, as the month of Ramadan drew near, Farah's anticipation level rose. Though she dared not voice her longing except in prayer, she hoped each year that this would be the time Allah would answer her petitions and make Himself real to her. She knew Allah was merciful. Why then should she not hope that He would extend his mercy to her, despite the fact that she was a female?

Perhaps it hadn't happened to her before because she had been so late in becoming a woman, far beyond the normal age for any girls she knew. As a result, she had only recently veiled. Now, shielded from prying, lustful eyes each time she left her home, she maintained her purity with honor, choosing to wear the most concealing *abaya* possible, as well as black gloves and stockings so that even the smallest portion of her skin would not be visible. Even the soaring temperatures of the desert summer hadn't deterred her, though she opted to wear abayas made of cool silk during the year's hottest season rather than one of the heavier materials more common to the winter months. She personally could not imagine why some women complained at the need to cover themselves in public. It was, after all, what the beloved Prophet Muhammad had commanded so that faithful Muslim women might remain chaste and virtuous. And wasn't that much more important than wearing something only slightly more comfortable?

Ease and comfort were not Farah's primary concerns. The stories of the great Prophet and his faithful followers were her passion, and she pursued her religion with a fervor seldom seen in Saudi women, including Farah's younger sister, Nadia, and their mother, Sultana. As a result, Farah was her father's favorite—next to his only son, of course. Kareem was the firstborn, just a year older than Farah; he was also a male. That in itself was enough; he would always be the preferred child. But Farah's devout and submissive spirit had earned her a place in her father's heart as well, though he was restrained in his affections and compliments toward her. She understood without question that should she ever disobey or shame her family in any way, she would lose that favored spot and would be severely punished. But why should that concern her? She had no intention of ever

10

being anything but the most dutiful daughter—and some day soon, a dutiful wife.

For now, as she observed her first Ramadan as a woman rather than a child, she concentrated on her prayers, ignoring the growling of her stomach as she fasted according to the requirements of the holy month. Who knew what Allah might choose to do on her behalf before the month was over? The possibilities transformed Farah's gnawing hunger pangs to butterflies of anticipation. Surely this would be the year when she would draw closer to Allah and her life would change, once and for all!

∽৩৫ ∽৩৫ ∽৩৫

Kareem knew that second only to his father, he was ruler in their home. His wants and desires would be met at the cost of his mother or sisters, and his word was considered law, so long as it did not contradict the teachings of Islam, the strict traditions of the Saudi Kingdom, or his father's wishes.

Kareem knew too that though the family wasn't wealthy, they were financially comfortable enough that he would have no problem obtaining the wife—or wives—of his choice when it came time to marry. He was also well aware that his tall, muscular stature and chiseled features created quite a stir among the eligible young women of Riyadh, and that they would welcome the possibility of becoming his bride, though in reality they would have little say in the matter. The mothers of the prospective couple would be instrumental in the matchmaking, but it would be the men in the families who would agree to and finalize the betrothals; brides were simply the chattel that completed the agreements.

But none of that was enough for Kareem. Though his father gave him the respect and honor due the firstborn and only son, and his mother nearly worshipped him, as did his youngest sister, it galled Kareem that his other sister, Farah, seemed content only to love and respect him. Unlike the other two females in the household, she did not worship him or hang on his every word. It was apparent to Kareem from an early age that Farah was much more devout in her religious beliefs and devotion to Allah than

11

most females, reserving her worship for Allah. Though Kareem believed, as did all good Muslim men, that their women should be faithful and chaste, he also felt that too much devotion to religion would prevent women from serving men as they were so obviously created to do.

For that reason, he hated Farah, though she had never done anything but be kind to him. He also hated her because she had managed to earn a place in their father's affections. Kareem knew it was lower than the place he owned, but it was higher than a woman deserved—higher even than Kareem's mother or youngest sister. Therefore it was unnatural, and it bothered Kareem nearly to the point of obsession.

Even now, as he knelt on his prayer rug, his face to the ground, reciting his praise and petitions by rote, his mind was not on Allah or anything associated with the observance of Ramadan. It was focused on Farah, who no doubt at this very moment was herself kneeling in prayer in the solitude of her room. The darkness of his thoughts blocked out all else.

❧ ❧ ❧

Ramadan. The very word sent a shiver of excitement down Farah's spine, even as she knelt and listened...for what? She had no idea. *Will Allah speak to me? If so, how? Will I recognize His voice? Understand His words?*

She shook her head and squeezed her eyes shut to block out all distractions. The very thought of hearing from Allah was overwhelming. Better to concentrate on the meaning of the holy month that was now well underway.

It had been an especially hot day throughout the sprawling capital city of Saudi Arabia, with temperatures far exceeding 100 degrees Fahrenheit. But that was no surprise. Ramadan occurred during the hottest season of the year, and the very meaning of the word denoted intense heat and scorched ground. The residents of this part of the world expected nothing less, and the teeming millions who called Riyadh home were no exception.

Like the rest of her family, Farah had risen long before daylight so she would have time to eat *Suhoor* before the call to first prayer sounded from the minarets and the day's fast officially began. Even the lightweight material of Farah's *abaya* made breathing an effort, and sweat poured from her body as the blazing sun bore down from a merciless sky each time she stepped outside the confines of air-conditioned comfort. But Farah bore the difficulties without complaint, listening and waiting for the answer to her prayers. She hoped it would come before the end of the fourth prayertime, *Maghrib*, and the breaking of the day's fast with dates and coffee prior to a complete meal known as *Iftar*. But if no answer came by the setting of the sun, she would not grow impatient. After all, the month was only slightly half over. Who knew what Allah might grant to her before Ramadan's end at *Eid ul-Fitr*? And if she had no answer by then, she would continue fasting and praying throughout the six additional days of *as-Sitta al-Bid*. Surely Allah would honor her extra effort and reward her with a special blessing.

She smiled and prayed as her fingers
flew across the keyboard,
an open Bible at her side.

## Chapter 2

SARA COULDN'T SLEEP. SUMMER HAD EXPLODED ON RIVER Crest's unsuspecting residents, and the temperature hadn't cooled off much during the night. Grateful that the Pacific Northwest summers were relatively short and normally quite mild, Sara was nonetheless uncomfortable and restless, as she tossed and turned, cooled only by the oscillating fan at the foot of her bed.

*At least if we lived where the weather was warmer most of the time, we'd have air conditioning,* she thought. *But all we have are these fans to keep the hot air moving.*

She sighed. Should she stay in bed and hope to drift off soon, or give up and see if she had any interesting email?

Smiling at the no-brainer question, she rolled out of bed and slipped her feet into her slippers before she thought better of it and slid them off again. Right now even slippers were too confining, and the coolness of the hardwood floors was a welcome relief.

Sara crossed the room and flipped the switch on her desk lamp before sitting down and booting up her computer. In moments she was scrolling down the inbox list, eliminating the majority of impersonal notes as she went. Disappointed to find nothing worth pursuing, she decided to visit the chat room she'd frequented lately—the one where Christian believers of Muslim backgrounds tended to gather, as well as Muslims seeking to connect with these non-practicing Muslims for various reasons.

She was pleased to find several people already online and discussing the importance of Ramadan, since the annual holiday had just begun. Though Sara had never lived in a Muslim country and no one in her immediate family was a practicing Muslim, her parents had taught her about the faith of her ancestors and relatives. As a result, she felt drawn to use her knowledge of Islam to connect with Muslims who might be open to hearing the true gospel.

Sara greeted the others in the chat room and was quickly acknowledged by Nura, a young woman in Saudi Arabia with whom Sara had corresponded on various occasions. It was obvious that Nura was more than just mildly interested in learning about the "people of the Book," as she and so many other Muslims referred to Christians and Jews. Primarily, however, Nura's questions seemed to focus on the prophet Isa, or Jesus. Sara had prayed more than once to have the opportunity to lead Nura from her limited understanding of Isa as one of the prophets of Islam to a full acceptance of Him as the Son of God. Perhaps tonight would be her opportunity.

As the two young women, separated by thousands of miles and drastically opposing cultures, began to communicate, Sara felt the first puff of cool breeze blow through her open window. She smiled and prayed as her fingers flew across the keyboard, an open Bible at her side.

❧❧❧ ❧❧❧ ❧❧❧

Farah didn't enjoy browsing the outdoor *suqs* or even the air-conditioned malls in the same way her mother or sister did. Shopping was a joy for most Saudi women, as they had so little else to entertain or amuse them. Though some of the more progressive fathers allowed their daughters to receive an education, even sending them to college or university, few of these educated women were able to find jobs when they graduated, though Farah knew that was changing ever so slightly. But for the most part, they continued to be dominated by the men who ran the country—and the lives of everyone in it. Those women fortunate enough to be married to men who treated them with kindness devoted their lives to caring for their husbands and children, gathering together with other women to socialize at every opportunity. Shopping was at the top of their list of pastimes, though the family income level dictated how much of that shopping time was actually spent in making purchases.

Farah understood and appreciated that her father provided them with sufficient funds for all their needs and more than a few extras besides. But none of that really mattered to her. She would rather have stayed at home, continuing in prayer through the night and sleeping a little besides. Her mother, however, had insisted that the three of them take advantage of the all-night restaurants and shopping available to them during Ramadan. It was a festive season of celebration, where gift giving to those less fortunate was required alongside prayer and fasting. And so Farah meandered through the various shops and stands, with her mother on one side and Nadia on the other, as they eyed the merchandise for sale and smelled aromas of incense and spices mixed with lamb and chicken cooking on spits. All three of the women, even Nadia who had developed early and been veiled at nearly the same time as Farah, were now cloaked in black, their faces covered and their honor intact.

As they rounded a corner and spotted their favorite restaurant across the street, Farah thought she recognized her aunt and cousin waiting for them at an inside table by the window. Though their *abayas* made it impossible to be sure, Farah's mother and aunt had prearranged the meeting, with their husbands' approval, and so it was logical to assume that the women in black who sat at the table, their heads turned in their direction as if watching for their arrival, were indeed their relatives.

Soon after the mutual identification was established and the curtains drawn over the window and around the booth, the five of them removed their veils and relaxed, sipping coffee flavored with cardamom, eating delicate pastries, and enjoying the air-conditioned comfort of the restaurant. Though it was already after midnight, it was still nearly 100 degrees outside. Visiting with friends and family and enjoying a snack or meal at this unusual time was one more aspect of Ramadan that most Muslims enjoyed. Because they fasted throughout the day, many made it a point to go out at night and take advantage of the special late-night hours offered by many restaurants and shops throughout the month. For Farah, it was but one more distraction from the goal she had set for herself during her first official observation of Ramadan as a woman.

She wanted to connect with Allah, to hear from Him, if that was possible. She wasn't sure if it could happen, and there seemed to be no one she could ask without being dismissed or worse. There were some topics best left unspoken, and a female seeking a deeper relationship with Allah was no doubt one of them.

Farah sighed as the female chatter continued around her, and she noticed once again the resemblance between her mother and aunt. Farah's mother, Sultana, was only one year older than her sister, Sakeena, but it would be easy to mistake them for twins. Only in the last few years had Sakeena's thick black hair begun to show a little gray around the temples, making the sisters slightly more distinguishable from one another.

Farah's glance shifted to her younger companions. Nadia, scarcely thirteen, was the true beauty in the group. Her large dark eyes sparkled like shimmering pools, inviting and entertaining, mirroring her optimistic personality. No doubt she would marry young; Farah prayed she would also marry well and be happy.

Farah's cousin Nura, nearly seventeen now, expected her parents to arrange a marriage for her soon. The attractive young woman sat directly across from Farah, her dark eyes cast down-ward, speaking little. Farah had always liked Nura but never felt close to her because she was so quiet and reserved. Farah wondered even now what was going on behind her cousin's subdued appearance.

The conversation droned on, despite its animated tone, while Farah picked at her refreshments, saying little but smiling now and then to indicate her interest and attention. How she longed for a trusted companion who would understand her quest! But she had long since ruled out her mother and sister, since they had no real interest in spiritual matters. They followed the law and obeyed those in authority over them; wasn't that enough?

For most women it was. But Farah was not most women, though she refused even to let herself think those words, let alone say them out loud.

❧ ❧ ❧

Nura's mind whirled with the many new ideas she had accumulated since connecting with the young American of Saudi heritage. Sara was an enigma to Nura, her words showing her to be a humble and gentle young woman. *How can that be*, Nura wondered, *when the girl lives without any of the proper constraints of a Muslim female in the kingdom?* The primary source of conversation between the two when they met online was Islam and Christianity, Muhammad and Isa, whom the American sometimes called Jesus. But at times they veered from the subject and spoke of more personal topics, learning in the process that they were very nearly the same age. Nura would be seventeen in a few weeks, as would Sara a couple of months later. Beyond that, their lives couldn't have been more different.

Nura told herself she was glad she didn't have to contend with such frightening issues as women driving their own cars, starting their own businesses, dating and marrying men of their own choosing. The list was endless. How could a woman make such decisions and carry such responsibility? Nura knew that an increasing number of women from more liberal families in the kingdom had begun to practice such things — except for driving cars, of course — but she had also been taught that females simply were not equipped to do so, nor were they meant to. Allah had created them for their husband's pleasure, and they would only find fulfillment in serving them and bearing their children. For a woman to desire more was evil, and the punishment sure and swift. And it was all for their own good. How else could women be protected from themselves? Without the control of

19

men, women would destroy themselves and everyone around them with wanton and lewd behavior. Their only hope for paradise was to be faithful to Allah by obeying their male authorities without question.

*And yet Sara appears to flourish without such restraints. At least, it certainly seems so from what I've come to know of her online. Is it truly possible that this young woman who lives in such a heathen land could be happy and fulfilled by pursuing her own dreams and making her own choices?*

The very thought seemed blasphemous, and Nura shuddered at the implications. Pulling her thoughts from her earlier discussion with her American counterpart, Nura tried to focus on the conversation between her mother and her aunt, as they chatted nearly nonstop. Nura's younger cousin, Nadia, seemed to hang on the women's every word, but Nadia's older sister appeared nearly as disinterested as Nura felt. Was it possible the two cousins had similar feelings and concerns? If so, how could Nura be certain? To broach the subject would be dangerous. Still…

No. She would keep her thoughts to herself and speak only with Sara online. No one else must ever know the traitorous questions that danced through Nura's head.

Forcing a smile, she took a deep breath and determined to pay attention to the conversation between her mother and aunt. It was anything but fascinating, but at least it was safe.

Once in the chat room, Nura was
disappointed to see that Sara
wasn't there.

## Chapter 3

SARA WONDERED WHY SHE'D BOTHERED TO SHOWER. SHE hadn't been dressed for more than five minutes, and already she felt nearly as sticky as when she'd first rolled out of bed. Of course, staying up for hours to talk with Nura certainly hadn't helped overcome her feeling of being ill-prepared to face the day.

An impatient knock on the door snagged her attention, and she knew it was her brother, Emir.

"You going to be in there all day?" he groused. "You're not the only one that needs to get ready for school, you know."

She smiled. Her brother was slightly over a year younger than she was, and the two of them had spent their growing-up years verbally sparring with one another, and yet they were as close as any two siblings could ever be. Emir was a pain at times, but Sara loved him unconditionally.

"I'll be out in a minute," she called.

Peering into the bathroom mirror, she grudgingly admitted that her few dabs of makeup weren't going to hide her red-rimmed eyes. This was definitely going to be a rare sunglasses day in a corner of the world that was much more used to seeing umbrellas and raincoats.

*If only I'd been able to get through to her*, she thought. *She'd seemed so interested at first, but she always does. And then, just when I get her to the point of making a choice to receive Jesus as her Savior, she backs off and says she has to think about it some more.*

Sara sighed. She couldn't really blame Nura. After all, the girl lived in the Saudi Kingdom, and making such a decision was not something that was done lightly. Though Sara had never been to Saudi Arabia, her mother had told her many stories of what it was like for women in such a repressed country. Sara understood to a point, but it was nearly impossible to put herself in her counterpart's shoes and imagine life without the many freedoms she herself enjoyed.

She shrugged, giving her shoulder-length black hair one final shake before heading downstairs to grab a quick breakfast. If she hurried, her dad would be able to drop her at school on his way to work, and she could avoid arriving at her destination feeling any more damp and disheveled than she already did. How glad she would be when this onslaught of late-summer heat moved on and the little southwest Washington town of River Crest returned to its normal gray, cloudy, wet weather. Sara had never lived anywhere else, and she had no problem dealing with cool summers and even cooler winters. The occasional sun breaks were nice, but anything over ninety degrees was simply not acceptable to Pacific Northwest natives like Sara and her family.

❧❧❧ ❧❧❧ ❧❧❧

Another day of fasting and prayer was nearly at an end, and Farah fought disappointment at not having sensed anything different. She had been so hopeful going into this Ramadan season that this would be the year she would experience a new level of faith in Allah. Though she would never say the words aloud, as she didn't want to imply that Allah had made a mistake by creating her as he had, there were times she couldn't help but wish she had been born a male. How different her life would have been, and how much more open she could be in her pursuit of worship and religion!

She lifted herself from her prayer mat and stepped slowly toward the open window, gazing outside from the second story of her family's modest but comfortable home. Though no longer as visible as during the hours of mid-day, Farah knew that lingering heat still shimmered upward from the baking pavement. She imagined it rising to the skies, along with the prayers of the faithful Muslims of Riyadh and elsewhere, and her heart cried out for a touch from the great creator, Allah himself.

Startled by the thought, she wondered if indeed it was a blasphemous desire. How could someone like her expect anything in the way of a personal touch from one so mighty as Allah? Was she being prideful and vain even to imagine it? Ashamed and frightened, she returned to her prayer mat, bowing with her face to the ground, her heart more troubled than ever before.

◆◈◆ ◆◈◆ ◆◈◆

It had been a long day, but the final bell had at last released the antsy students. Relieved, the high schoolers burst through the double glass doors of the school building and flowed out onto the streets of River Crest, spreading out in all directions as the scorching afternoon sun enveloped them in stifling heat.

Sara trudged in her usual direction toward home, her full backpack resisting her every step.

"What are you going to do the rest of the day?" Joni asked, plodding along beside her.

Sara answered her friend while keeping her eyes straight ahead. "Homework, I guess." She shrugged. "What else?"

She heard the younger girl sigh. "Yeah, I know. It's too hot to do anything outside."

They continued in silence for another moment before Joni spoke up again. "We could go to the mall. At least it's air conditioned."

Sara had to admit that anywhere cool sounded good at the moment. But the mall? Nah. She just wasn't in the mood to go anywhere with a lot of people, and the mall was always crowded. Today would be worse than usual, as everyone sought a respite from the unusual heat wave.

"I don't think so," she said. She knew she should say something more, offer an alternative or reasonable option, but her mind was blank. She had no idea what she wanted to do; she only knew that she didn't want to go to the mall.

*Somewhere quiet,* she thought. *Somewhere I can think and pray.* But Joni wouldn't understand. Sara liked Joni. They lived on the same block and had been friends since grammar school, though Joni was actually a couple of years younger than Sara. Also, Joni wasn't a believer—well, at least not one who showed any serious commitment to what she claimed to believe. And lately Sara had felt the need to connect with believers who shared her passion. She was sick of compromise and lukewarm faith, tired of Sunday-only worship. She wanted more. She wanted her life to count for something, to make a difference somehow. How could she do that if she hung out with people whose primary topic of conversation was what to wear the next day?

Keeping her thoughts to herself, Sara pressed on, with Joni walking silently beside her. The heat was so oppressive that it made it easier not to talk. By the time they reached Joni's house, Sara wanted nothing more than to plunk down in front of her fan with a cold drink and listen to the quiet for a while. Maybe later she'd log into the chat room and see if she could make a little more headway with Nura.

Sara said good-bye to Joni as the slightly chubby blonde girl who was so opposite Sara in nearly every way veered off up her walkway toward her front door. The new school year was only a couple of weeks old, but already it seemed they were falling into a routine of walking to and from school together, though they had little in common anymore beyond that. As Sara watched Joni step inside her house and close the door behind her, she shot up a silent prayer that one day soon Joni would at last see the need to get serious about her faith. She just hoped her childhood friend wouldn't put it off too long.

Nura couldn't wait for the night to end, not so much because she was looking forward to another day of fasting and prayer but because her American friend often logged in to the chat room at that time. As Nura's day began, Sara's was drawing to a close, and it seemed she nearly always allowed for some Internet time. Occasionally the two girls chatted about their days, and though Nura hated to admit it, she was fascinated at hearing about Sara's life at school and with her friends, particularly now that Sara had started her senior year of high school. In fairness, Sara also asked Nura about her life and seemed interested in her replies, including the fact that Nura's studies were done at home, under her mother's watchful eye.

Once in the chat room, Nura was disappointed to see that Sara wasn't there. Still, there were others she could talk with — or just "listen in on" for a while — until Sara arrived.

Nura smiled. *I should be grateful that I have a father who allows me such a luxury as my own computer! If he didn't trust me, he would never have given me such an amazing gift.* She knew that many of her friends were only allowed to use computers in their homes under strict supervision, and some couldn't use them at all. Nura appreciated her freedom and didn't want to abuse it, yet she knew she was dancing dangerously close to the edge by visiting this chat room. If her father ever found out...

But how could he? She certainly wouldn't tell him, and he never came to her room and checked up on her, simply because she had never given him reason to do so. Her mother, on the other hand, came to her room quite often, but never without knocking. Even if she did come in uninvited, she wouldn't know how to turn on her daughter's computer, let alone find her way to a chat room. Nura was safe in her explorations of Western life and discussions with nonpracticing Muslims — though she knew her parents would consider such people traitors to the faith.

Sara's name popped up on the screen, snagging Nura's attention and causing her heart to leap with anticipation. It was as if the girl in America had become her closest friend and confidante, though the two had never met.

*But I was born a female, she*
*reminded herself.*

## Chapter 4

Another day of Ramadan had come to an end, and Sultana was busy with last-minute preparations for *Iftar*, the meal that would officially break the family's fast. She had tossed most of the ingredients — cubed lamb, onions, garlic, potatoes, and various spices — into the pot early that day, so it was now ready to serve. The aroma had been making her mouth water for the last several hours, as she suffered through yet one more day of fasting. Sultana enjoyed the special celebrations that went along with Ramadan, but she had always hated the long daylight hours without food. Whenever possible, she spent much of the day sleeping to make the deprivation easier.

She smiled at the thought that her family would be gathering soon. There was nothing Sultana liked better than having her husband and children around the table, safe and healthy and enjoying each other's company. She knew she was fortunate to have a husband who, though a strict Muslim, treated his wife and two daughters with kindness and affection, so long as they were obedient and submissive. Sultana knew from personal experience that such was not always the case, though she tried to block out the memories of her childhood and concentrate on the blessings of today.

Nadia was the first to join her mother in the kitchen, and Sultana immediately put her to work setting the table. As she watched her younger daughter move about her simple tasks with such grace and agility, she was struck as she often was by Nadia's exceptional beauty. No doubt the girl would marry early, though Sultana's heart squeezed at the thought. True, there was a time when Saudi girls were married at Nadia's tender age of thirteen, but Nadia was her youngest—her baby—and Sultana wasn't ready even to consider letting her go, at least not for quite a while.

*Besides*, Sultana told herself as she handed the china plates to Nadia, *Farah is the oldest. She should marry first.*

She sighed, realizing that once again her older daughter had not arrived to help prepare for the family meal. Farah was the most cooperative of young women, and neither Sultana nor her husband could fault her on points of obedience or submission. If anything, the girl was devout to a fault.

*Which is undoubtedly what has held her up now*, Sultana fussed, excusing herself from Nadia's presence to go and check on Farah. *It is nearly time to break the fast, and yet the girl has not emerged from her room. If we did not insist she come to join us for the* Iftar *meal, I do believe she would continue in prayer throughout the night.*

She shook her head as she approached Farah's closed door. *Too much religion is simply not good for a young girl, but how do I convince her of such a thing when praying and reading the Quran is all she wants to do? Though she is submissive, she is also quite dedicated.*

∞ ∞ ∞

It took a moment before Farah recognized the sound that had invaded her seclusion. A knock on the door. It could only be her mother. Was it really time for prayer and fasting to end? It seemed the day had just begun.

Rising from her prayer rug, she went to open the door. Farah smiled when she realized her door was unlocked, but her mother was so respectful and considerate of her that she never entered without knocking. Her sister offered her the same courtesy, and even her father rapped before turning the knob. Kareem was another story entirely.

Pulling the door open, Farah welcomed her mother with a quick hug. "Forgive me, Mother. Is it time already?"

Sultana raised her dark eyebrows, but Farah knew her feigned disapproval did not override her caring heart. "Already? Your sister has been helping me prepare dinner for the last fifteen minutes."

Farah's contrition was genuine. "I'm sorry. I truly didn't realize the time. I will come and help immediately."

Sultana nodded. "Thank you."

Farah followed her mother toward the kitchen, noticing for the first time the delicious aromas that wafted through the house. Had they penetrated Farah's bedroom and she simply hadn't noticed?

"You've fixed *khorma*, haven't you, Mother?"

Sultana stepped into the kitchen and turned back to her daughter, her dark eyes twinkling. "Surely the smells of lamb cooking haven't tempted you," she teased. "I thought such a devout Muslim girl did not even need such mundane things as food to sustain you."

Farah smiled. "You know I would have preferred to remain in prayer, but the instant I smelled your cooking, I wanted nothing more than to sit down with my family and break the day's fast."

"Then come and help me finish," Nadia interrupted. "I'm starving! Unlike you, I've been smelling the food for hours, and I can't wait to eat."

Sultana laughed. "She's right, you know. The entire family is hungry. Your father and brother will be home from the mosque shortly and will want their food on the table when they arrive."

Farah nodded, picking up the pile of silverware to carry from the kitchen to the dining area. Though she complied outwardly, her thoughts had been transported from the *Iftar* meal to the mosque, where she so wished she could go to pray with her father and brother.

*But I was born a female*, she reminded herself. *It is enough that I can pray at home. I must learn to be satisfied with serving the men in my life—now, and also once I am married.*

A slight shiver passed over her at the thought. How many times had she implored Allah that she be blessed to marry a man who would allow her to pray and study the Quran without limits? It was a prayer she so hoped that Allah would choose to answer.

෯෨ ෯෨ ෯෨

Though the day was nearly at an end, the heat still simmered above the sidewalks. Kareem and his father Ahmed, their cool white *thobes* flowing behind them as they moved, made their way home from the mosque, only a few blocks away. Kareem knew his father took the observation of Ramadan seriously and always seemed a bit subdued as they returned home after a long day of fasting and prayer. It was a sentiment Kareem did not share.

Two more blocks. That was all Kareem could think of—the food that awaited them when they arrived at home and how far they had to go before they got there. He hated fasting and found ways to avoid it when his father was not nearby. But he'd had little chance to cheat today, as Ahmed had spent nearly every moment throughout the day at Kareem's side, whether at their small family-owned factory or the mosque.

"Are you hungry, my son?" Ahmed asked, his eyes still fixed straight ahead as they walked.

Kareem marveled that his father always appeared to know what he was thinking. He hated it as well. It seemed an invasion of his privacy, just one more thing that his father could control in his life. Perhaps that was why Kareem enjoyed being around his mother and sisters when his father was away. It was one of the few times he felt the ability to rule others without interference, and he thrived on the sensation. One day he would exert such control over his own wife and children, and he anticipated that time with excitement.

"Yes, Father," he answered, "though not excessively so."

Ahmed chuckled, and once again Kareem suspected his father knew what he was thinking. His expression of moderation had not fooled the older man for a moment. Ahmed knew Kareem was ravenous, but neither of them spoke of it again.

Kareem attempted to move the conversation from himself, even as he blinked away the sweat that trickled from his brow into his eye. "The women should have the food on the table by the time we arrive," he observed.

Ahmed grunted. "Unless your older sister is late in coming to help again. Your mother tells me she gets caught up in her prayers and forgets to leave her room at the end of the day."

Kareem took a deep breath, reminding himself to show restraint in his response. "Farah spends too much time in prayer," he commented, glancing toward his father for affirmation. "It is unnatural for a woman."

Ahmed nodded. "True. Yet how can I fault her for being too devoted to Allah? And she is certainly submissive in all her actions and attitudes." He paused before adding, "She is truly remarkable for a female, do you not agree, Kareem?"

They arrived at their front gate then, and Kareem was spared from answering his father's question. Relieved, he followed Ahmed into the house, his mouth watering at the smells that greeted them.

*Oh, why had she ever visited the chat room in the first place?*

## Chapter 5

BEFORE SARA OPENED HER EYES, SHE KNEW SOMETHING WAS different. She searched her mind until she found the answer. The heat! It was gone at last. It must have dissipated sometime during the night, for though she didn't remember doing so, she had quite obviously pulled a cover over herself at some point.

Now, as she lay on her side huddled under that blanket, her knees pulled up for added warmth, she marveled at how something as seemingly insignificant as a warm bed on a cool morning could produce such a sense of luxury. If only she didn't have to get up for school this morning, she'd pull the cover over her head and go right back to sleep.

Peeking at her alarm clock, she resigned herself to the fact that it would go off in a matter of minutes. What was the point of lying there until it did? Why not just throw off the blanket, slip into her robe, and turn off that annoying fan?

She smiled. The air blower at the foot of her bed had been her only source of comfort during the recent heat wave, but now that their more normal Pacific Northwest weather had returned, the fan was no longer needed—or welcome.

Pulling herself to a sitting position and throwing her legs over the side, she found her slippers and quickly stepped to the foot of her bed and hit the OFF button before reaching for her robe. As she shuffled toward the doorway, anxious to get to the bathroom and claim the shower before her brother beat her to it, she paused when her eyes landed on her computer screen.

Was Nura still awake, or had she gone to bed for the night? Because it was Ramadan, Sara suspected Nura was up and might even be at her computer, dropping in to say hello in the chat room.

The temptation tugged at Sara's heart. She really should take advantage of the fact that she was awake a few moments early and get started on her shower. But the memory of her conversation with Nura the previous night restrained her. They had come so close—again—to a place of decision for Nura. But just as Sara had been so sure her friend was about to pray with her to receive Isa as her Savior, the girl had changed her mind and signed off. Now Sara couldn't help but wonder if perhaps Nura had regretted her decision and might be back online, waiting for her American friend to talk with her again.

With a sigh, Sara plopped down in her chair and booted up the machine. There was only one way to find out. Besides, while she'd hesitated, her brother had obviously beaten her to the shower, as she could now hear the water running. Might as well use the time to try to reconnect with the Muslim girl who was so close to discovering the Truth.

❧ ❧ ❧

The fast had been broken and the dishes from the *Iftar* meal washed and put away. Nura's mother Sakeena had suggested that the two of them browse the *suqs* for a while and then stop for some cool refreshments, but Nura had declined, citing the oppressive heat as an excuse. She was glad her mother hadn't offered the alternative of going to one of the air-conditioned malls, as that would have defeated Nura's reason for declining the outing. But she had counted on the fact that her mother had always preferred the outdoor *suqs* to the malls, though the merchandise was often inferior. It seemed Sakeena just enjoyed browsing outdoors, though she seldom bought anything.

Now, seated in front of her dark computer screen, Nura fidgeted, trying to convince herself to go to her mother and tell her she had changed her mind and would love to go shopping with her after all. But still she sat, ignoring her own arguments and fighting the temptation to reconnect with the American girl named Sara.

Oh, why had she ever visited the chat room in the first place? She, Nura, a faithful Muslim girl, had no business intermingling with infidels who no longer practiced the true religion and even went so far as to believe that Allah could exist within a man. What nonsense! What blasphemy! Could there be a worse sin? And now she had allowed herself to be influenced by such people. Surely Allah was furious with her! And what would her father say if he knew?

Nura shuddered as a dim memory danced in the shadows of her mind. She hadn't been more than four or five years old, and though she couldn't recall details, she would never forget her father's words: "Remember this day, my daughter. This is the just punishment of one who disobeys Allah and turns against her own family and religion."

She had stood between her parents, pressed up against her mother's *abaya* and wishing she could hide her eyes in its folds but forced instead to watch as the girl, who couldn't have been more than fourteen or fifteen, was dragged into the swimming pool by her father and brother. The mother stood at the side of the pool, weeping but silent, as the doomed girl cried and pleaded for mercy. But Nura learned that day that despite the Muslims' claim that Allah was merciful, none would be extended to those who betrayed their faith.

Nura had felt as if she were drowning with the girl, as she watched her flailing and struggling while the men in her family held her head underwater until her fighting stopped and she was still. It was nearly a week before Nura was able to speak again, and after that she was very careful what she said.

Staring now at the dead computer screen, she shook her head. No. She was neither brave enough nor foolish enough to talk with the American again. She could only pray that Allah would forgive her and never allow her father to discover her infidelity.

&#8766;&#8766;&#8766;  &#8766;&#8766;&#8766;  &#8766;&#8766;&#8766;

Farah was full and content. She had enjoyed the meal with her family and dutifully cleaned up afterward. Now she had returned to her room to rest and reflect on the day—and to meditate on why her prayers and fasting had not yet fulfilled her longing for a deeper spiritual experience.

As she leaned against the pillows of her bed, the Quran resting beside her, she smiled at the memory of her father's attention as they ate. Though he had reprimanded her for not coming to help her mother more quickly at the end of the prayer time, he had done so with a trace of pride in his voice and a twinkle in his eye. Farah knew her father loved her, and she also realized how blessed she was that it was so. Not all girls, particularly in the kingdom, had such a relationship with their fathers.

At the same time, she had noticed the angry squint of Kareem's eyes, as his wordless disapproval hung in the air. Why didn't Kareem like her? Hadn't she always shown him respect and submission? He seemed to hold some affection for his mother and at least tolerated Nadia. But there was little doubt in Farah's mind that her only brother despised her, and there seemed to be nothing she could do to change it.

Her mother was aware of it too, she was certain, for even as Kareem had glared at her across the table, Sultana had reached over and patted Farah's leg in a gesture of encouragement. How she loved her mother! Whatever would she do without such a caring woman as her role model and mentor? Apart from Kareem's simmering discontent, Farah imagined that she had been blessed with the best family anywhere.

Smiling at the thought, she soon gave way to the contented feeling of a full stomach and drifted into a deep sleep. In a matter of moments she found herself in the most beautiful garden she had ever seen, where colors were brighter and fragrances sweeter than anything she had ever experienced or imagined. The sound of water bubbling over rocks sang to her as she wandered the grounds, more enchanted at every turn or step.

Then, quicker than her breath could register, He was there, standing in front of her, draped in a long white robe with a hood.

She swallowed, fear mingling with inexplicable joy. Fighting the urge to fall to her knees and worship, she instead forced herself to speak.

"Who are you?" she asked, though she was certain no sounds had come from her lips.

"I am Isa," came the answer, nearly knocking her to the ground with its power yet wrapping her in a sweetness she could not explain. "I have come to call you to My heart."

*Heart.* At the word, her own heart began to pound so loudly she could no longer hear the water flowing nearby. Struggling to breathe, she strained to see the face beneath the hood. She knew at that moment, the secret was in His eyes! If only she could see them.

And then she was awake, bolting upright in her bed, gasping for air. A dream! Of course. It had been nothing more than a dream. It meant nothing. Nothing at all, except...

Except that she could still smell the fragrance of the garden—faint but floating in the air around her. How could it be? How could any of this be? She had been fasting and praying, reading the Quran, doing good deeds, and seeking Allah. Why, then, would she be visited by the prophet Isa?

The thought came to her that she could ask her mother, but she imagined the terror it would cause the poor woman to realize her daughter was even thinking in such a way. No. She could not ask her. She couldn't ask anyone. She must keep the dream to herself, and never, ever mention it. Perhaps, if she prayed more and studied the Quran more diligently, she could even forget it entirely.

*Had something happened to her?*

## Chapter 6

Sara was frustrated. She had been so sure Nura would be back online that morning, but she hadn't checked into the chat room by the time Sara had to shut down her computer and get ready for school. All day long she had prayed for Nura and looked forward to talking with her as the evening hours approached. But now the day was nearly gone, and still she'd heard nothing, though she'd checked several times.

She sighed, plopping down on her bed and staring at the ceiling. Homework had consumed the majority of her time since returning from school that day, but she'd had to remind herself to stay focused, as her mind kept drifting to her friend in Saudi Arabia. Had something happened to her? Had Sara said something to alienate her? True, it was Ramadan, which changed nearly everyone's schedule in the Muslim world, but it hadn't kept Nura from her computer before today.

As she lay there, she noticed for the first time that the house was unusually quiet. Her fifteen-year-old brother Emir hadn't come down for dinner, claiming he didn't feel well. But even an upset stomach or headache didn't usually keep him from playing his music just loud enough that she had to ask him to turn it down at least once during the course of the evening. Maybe she should go check on him and see if he was all right or if he needed anything.

Pulling herself from her bed, she padded barefoot to Emir's room and was surprised that no light shone under the doorway. It was only a little after eight, and Sara couldn't remember the last time her only brother had gone to bed that early.

Knocking on his door, she waited. When he didn't answer, she tried again, a bit louder this time, but still she got no response. Though she and Emir had long since reached the age where they no longer burst into one another's room without invitation, a sense of unease was beginning to invade her heart and wrap itself around her throat. Should she ask her parents to check on him, or go ahead and peek in herself?

*No reason to upset Mom and Dad*, she reasoned. *If I go in and find out he's sicker than we thought, then I can tell them.* Her mind made up, she turned the knob, knowing it would open because her father had insisted they had no need for locks on their doors, so long as they all respected each other's privacy.

*But this is an emergency*, she thought, pushing the door open and listening for Emir's breathing while her eyes strained to see outlines in the near darkness. When no sound came, she called to him in a whisper.

"Emir? Emir, are you awake? Can I come in?"

Nothing. The sense of alarm that had begun to invade her peace only a few moments earlier now grew to monstrous proportions. What had happened to Emir? Why didn't her brother answer her?

Heart racing, she felt along the wall until she found the switch, then flipped it on. The empty bed nearly took her breath away. Where was he? Had he gone downstairs after all?

And then she saw the open window—not just the pane slid upward to let in the cool evening air, but the screen removed as well. It was apparent that Emir had gone out the window, but why? Where could he possibly need to go that he couldn't just leave by the front door?

The possible answers swirled through her mind, all seemingly implausible and none serving to calm the anxiety that was quickly getting the best of her.

෴ ෴ ෴

It had been a long and sleepless night. Nura had struggled to join the family in the celebratory eating during Ramadan's hours of darkness between the daylight fasting. Her thoughts warred with one another, one moment calling up horrifying memories of a young girl struggling in the family pool until her body went limp, and the next calling Nura to return to the chat room and try to reconnect with Sara.

All this talk of Isa, particularly Sara's claim that He was more than a prophet—that He was, in fact, the very Son of God Himself—was nearly more terrifying than the realization of the price that could be paid for believing such a claim. *Why do I even consider it?* she asked herself. *Why don't I just dismiss it and never return to the chat room again? After all, it's populated by nonpracticing Muslims and infidels who claim that the Spirit of God can actually inhabit a human being. What blasphemy! And what treachery on my part if I chose to accept it! Even dabbling with the infidel's religion could get me into serious trouble. Why can't I just forget it and move on?*

Sitting on her bed in the quiet of her room, where the dark computer screen beckoned, Nura told herself she should go to another room and rest within the safety of her family's presence. Oh, how much easier life had been before she'd made the foolish choice to begin a dialogue with Muslims who no longer practiced their religion! What kind of Muslim did such a thing anyway? Why would anyone want to leave the true faith and get involved in something that was so obviously false? How could anyone believe the story of God's Son dying on a cross? The whole premise was faulty; every true Muslim knew that Allah had no son. How, then, could a son who did not exist come to earth as a mere mortal and shame himself by dying such an ignominious death? And for what? For the sins of mankind? It made no sense. Good Muslims knew that they were responsible for their own sins and their own eternal destiny. That's why they worked so hard at praying and fasting, doing good deeds and studying the Quran. True, they couldn't be absolutely positive of a place in Paradise unless they martyred themselves for their faith, a thought that caused Nura to shudder. But surely she was a good Muslim girl, wasn't she? She tried to obey her parents; she was modest and did not entice men to look at her; she was submissive and—

She sighed. Why was it that the harder she tried to convince herself that she was a good Muslim girl and that was all she needed, the more she was drawn to the American girl named Sara and her words about the prophet Isa?

Closing her eyes, Nura told herself she would spend the next day of Ramadan in more devoted prayer, focusing only on Allah and the words of the Quran. *If I can be faithful enough, surely my impure and treacherous thoughts of the infidel religion will fade away, and I will be at peace again.*

❧ ❧ ❧

Sara stood rooted to the spot, her heart screaming at her to alert her parents and tell them that Emir's room was empty, but her feet refused to move. Surely her brother was just downstairs in the kitchen, looking for something to eat because he was feeling better and had missed dinner. Or perhaps he was talking to their parents, or...

She turned toward the hallway, her gaze coming to rest on the open bathroom door. She had so hoped it would be closed, explaining Emir's absence from his room. But the open window explained it far too well, and as much as she didn't want to believe it, she knew her brother was not in the house. He had gone out through the window—for whatever reason, she had no idea—and had therefore probably lied about feeling too sick to come down for dinner earlier.

But didn't he realize their mother would be up to check on him soon? She would never go to bed without making sure her children were all right and didn't need anything. What had Emir been thinking when he climbed out that window?

Before she could come to a decision about whether or not to tell her parents of her discovery or to wait awhile to see if Emir returned, a noise at the window spun her away from the hallway and back to face into her brother's room once again. Already Emir had climbed halfway inside and appeared stunned to discover his sister standing in the doorway, waiting for him.

"I wondered why the light was on," he said, climbing in the rest of the way. "I was sure I left it off. What are you doing in here?"

"I came to check on you," she answered. "It was quiet, and I thought..." She stopped, realizing she had allowed Emir to put her on the defensive. "Wait a minute," she said, her voice growing stronger as she drew herself up straight. "I'm not the one in the wrong here. What are you doing sneaking in and out of your window? I thought you weren't feeling well."

A brief flash of contrition swept over Emir's handsome face, bringing a slight blush to his otherwise swarthy complexion. But he recovered quickly, a haughty expression preceding his words. "It's none of your business," he answered. "Since when are you my keeper?"

A flash of irritation fueled the rising volume of Sara's words. "Since you lied to Mom and Dad. That's not right, Emir, and you know it. I was just about to go down and tell them you weren't here when you came in the window. How would you have explained that to them?"

Emir's dark eyes widened before he hurried to her side and pulled her the rest of the way into the room, closing the door behind her. "Not so loud," he hissed. "Do you want them to hear you?"

"Maybe I do," she said, lowering her voice only slightly. "After all, they have a right to know that their son is up to something." She squinted her eyes and glared at him. "What is it, Emir? Why were you out there? What's going on that you don't want anyone else to know about? Are you going to tell me, or do I have to go downstairs and get Mom and Dad?"

Emir's anger was apparent, but Sara saw his chest rise and fall slowly, as he breathed deeply and calmed himself. Then he went to the side of the bed and plunked down, patting the mattress beside him. "Sit down," he said, "and I'll tell you about it. But you have to promise that you won't say anything to Mom and Dad."

"That's a promise you know I can't keep," Sara said as she joined her brother on the edge of the bed. "Not until I hear what you have to say."

Resistance flashed in Emir's eyes, but then he dropped his head and nodded. "All right," he said. "I guess I have no choice. But please try to understand." He looked up, his gaze pleading. "And at least consider keeping it to yourself. It's not any big deal. And it's definitely not anything Mom and Dad need to know about—at least not right now."

Sara raised her eyebrows. She supposed she could at least give him that much, but if he was involved in something dangerous or illegal, there was no way she was keeping it from her parents. "OK," she said, nodding. "I'll try, depending on what you have to say."

Would it help to read more
of the Quran?

## Chapter 7

FARAH HAD REMAINED WATCHFUL ALL NIGHT, AFRAID EVEN TO doze off for fear of returning to the garden in her dream — and to the vision of the man who had identified Himself as Isa.

Even now, after her father and brother had gone out for the day and she was once again in her room, her prayer rug beckoning, she paced, her heart uneasy. Would it help to read more of the Quran? Surely the sacred book would hold the answers she sought. Surely they would help her put the disturbing dream behind her and dispel the yearning it had birthed in her heart.

"Oh, if only there was someone I could talk to about this," she whispered, afraid to speak any louder, though she knew no one was listening. "I feel so alone, so confused! I don't want to be unfaithful, and yet . . ."

She stopped and gazed out the window as the shadows of early morning came into focus in the rising sunlight. Her stomach churned at the memory of the sweet fragrances that had surrounded her in the garden, lingering even after she awoke. The longing to smell them again tugged at her resolve to never return to that mysterious place. Even more so, the desire to speak to the Man with the soothing voice was almost more than she could resist.

The call to prayer, echoing from the minarets and reverberating across the city, interrupted her reverie and reestablished her focus, as she took a deep breath and dismissed the traitorous thoughts of a Man named Isa whom the infidels believed was more than a prophet and who had spoken of calling her to His heart. Dropping to her knees on her prayer rug, she asked Allah to forgive her and to show her the truth, whatever the cost.

～✺～ ～✺～ ～✺～

Sara waited, as Emir squirmed and appeared to be struggling with summoning up the courage to confess what he'd been up to when he climbed out his bedroom window. At least, Sara hoped that was the cause of her brother's hesitancy. In the back of her mind was the thought that perhaps he was stalling for time so he could come up with a plausible lie, but she scolded herself for even considering it. Emir had never lied to her—not that she knew of—and she had no real reason to believe he would do so now. She shoved the suspicion as far from her thoughts as possible.

At last Emir raised his head and fixed his dark eyes on hers. Sara had always thought her little brother was the most handsome boy on the planet, and she wondered how she would ever find a boyfriend to compare to him. Some young woman was going to be quite blessed to land Emir as a husband one day, though Sara conceded that the young man who had shared her life since he was born fifteen years earlier still had a lot of growing up to do.

"I went to see Joni," he said, his voice husky as if trying to hold back tears or cover his embarrassment.

Sara frowned. "Joni? Why would you do that? And why go through the window? You could have called her, or just gone out the door and—"

Emir raised his hand to interrupt her. "Let me finish. Please. I know it doesn't make sense, but..." His voice trailed off, as he took a deep breath and once again seemed to be stalling. At last

50

he plunged ahead, his eyes imploring her to understand. "We're only fifteen. I know we're too young to be in love, but we have feelings for each other. I've known it for a long time, but I didn't have the nerve to tell her. When I finally did, she told me she felt the same way. I wanted to see her tonight—alone, so we could talk with no one around. I was so nervous that I really did feel sick earlier. That's why I didn't eat dinner. I should have waited until it was completely dark, but I got impatient. And besides, I wanted to go see her and get back before Mom came up to check on me and say good night. I was only gone for a few minutes, honest. Just long enough to..."

His voice trailed off once again, and his cheeks reddened. He cleared his throat. "Are you going to tell Mom and Dad? I really don't want them to know—not yet. They'd probably just say something to Joni's parents, and it would turn into a big mess. There's no need for it, Sara. Really. Joni and I are young, and we don't know what's going to happen. Probably nothing. But we just want it to be our secret for now."

Sara was stunned. She had sat perfectly still, letting Emir ramble while she questioned if she was hearing him correctly. Joni? Chubby little Joni, whom they'd all known forever and who was almost a member of the family? How could it be?

"I don't get it," she said at last, taking the opportunity to respond when Emir took a breath. She shook her head. "It just doesn't make sense. Joni? Seriously? I mean, you know I love her. She's almost like a sister to me. But it never occurred to me that you would be attracted to her. I didn't think you even noticed her."

Emir hung his head for a moment before lifting it and gazing at her once again. "I ignored her on purpose," he said. "I didn't want anyone to know how I felt, not even her. But when I finally told her, she said she'd had a crush on me for years."

Sara hesitated. Though it was true she'd never seen Emir show the least interest in Joni, the girl had exhibited several signs that she might be interested in him. Was it possible that Emir was telling the truth after all?

Sara wanted to believe him, but it was a stretch. "So you're telling me you crawled out the window to go see a girl who lives a few houses down the street, just to be alone with her for a few minutes, and then came right back."

Emir nodded. "I know. It doesn't make sense, but..." He shrugged. "I don't know how to act," he confessed. "Don't forget, I've never had a girlfriend before."

Sara raised her eyebrows. What he had said was true. She knew several girls who had confessed to having a crush on Emir over the years, but at their young age it meant nothing. This was the first time Sara was aware of that Emir had been the one to express an interest in someone of the opposite sex. That it was Joni was beyond surprising, but who knew about this sort of thing?

"I suppose you're right," she said. "But I must admit, I would never have expected your first crush to be on Joni, of all people. We've known her forever!"

Emir smiled. "Exactly. I think that must be part of the reason I'm attracted to her. I feel... I don't know, safe with her, I guess. Does that make sense?"

Sara smiled. "As much as anything about this situation." Her smile turned to a chuckle. "It will be interesting to get Joni's take on this. I'm looking forward to talking with her on the way to school tomorrow."

Emir's eyes widened. "Oh no, you can't! I mean, please, don't embarrass her—or me. I promised her I wouldn't tell anyone, not even you. At least wait until I tell her that you know so it won't catch her by surprise. Please?"

The pleading in his eyes was more than Sara could resist. She nodded. "OK, I promise. I'll hold it in as long as I can. But you know Joni and I have started walking to and from school together most of the time. It won't be easy to keep from saying something, so you'd better tell her soon. Deal?"

Emir grinned, the relief evident on his face and in his relaxed shoulders. "Deal," he agreed. Then he leaned over and kissed her cheek. "Now get out of my room, will you? A guy's got a right to at least a little privacy, you know."

Sara smiled and stood to her feet. Her brother's words sounded sincere, and she told herself there was no reason not to believe him. But the suspicion she had shoved away at the beginning of Emir's explanation was coming back to cast doubt and question on the entire conversation.

≈≈≈ ≈≈≈ ≈≈≈

"Nura?"

Her mother's voice at her door startled Nura, and she realized she had drifted off to sleep as she leaned against the propped up pillows on her bed. What time was it?

She glanced at her watch. It was nearly noon, and she'd spent little if any time in prayer that day, instead using all her energy to keep herself from her computer.

"Come in, Mom," she called.

The door opened, and Sakeena entered, her smile nearly as warm as her eyes.

"Were you sleeping?" she asked.

"Just dozing." Nura patted the bed. "Come and sit by me."

As her mother joined her, Nura marveled at the middle-aged woman's beauty. She so resembled her sister, Sultana, and also Sultana's younger daughter, Nadia. They were truly the beauties in the family, while Nura and Farah could best be described as somewhat attractive. Nura had often wondered if that was why the two of them were quieter than Nadia, more introspective. Was there any chance that Nura's cousin Farah, who was so like her outwardly, might wrestle with similar questions about her faith and religion?

Blocking the thought from her mind, Nura smiled. "Were you able to get some rest this morning? You fixed such a lovely meal last night, but I know you were tired. Tonight I'll do all the cooking, and you can relax."

Sakeena returned her daughter's smile. "Neither of us will need to cook tonight. Your Aunt Sultana has invited our family to join them for the *Iftar* meal this evening. Won't that be nice?"

Nura nodded, wondering at the sudden tension she felt in her stomach. She always enjoyed going to her aunt and uncle's home and visiting with her cousins, though they never spoke of anything important. Nadia was wrapped up in discussing clothes

53

and shopping, while Farah and Kareem scarcely said much at all. Why did Nura sense that tonight might be different?

Shaking off the thought, she said, "I'd enjoy that very much." She squeezed her mother's hand and wondered at what the next few hours might bring. At least being out of the house for the evening would keep her away from her computer and the chat room that even now wooed her to return.

But the presence only grew stronger,
and soon Zarah was weeping on
her prayer rug.

## Chapter 8

THE MORE FARAH TRIED TO CONCENTRATE ON HER PRAYERS throughout the day, the more her mind wandered to the Man in the garden. If He was indeed trying to call her to His heart, He was certainly doing a good job of it! Farah pounded the floor in frustration, trying to drive the Man's image and voice from her mind, but they refused to budge. Angry, she spoke aloud without thinking: "Leave me alone, Isa! I want no part of the false religion that worships You as one of their gods! You are a prophet of Islam, nothing more!"

But the presence only grew stronger, and soon Farah was weeping on her prayer rug. Was there no escape from this vision that haunted her? For surely that was all it was—a vision from a dream, nothing more. Oh, the ache to speak to someone else about it! How grateful she was that no one was there at that moment, or she might well have said something she would regret for the rest of her life.

*It is Ramadan,* she reminded herself. *The holiest of holy seasons. It is a time to pray and read the Quran, not explore false religions. How can I be so unfaithful, so foolish? Help me, Allah! Forgive me and help me, please!*

She remembered then that her aunt and uncle, as well as her cousin Nura, were coming to share the *Iftar* meal with them that evening, and somehow the thought that they would be there in a couple of hours comforted her.

*Why?* she wondered, though no explanation came to her. She supposed, if for no other reason, their presence might help keep her mind off the strange dream that had interrupted her life and refused to let her go. She hated that her love of the holiday and her seeking of Allah had been disturbed. She also longed to return to the comfortable knowledge that her Muslim faith was right and that she needed nothing more, but her fear that perhaps that would never happen made her cry all the harder. For the very first time, she found herself wishing for the day of prayer and fasting to come to an end.

❧ ❧ ❧

Sara found herself looking at Joni in an entirely different way as they walked to school in the cool morning air. There was a hint of moisture surrounding them, but scarcely enough to be noticeable to two teenaged girls who had been raised in the Pacific Northwest. Rain was simply a way of life, and unless it came as a deluge, they seldom even bothered with umbrellas. Even the little old lady walking her Chihuahua seemed oblivious to the weather, as they tottered along on the opposite side of the street. Sara smiled at the sight of them. They were a familiar fixture in the neighborhood, though she'd never spoken to them.

Sara pressed ahead, scarcely noticing the neatly manicured lawns to their right, or the multicolored profusion of late summer flowers, including the rich bursts of roses and violets that bloomed for such a short season in their corner of the world and would soon die out with the arrival of fall. She was too busy sneaking peeks at her younger friend.

Joni seemed oblivious, no doubt unaware that Emir had revealed their secret to Sara. Would she be embarrassed when she learned that Sara knew of the budding romance? Might she be angry at Emir for divulging the information, even under pressure? Sara was certain he would never have volunteered the information if she hadn't caught him sneaking in his window. But she had, and so he had told her the nearly unbelievable story—a story that Sara still struggled with accepting.

Turning her head sideways, she glanced once again at the pudgy girl with the short blond curls that bounced when she walked. Apparently Joni sensed Sara's gaze and turned her head, her blue eyes questioning. "What?" she asked, raising her eyebrows. "Is something wrong?"

Sara felt her cheeks grow hot, and she quickly shook her head. "No, nothing. Why do you ask?"

Joni shrugged and grinned, her dimples lending a light mood to the conversation. "Oh, I don't know. Maybe because you keep looking at me weird. What's up anyway?"

"Nothing," Sara repeated, returning her gaze to the straight forward position. "Really. I was just... wondering how things were going with you. You know, with school and all. We've been back for a couple of weeks now, and it's your first year of high school, so I thought..."

Her voice trailed off as she wondered what to say next, but Joni rescued her, apparently accepting Sara's explanation. "I'm fine," she said. "High school is OK, I guess. There's more homework, and I don't like one of my teachers very much, but otherwise, no problems. What about you?"

Joni's question caught Sara off guard. She frowned and risked another quick glance at her companion. "Me? I'm fine too. But this is my senior year. I'm used to things at high school. They're not new to me like they are for you."

Joni nodded. "You're right. And thanks for asking." She offered another smile. "You're a good friend, Sara, especially since you're so far ahead of me in school and everything. Most seniors don't want anything to do with the younger students."

"That's silly," Sara countered. "We've been friends for years. That's not going to change just because we're growing up." She paused, considering a thought that had popped into her mind before deciding to voice it. "In fact," she ventured, "who knows what the future might hold for our relationships as we get nearer to adulthood? It's possible our families could grow even closer, don't you think?"

Joni shrugged. "I guess so," she answered, though Sara heard no conviction in her voice. She had so hoped Joni would take the bait, but apparently that wasn't going to happen. Sara would just have to wait until Emir told Joni that Sara was on to them, and see how the girl reacted then.

∽∾ ∽∾ ∽∾

The meal had been even tastier than the night before, with Sultana and her daughters having prepared a delectable fish stew, along with eggplant and yogurt salad, causing everyone except Farah and Nura to reach for second helpings and rave about the cooking. Farah smiled and accepted her portion of the compliments; but while Sultana and Nadia beamed at the attention, Farah couldn't help but notice that Nura picked at her food, even as Farah did. Was it just a coincidence that neither of them was hungry? Oh, if only she had made more of an effort to get closer to her cousin through the years! Perhaps Nura could have been the confidante Farah so desperately needed right now.

"Are you feeling all right, Nura?" Farah asked, surprised at the sound of her own voice. Had she really spoken aloud?

Farah's surprise seemed mirrored in the responses around the table, as the women examined Nura as if they had just noticed she was there. Sakeena seemed the most concerned.

"Nura, are you ill? You said nothing about not feeling well earlier." Because she was seated next to her daughter, she reached up and touched her forehead. "You don't seem to have a fever."

Nura's embarrassment was obvious. "Oh no, I'm fine. Really! It's just..." Looking down at her barely touched plate of food, her cheeks flushed and she stammered as she spoke. "The food is... wonderful. I..."

Farah thought she saw a flash of fear in her cousin's dark eyes before she continued. A chill traveled up Farah's spine as she realized the fear was familiar.

"I have a headache," Nura mumbled. "It came on suddenly, and—"

60

Immediately Sultana was on her feet, patting Nura's shoulder and gesturing to Farah. "Farah, get your cousin a couple of aspirin and take her to your room so she can lie down. Come, Nura, you'll feel better if you can rest a bit."

Sakeena smiled. "Thank you, dear sister. I'm sure that's exactly what Nura needs." Turning back toward her daughter she said, "Go with your cousin and lie down as your aunt suggested. I'll be in to check on you in a little while."

After only a brief hesitation, Nura nodded and stood to her feet, as Farah led the way to her room, a sense of excitement tinged with foreboding swirling around in her chest.

*She was drawn to that edge where
safety and danger met and lives
changed forever.*

## Chapter 9

THOUGH NURA KNEW SHE HAD BEEN WRONG TO LIE ABOUT having a headache, she was so nervous by the time she got to Farah's room that she truly was starting to feel sick. The cousins had spent time in one another's rooms on many occasions over the years, as the families visited back and forth, but always the conversations had been surface-related. Neither Farah nor Nura was overly interested in boys or clothes, jewelry or shopping, or any of the things that fascinated Nadia and most other young women their age, so they often found they had little to talk about other than their studies. And that didn't make for much of a solid foundation when it came to revealing innermost secrets.

Sitting down on the edge of Farah's bed, Nura was stunned that she was even considering opening up to her cousin. There was nothing safe or wise in the possibility, so why not dismiss it from her mind and simply lie back and rest, as her mother and aunt had suggested? She might not have a headache, but she was glad to be away from the busy chatter of the family at the dining room table.

Kathi Macias

"I'll get you those aspirin," Farah said as Nura lay back against the pile of pillows, sinking down into their softness and grateful for the sense of comfort they seemed to offer. She nodded as Farah left the room on her mission of mercy, returning in a matter of minutes with a glass of water and two white tablets.

Nura noticed that her cousin closed the door behind her, and she was grateful, as she dutifully swallowed the aspirin and smiled in appreciation. "Thank you," she said. "Really, I'll be fine. I just needed to rest a little."

Farah nodded, seated beside her on the bed. "I noticed you weren't very hungry."

Nura raised her eyebrows. "You weren't eating much yourself."

Farah's cheeks flamed. "I guess I wasn't hungry either."

"Strange," Nura observed.

Farah's eyes widened. "What do you mean?"

"Aren't you usually hungry at the end of a day of fasting? I am—most of the time."

The girls stared at one another for a moment, and Nura found herself biting her tongue to keep from blurting out the questions that nagged at her mind and nudged at her heart. If only Farah would say something to indicate that it would be safe for Nura to bring up the subject of the chat room and her American friend who talked so much of Isa! Sara had even told Nura that occasionally the chat room was visited by believers in Isa who actually lived within the Saudi Kingdom. Nura found it hard to believe that such people could exist within her own country, and she certainly wasn't going to bring up the possibility with Farah, at least not yet.

"I suppose I should get back to the others," Farah said at last, dropping her eyes before lifting them again to look at Nura.

Nura nodded. "Thank you. I appreciate your kindness. And please assure my mother and aunt that I am fine."

Farah stood up, looked down at her one last time as Nura waited, scarcely breathing...and then Farah was gone, closing the door softly behind her as Nura fought the tears that seemed to hover so close these days.

Farah fidgeted through the remainder of the meal, which went on for some time as they all sat around the table, visiting and enjoying a scrumptious dessert of pound cake smothered in strawberries. Yet even such a sweet delicacy, normally one of Farah's favorites, didn't tempt her.

She couldn't get her mind off Nura. Was it just her imagination, or had her cousin been about to say something — something beyond the normal pleasantries they exchanged, something secret and possibly even dangerous? Though Nura had never been one to invite Farah into her private world, the girl had seemed nervous and edgy, even stiff and almost formal just before Farah left her. Something wasn't right. Whatever it was, Farah was torn between wanting to know and being afraid to find out. The cousins' relationship was safe as it was. Why risk changing it and losing that safety factor?

And then there was Kareem. She glanced across the table, but her brother was ignoring her. Though he had said nothing as the little scene with Nura's headache played out earlier, Farah hadn't missed the glare of contempt that shot from his dark eyes. But was it more than contempt? Had she only imagined that suspicion clouded his features?

Farah sighed and forced herself to taste one of the berries. It was sweet and juicy, as she had imagined, but the flavor did nothing to make her want more. Her mind continued to return to the possibility of risking the safe level of her current relationship with Nura. Her entire life seemed to revolve around that thought these days. She sensed she was dancing on the edge of something dangerous, yet wonderful, and she was both terrified and intrigued by the possibilities.

No. It was more than terror and intrigue. She was drawn to that edge where safety and danger met and lives changed forever. And the drawing grew stronger each day, fueled by the memory of the prophet Isa in the garden of her dream. How desperately she wanted to tell Nura of that dream! Would she understand? If not, would she at least keep her secret? Or would she tell her parents, who would then tell Farah's parents?

She nearly choked on the berry in her mouth but managed to recover so no one noticed. Before she could talk herself out of it,

65

she excused herself to go check on Nura, knowing that her very life could change by the words she was about to speak.

Sara had drifted through her first-period class, feeling sleepy and fighting the urge to fade away into a daydream. The main focus of her thoughts continued to be Emir and Joni, still the most unlikely couple she could imagine. But who could predict who would be attracted to whom? She certainly was no expert on matters of the heart. Though she'd had a couple of crushes in her life and knew of a handful of teenage boys who had expressed an interest in her, that was as far as her romantic experience extended. For her to label a relationship as unlikely bordered on the ridiculous.

By the time the bell rang, excusing the students to go to their next class, she was grateful for the relatively cool air that greeted her when she stepped out the door. She needed to stretch and breathe and move around a bit if she was going to make it through five more classes by the end of the day.

After making a quick stop at her locker to exchange books, she hurried around the corner to cut across the lawn to the science building. She had no sooner set foot on the grass than a familiar sight caught her eye. Standing under a nearby pine tree was Emir, his face toward her but his eyes firmly fixed on the girl in front of him. That girl was Joni, her back to Sara, gazing intently at Emir as he talked nearly nonstop. Whatever he was saying to Joni, she was taking it in without interruption. Sara couldn't help but think her brother was filling Joni in on the events of the previous evening. What would Joni's reaction be? The walk home from school that afternoon was bound to be a revealing one.

Tucking her head to avoid their eyes and conceal her smile, Sara crossed the lawn without looking back. If her little brother and his first love needed their privacy, she wasn't about to interfere.

Farah knocked lightly, thinking Nura might be asleep and not wanting to bother her. But Nura's invitation to enter came immediately, so Farah opened the door without further hesitation. Her heart raced at the thought of what she was about to do, and her breathing was labored. Even her hands were clammy as she approached the bed and perched on the very edge. The small lamp on the dresser cast a dim light across the bed, making Nura's face appear to glow, though her expression was anything but joyful. Apprehensive? Nervous? Farah couldn't be sure.

She took a deep breath. "Are you feeling better?"

Nura nodded. "Yes. I think so."

"No more headache?"

Appearing surprised, Nura hesitated before answering. "Headache? Oh no, it's gone. Thank you."

Farah waited, the silence between them nearly crackling with anticipation. At last she opened her mouth and asked, "Have you ever had a dream?" When Nura frowned at the obvious absurdity of the question, Farah added, "I mean, a really strange dream. One that was so real you could nearly taste it — or smell it."

Nura's frown deepened. "I've had dreams that were much clearer than others, sure. Dreams that stayed with me the next day. Is that what you mean?"

Farah's eyes filled with tears, and she tried to will them away. She shook her head. "No," she whispered, wiping the tears with her hand before they could drip down her face. She swallowed, wondering if she could find the strength and courage to continue.

Nura's hand reached up to help Farah wipe away her tears, and Farah knew then that she could tell her story. In fact, she sensed that if she didn't, she would burst from the pain of holding it in.

At last Nura whispered, "Who? Who was He, Zarah?"

## Chapter 10

Nura thought surely her heart would explode out of her chest. Could Farah hear it, or was her own heart beating equally hard, causing the tears to flow from her eyes? Nura couldn't remember ever seeing her cousin cry before. Were they truly on the verge of something so life-changing that their very souls sensed it and responded?

Nura swallowed, praying Farah would speak first. She wished she weren't such a coward, but she simply couldn't bring herself to tell her cousin about Sara or the chat room, at least not until she knew what Farah meant about her dream.

"I've been praying and fasting," Farah said at last, her tears slowing slightly and her dark eyes shimmering as she spoke. "Of course, I realize we are all doing so because of Ramadan, but this is something more."

She dropped her eyes, and Nura found herself hoping that Farah wouldn't lose her courage. When Farah lifted her gaze again, Nura knew she would continue speaking.

Kathi Macias

"I'm sure you know that my family sometimes thinks I'm overly devout, that I pray and study the Quran more than most other girls or women."

She hesitated until Nura nodded, then continued. "This year I anticipated Ramadan more than in the past, though I've always enjoyed it more than any other time of year. But now that I'm older, I wanted to..." Her voice trailed off and she swallowed before going on. "I wanted to draw closer to Allah, to have a deeper and more meaningful faith. Does that make sense?"

It didn't, and yet somehow it did. Nura nodded again.

"Yesterday evening, after the *Iftar* meal, I dozed off while lying on my bed, and I had a dream." A flash of fear danced through Farah's eyes, and it appeared she was struggling to open her mouth.

*Oh, please don't stop,* Nura thought, nearly holding her breath.

"I was in a garden," Farah said, her voice lowered almost to a whisper, forcing Nura to strain to catch each word. "It was the most beautiful garden I had ever seen. The colors were so bright they nearly blinded me, and the wonderful smells...they stayed with me even after I woke up."

Nura wanted to cry out, to beg Farah to tell her what happened next, but she kept herself still and waited, not wanting to do anything that might interrupt her cousin's confession.

"And then I saw Him, standing there in a hooded robe. I don't know how or why, but I knew He was waiting for me."

For a moment neither of them spoke. At last Nura whispered, "Who? Who was He, Farah?"

Nura saw Farah's jaws twitch before she answered. "Isa. It was the prophet Isa. He said that He had come to call me to His heart."

The tears that had dripped from Farah's eyes now burned at the back of Nura's eyelids, as the thought that Isa was at the center of everything that was going on with both of the cousins. Her heart skipped a beat at the implications.

"What happened then?" she asked.

"I woke up," Farah said. "But it was as if I were still there, smelling the flowers and hearing His voice."

70

Nura swallowed and took a deep breath. "Do you still smell the flowers and hear His voice?"

Farah shook her head. "No. I remember the fragrances, but I don't smell them. And I don't hear His voice. But I do feel like He's still calling me."

Nura felt her eyes widen. What Farah had just said described what she had been feeling as well. Did she dare tell her about Sara and the chat room? Yes, of course! If Farah had taken such a chance to tell her of the dream, then she too must take a risk and tell Farah of her own struggles.

Taking Farah's hand in her own, she said, "None of this makes any sense, I know, but...somehow I understand."

The flicker of hope in Farah's eyes gave Nura the courage to continue. "I have something to tell you as well."

⁓ ⁓ ⁓

Kareem smoldered, scarcely able to enjoy his dessert. As usual his older sister had managed to take the focus off him and turn it toward herself, as the topic around the table was now Nura's headache and Farah's compassionate concern. Why did the others' reasoning not ring true to him? He was nearly certain that Farah's second absence from the family gathering was spurred by something other than compassion, but he couldn't put his finger on what it might be.

As much as he disliked Farah, he had never cared much more for his cousin Nura either. She wasn't quite attractive enough for his liking, though at least he had never heard that she was as overly religious as Farah. His sister's devotion to her faith was almost an embarrassment to him, and he wondered why she couldn't be satisfied to be a normal, obedient girl like Nadia. Besides, Nadia was absolutely beautiful. More than once Kareem had found himself wishing she wasn't his sister.

He quickly shifted his thoughts from Nadia to Farah. The more he thought of Farah and Nura, no doubt talking and scheming together about things they had no business discussing, the angrier he became. Why couldn't his father see that Farah was

71

not the perfect Muslim daughter he imagined her to be? Perhaps Kareem could enlighten him if he could find the right information.

With that thought in mind, he excused himself from the table, as his plan began to take shape.

∽✿∾ ∽✿∾ ∽✿∾

Farah was stunned. The more Nura's story unfolded, the more Farah's mind recoiled in disbelief. Farah knew that many Muslims used the Internet, most for legitimate study and research, some to spread their personal beliefs and recruit new followers, but... her own cousin, prowling around a chat room with infidels? What was she thinking?

And yet why was her experience so different from Farah's? True, Nura had actively sought out the contacts who had initiated her thinking, while Farah had not. The dream had come to her with no direct invitation on her part. But quite obviously the ultimate result was the same: both Farah and Nura faced serious questions about the identity of the prophet Isa. They had been taught from earliest childhood that He was no more than a prophet and certainly not on an equal plane with the ultimate prophet, Muhammad. To consider Isa anything more was blasphemy and punishable in ways too horrible to contemplate. But—and Farah shuddered at the thought—what if it were true?

Nura had stopped speaking, and Farah knew her cousin waited for a response. What should she say? Before she could decide, she heard her bedroom door open and saw Nura's eyes open wide at the interruption.

Icy talons gripped Farah's throat as she turned to face the intruder, praying she would see her aunt or mother standing in the doorway but knowing even before she looked that it would be Kareem. Her dread was quickly confirmed, as she beheld him glowering at her, the hatred in his eyes worse than anything she had seen there before.

What had he heard? Anything? Everything? Enough to report to their father and uncle? Whatever it might be, she knew the outcome would ultimately not be good for herself or Nura.

∞∞ ∞∞ ∞∞

Sara had found it difficult to concentrate during the last class of the day, even though she normally enjoyed English and admired her teacher. But today her only thoughts were of Joni and Emir, and what might transpire between herself and Joni on their walk home from school that afternoon.

The thought that Joni might try to avoid her brought a stab of concern, but only for a moment. Even if the younger girl considered walking home alone to avoid the conversation, Sara knew where Joni's last period class was and would have no problem intercepting her.

When the bell rang, Sara was out the door ahead of everyone else and standing in front of Joni's classroom by the time the girl had gathered her books and made her way outside. The surprise on Joni's face was quickly followed by resignation, and Sara smiled, knowing she was about to get some answers to her questions about the so-called relationship between Joni and Emir.

As the two girls fell into step down the familiar sidewalk toward home, Sara didn't give Joni any time to regroup. "I saw you and my brother talking together after first period," she said, darting a sideways glance to gauge Joni's reaction. A quick tensing in her shoulders was all that showed. "I guess he told you that I caught him sneaking in the window of his room last night."

Still staring at the sidewalk straight ahead, Joni nodded. "Yeah. He told me."

Sara hesitated only a few seconds before prodding for more. "What else did he tell you?"

At last Joni turned her head and looked briefly into Sara's eyes. "He told me that you know about . . ." Her gaze flitted away once again. "About us."

The words sounded as unnatural as the entire situation felt to Sara. But if both Joni and Emir insisted they had feelings for one another, how was Sara to prove otherwise?

"So you two are . . ." She couldn't bring herself to use the term *in love* for the unlikely pair, so she changed direction. "You have feelings for each other, I understand."

73

Kathi Macias

Joni nodded again, her blond curls bobbing. "Yes. I have for a long time, but I didn't think Emir felt the same."

The girl's voice cracked at the end of her statement, and Sara wondered if it was from the strain of lying or if she just might be overcome with the realization that Emir really did care for her. Whatever the case, it was obvious that Joni wasn't going to budge from her version of the story. Sara had hoped to come away from their conversation with a clearer picture of the truth, but apparently that wasn't going to happen. For now she would have to leave it alone and accept it for what it was. But if Joni and Emir were lying, what was going on that necessitated it? That was what bothered Sara most of all.

Emir watched his mother's back as
she exited the room, and then his
eyes met Sara's.

## Chapter 11

Emir raced home from school on his skateboard and nearly exploded through the front door. His heart pumped wildly as he took the stairs two at a time and plunked down in front of his window just as Sara and Joni came into view below. Walking side by side as they drew even with Joni's house, Emir wished he could hear what they were saying. Was Joni sticking to the story they'd agreed upon? Was Sara buying it?

As Joni turned at the entrance to her yard and Sara pressed on toward home, Emir's thoughts were interrupted by a rap on his door. Jerking his head away from the window and toward his visitor, he swallowed his sense of guilt and smiled at his mother.

"Mom," he said, reminding himself to act naturally but knowing he wasn't doing a very good job, "I didn't see you when I came in."

Emir's mother, Layla, was in her early forties, but according to Emir's father and others who had expressed similar opinions, looked several years younger. Her thick black hair was cut in a short, trendy style, and her wide eyes gave her an appearance of innocence. Yet Emir knew she was anything but naive. He'd seldom been able to get much past her in his fifteen years of life; he could only pray that this would be an exception.

Layla raised her perfectly sculpted eyebrows. "I'm not surprised," she said, a hint of annoyance in her voice. "You burst through the front door and ran upstairs as if the devil himself were chasing you. Whatever was so important that you had to race to your room without even saying hello?"

Emir felt his cheeks flame. "I'm sorry, Mom. Really. I was just glad to be home, and—" He shrugged, repeating himself as he looked away from his mother's questioning glare. "Sorry."

Layla hesitated before answering. "I should hope so," she said at last, walking toward him and giving him a quick embrace. "Well, now that you're here and no longer running for your life, why don't you tell me about your day? How was school? Is everything going well with your studies? Are you adjusting well to your new schedule?"

*Running for your life.* Why had she chosen such a phrase? What did she mean by it? The possibilities swirled through his mind and churned in his stomach, nearly incapacitating him until he couldn't speak. But he knew he'd better answer quickly if he didn't want her to really start grilling him and giving him the third degree.

"School was great," he said, trying to keep his gaze steady and to appear as nonchalant as possible. "Nothing new or exciting. Just the usual. You know, homework and football tryouts, stuff like that."

His mother's smile was still a bit tentative, but he was fairly sure she was coming around. "Good," she said. "You love football, and you're good at it." Her smile widened, and this time her dark eyes joined in. "I'm glad you're trying out for the team. Your father and I look forward to watching you play—just so long as your grades don't suffer because of it."

Emir nodded, searching for a way to steer the conversation away from football and grades. He wasn't ready for his parents to find out that he hadn't even tried to make the team, and that his grades were shaky at best. Before he could change the subject,

Sara stepped into the open doorway, her eyes darting from Emir to their mother and back again.

"Hi, family," she said, her greeting turning Layla around to face her. "Is this a private meeting, or can anyone join?"

"I was just asking Emir about school and trying to find out why he raced in the door and up the stairs without even saying hello to me." Layla shifted her gaze back to Emir. "That is very rude, you know."

Emir blushed again. "I know," he said, his shoulders and head hanging. "I'm sorry, Mom."

"Forgiven," Layla said. "But don't let it happen again. Now, I've got to get back downstairs and start dinner. Your father will be home soon, and he needs to eat right away so he can go back to work for a meeting."

Emir watched his mother's back as she exited the room, and then his eyes met Sara's. Something told him he was in for yet another confrontation, and he felt his shoulders tense. Life had become far too complicated lately, and he couldn't even let himself picture how it might all turn out. He could only hope he would finally find the acceptance he was looking for, despite the dangers involved in the process. Most of all, he had to make sure his parents didn't find out. It would kill them to know.

Farah had been unable to sleep or even pray as the night hours wore on. Nura and her parents had said good night and left soon after Kareem burst in on the two cousins, and still Kareem had said nothing. After watching the girls in silence from the doorway, he had simply turned and walked away, leaving Nura and Farah to ponder their fate. Terrified, Farah had rushed to close the door, whispering reassurances to herself as much as to her cousin that Kareem couldn't possibly have heard anything they said. Though the girls had agreed that they hadn't spoken loudly enough for anyone to hear them through the door, neither seemed fully convinced.

Several times after their company left and before Farah had returned to her room, she had looked up to find Kareem glowering at her. Each time she told herself he knew nothing, but her heart pounded wildly in her chest at the thought of what could happen if he did. She had long known that her brother didn't like her, but never before had she given him anything he could use against her. Now she wasn't so sure.

Throughout the night, Farah had tried, over and over again, to pray and to read the Quran, but her mind would not focus. The hatred in Kareem's eyes turned the blood in her veins to ice, as she thought about Nura and imagined that she too was spending a restless and fearful night.

At last, toward the earliest morning hours and before the first rays of dawn, Farah drifted away as she lay on her bed, her head resting on the very pillows where Nura's had lain only hours earlier. And though the dream was not as clear this time, there was no mistaking the voice. *Come, Farah,* He said. *I am calling you to My heart. You will find much peace and joy there.*

But when she exploded back into reality, jerking upright on her bed and gasping for air, there was no peace or joy to welcome her, and Farah began to weep.

⋘ ⋘ ⋘

Sara waited until she was certain her mother was back at work in the kitchen before stepping inside Emir's room and closing the door behind her. She sensed that she was about as welcome as a case of poison oak, but she didn't care. Something was going on with her brother, and she was relatively positive that it had nothing to do with Joni.

"So what's up?" she asked, plunking down on the edge of the bed.

Emir met her gaze, though it was obvious he would have preferred not to. He shrugged. "Not much. Why?"

She shrugged in return. "Oh, I don't know. Just wondering, I guess. I mean, since I caught you climbing in your window last night, and now you expect me to believe your story about you and Joni, and then you race past Mom without even saying hello. Seriously. What am I supposed to think?"

Their eyes locked for several seconds until Emir finally glanced away, though Sara hadn't missed the look of alarm that had darted across his face when she made her remark about the story with him and Joni. Though Joni had confirmed Emir's account of their relationship almost verbatim, Sara was still having a hard time buying it.

The silence in the room was growing thicker, even as Sara grew impatient. "What's going on, Emir?" she asked at last, determined to get an honest answer.

But this time when Emir met her gaze, she saw determination in his eyes. "Nothing is going on," he said, his voice steady and even. "Nothing that I haven't already told you about. Listen, Sara, if you don't want to believe me or Joni, then I don't know what to tell you. We care about each other, OK? Maybe we're even in love. What's it to you, anyway? Why do you care? What difference does it make?"

Sara wasn't sure if it made any difference at all, if the words Emir spoke were true. But were they? As hard as she was trying to believe them, it just wasn't working.

"It matters to me," Sara said at last, "because you're my brother and I love you. I don't need any other reason."

Emir's gaze held steady, but Sara saw his Adam's apple bob more than once. Was he choking back tears? She wouldn't doubt it, though her macho brother would rather be skinned alive than admit it. At last she sighed in resignation and stood to leave. On her way out of the room, she turned back and caught him wiping something from the corner of his eye.

"You know where I am if you need me," she said, her voice just loud enough to be sure he heard. Then she closed the door and went next door to her own room.

The chat room, she thought. I haven't talked with Nura in a while. Will she be there?

## Chapter 12

FOR THE FIRST TIME SINCE SHE'D BEEN OLD ENOUGH TO understand what the holy month of Ramadan meant to her as a Muslim, Farah did not bow down on her prayer rug to seek Allah. She had already been awake when the morning call to prayer echoed across the skies of Riyadh, but though she tried to behave as usual, she had been unable to do so. The very sight of the prayer rug made her cringe. Was it her excessive prayer and reading of the Quran that had caused her to have such vivid and blasphemous dreams? If so, she wasn't going to aggravate the situation further.

But though the disturbed young woman did not participate in the daily prayers, she had no problem maintaining the fast. She couldn't imagine eating even if it wasn't a day of fasting. The very thought of food revolted her, turning her stomach to knots. The memory of her revealing conversation with Nura haunted her, exceeded only by the memory of the look in Kareem's eyes as he had stood in the doorway, silently accusing them and promising revenge.

Nura. Just yesterday she had been nothing more than a cousin and casual friend to Farah; now Farah felt as if she were bonded more closely to her than she'd ever been to anyone in her entire life. The thought that their lives could abruptly end together sent a shiver of fear up her spine, and she nearly cried aloud at the pain of it.

Kareem. Why did he hate her so? And why had she given him reason to cause her trouble? For there was no doubt in Farah's mind that her brother would do so gladly if the opportunity presented itself. Though she continually told herself that he couldn't possibly have overheard the words she and Nura spoke to one another, she also knew that Kareem was now suspicious of the young women's conversation and motives. They would have to be extremely careful if they ever spoke of their questions about Isa again. And somehow Farah was certain that they would.

๛ ๛ ๛

Ahmed and Kareem had no sooner left for the day than Sultana flipped open her phone and punched in her sister's number. Sakeena had scarcely answered when Sultana asked about Nura.

"How is my niece feeling today? Is she better? Did she sleep well?"

"Somewhat," Sakeena answered, "though she still looks a bit pale and drawn. I'm keeping a close eye on her."

Sultana nodded. "Good. We are all quite concerned. Even Kareem asked about her this morning."

A slight pause on the other end alerted Sultana to the fact that her sister probably didn't believe Kareem's concern but rather suspected another motive. Sultana had her doubts as well, but neither would voice them.

Sensing the need to change the subject, Sultana asked, "Shall we go shopping tonight? You know how I enjoy browsing the *suqs* during the late-night hours of Ramadan, and I want to take advantage of it as often as possible before the month is over."

"I'll have to see how Nura is feeling," Sakeena responded. "If she's not better, I may stay home with her."

"I understand," Sultana said. And she did, of course. With three children of her own, she knew that she too would stay home if any of them needed her. As a matter of fact, she had done so on many occasions.

After making a tentative date to call back before the *Iftar* meal, Sultana clicked off, suddenly desirous to go check on Farah. Until that moment she hadn't realized that her older daughter had also seemed a bit withdrawn and out of sorts that morning. Sultana hoped Farah wasn't coming down with whatever Nura had, but there was only one way to find out.

Headed for her daughter's room, she hoped Farah wouldn't be too annoyed at being interrupted during her Ramadan prayers.

&#x2766; &#x2766; &#x2766;

Sara had somehow managed to complete her homework, despite the fact that her mind continued to wander to the situation between Emir and Joni. She had stopped working only long enough to have dinner with her family and then returned immediately to her room, occasionally catching herself wondering if Emir might be sneaking out his window again.

*Stop it*, she scolded herself. *You're not his keeper. He gave you an explanation for his behavior, as ridiculous as it seems, so why not just accept it? Unless he shows you otherwise, just leave it alone!*

Her admonitions worked for a short time, but then the nagging suspicions returned, threatening to derail her research for her term paper. But at last she had accomplished her goal and completed the work that needed to be done for the evening. Now she was free to use her time as she wished.

*The chat room*, she thought. *I haven't talked with Nura in a while. Will she be there?*

Logging in, her heart skipped at least one beat when she saw that Nura was already online. Had she been waiting for her? Sara hoped so, even as she greeted her friend who lived so very far away.

&#x2766; &#x2766; &#x2766;

Nura's palms were sweaty. She was scarcely able to type, as she found herself hoping that Sara would appear. In less than fifteen minutes, she did, and Nura breathed a sigh of relief. Though she had opened up and talked with Farah, she needed someone detached to talk to now, someone who wasn't restricted by the same boundaries within which she and Farah existed. That meant Sara, for Nura knew no one else who fit that description.

*Hello,* Nura typed. *How are you, Sara? I've missed you.*

*I've missed you too. Where have you been?*

Nura hesitated. How did she answer that question? Sara had no real concept of what life was like for a young woman in the Saudi Kingdom, and Nura could only imagine the freedoms Sara enjoyed. There was no reason to get into all that.

*I've been busy,* Nura typed. *How is school?*

*Good, but lots of homework. How are your home studies?*

*Also busy, though the schedule is much lighter during Ramadan.*

*I can imagine—or at least I think I can. Do you do most of your work on the computer?*

*Nearly all of it, yes.*

*So do I, even though I go to school during the day. I just now finished my research for the term paper I'm working on, so I thought I'd check in and see if I could find you.*

*I'm glad you did.* Nura hesitated. What should she say now? How much should she tell Sara? She knew she had to tell her something, so she began typing once again. *Our family shared the Iftar dinner at my aunt and uncle's house last night. I was able to spend some time alone with my cousin Farah. She's a little older than me—eighteen—but we have a lot in common.*

Stunned at what she had just written, she realized it was true, though she wouldn't have thought so just twenty-four hours earlier.

*How nice that you have such a close relationship with your cousin,* Sara wrote. *My only relative who's near my own age is my younger brother, Emir, and I'm afraid we don't always have much in common. Right now I think he's hiding something from me—from the whole family, actually.*

Nura raised her eyebrows. Interesting. Should she follow up? Yes. It might just help her find a lead-in to her own family concern.

*Why do you think that about your brother?* Nura asked.

*I caught him climbing in his window last night. He says he went to see the girl down the street, a girl named Joni that we've known for years. He claims they care for one another, but somehow I don't believe him.*

Nura smiled as she typed her response. *Ah, Westerners and their dating. A little of that goes on here in the kingdom, but not much, and certainly not with my family. My parents will choose my husband, so I'm afraid I don't know anything about boyfriends or girlfriends or anything like that. Sorry!*

*LOL! Don't worry about it, my friend,* Sara wrote. *Sometimes I think your prearranged marriages aren't such a bad idea. At least they avoid a lot of problems and heartaches.*

*Maybe,* Nura conceded. *Though I know women who have been married against their will to men who cruelly abuse them, and they have no say in the matter. Thankfully, that's not the case in our family.*

*That must be terrible. I'm glad you don't have that problem, though I'm sure you have other problems to deal with . . . as we all do.*

Nura hesitated. Was this her opening? Yes. If she didn't take it, she might not get another one.

*Now that you mention it,* she wrote, *I do have a problem, and I'd like to tell you about it. Have you got time?*

*I've got all the time you need. Please tell me. I'm listening.*

Nura took a deep breath, and though her fingers were shaking, she began to tell her American friend about the conversation with her cousin the night before. The only thing she left out was the wordless confrontation with Kareem. Perhaps she would tell Sara about that some other time; for now, she just wanted Sara's reaction to Farah's dream.

Guilt washed over Zarah in waves
as she forced herself to answer.

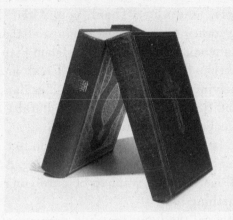

## Chapter 13

THE KNOCK ON HER DOOR CAUGHT FARAH BY SURPRISE, THOUGH she was relatively certain that the visitor had to be her mother. Seldom did anyone come to her room during the daylight hours of Ramadan, as they all knew how much the season meant to her and how seriously she practiced its disciplines. This morning, however, Farah lay quietly on her bed, wrestling with memories of her conversation with Nura the night before, the silent hostility of Kareem, and the possible scenarios that lay ahead as a result.

"Come in," she called, placing her hand on the Quran that sat open beside her on the bed. She felt badly about the attempt to deceive her mother into thinking she'd been reading, but it seemed the wisest move at the moment.

Sultana opened the door and smiled at her daughter, pausing briefly before advancing to Farah's bedside. As happened so often, Farah was struck by her mother's beauty, which she believed had bypassed her and been inherited by Nadia.

Farah returned her mother's smile as the older woman sat down on the edge of the bed. "Forgive me for interrupting you,"

Sultana said, her eyes darting to the Quran and back at Farah. "I see you are reading. You are so faithful, Farah—more than any young woman I have ever known."

Guilt washed over Farah in waves as she forced herself to answer. "*Shukran*," she said. "Thank you, Mom. But I'm sure there are many other women more dedicated than I am. And truly there is no woman more faithful to Islam than you."

Sultana's cheeks flushed briefly, and Farah imagined it was with joy at receiving such a compliment. Her dark eyes turned serious then, and Sultana laid her hand on Farah's as she spoke. "How are you feeling this morning?"

Farah lifted her eyebrows in surprise. "I'm fine. Why?"

"You seemed quieter than usual this morning. And with Nura not feeling well last night, I want to be sure you're not coming down with something too."

Farah swallowed the lump that had popped into her throat. "No, no. I'm fine, really. And I imagine Nura is too. Have you talked to Aunt Sakeena today?"

Sultana nodded. "Yes. I called her earlier, and she said she's keeping a close eye on your cousin. But if Nura feels better later, we thought we might all meet for shopping and something to eat tonight. Would you like that?"

Farah recoiled at the thought. She wasn't crazy about shopping under the best of circumstances, and now...

But if Nura felt well enough to come, perhaps the two of them would have a few moments alone to talk about what had happened the night before. Farah imagined that her cousin had as many questions and concerns as she did.

She smiled. "That would be nice, Mom—if Nura's feeling well enough to go, that is."

"Exactly." Sultana patted Farah's hand and smiled warmly. "I told your aunt I'd call her back later today to see how Nura is doing. We'll decide then." She rose from the bed and looked down at her daughter. "But now I must leave you alone to your reading and prayer. I'll let you know about Nura later."

When the door closed behind Sultana and Farah was once again alone, she felt the familiar tears that had threatened throughout the night, and this time she let them flow. She was simply too tired to fight them any longer.

∽❀∾ ∽❀∾ ∽❀∾

Nura was exhausted. She'd been at the computer most of the morning, talking with Sara about the conversation she'd had the night before with Farah. The two chat room friends had discussed Farah's dream, and Sara had told Nura that she'd heard rumors of many in the Muslim world being visited in their dreams by Isa. Could it be true—not only that Isa was appearing to other Muslims in their dreams, but also that He was more than one of the prophets of Islam, that He was actually the Son of God, as Sara claimed?

That was the stumbling block for Nura. Everything else Sara explained to her had made sense, and each time Nura had come to the point of accepting Sara's teachings, she stopped. *To accept Sara's beliefs is to commit the monumental sin of shirk—believing that God could actually indwell a human being. How is that possible? And yet...*

Nura shook her head and blinked her eyes. Oh, how she wrestled with these ideas so foreign to everything she had been taught her entire life! The wrestling went beyond the fear of what might happen to her if she did accept them, though that was surely a part of it. But to accept these teachings meant she would either have to keep her newfound beliefs to herself—or risk everything by changing the way she lived and worshipped. It was just too huge to contemplate!

Her mother had just told her about her aunt's invitation to meet them for shopping that night. Apparently it all depended on how Nura felt. How could she tell them she felt excited, terrified, confused? Yet there was nothing she wanted more than to see her cousin and try to find some time to talk with her alone. She had to sort this out with someone before she came to a final conclusion, and she knew she couldn't put it off much longer.

∽❀∾ ∽❀∾ ∽❀∾

This time Emir had waited until he was certain everyone had gone to bed for the night and he wouldn't have any more surprise visitors to his room. It was nearly midnight when he slipped from his bed and removed the screen from his window. How many times through the years had he climbed out onto the eaves and then onto the overhanging branches from the huge old apple tree that stood as a silent sentry in the yard? From there it was a short, simple slide to the bottom—and nearly as easy a climb on the return trip.

He was on the ground and racing to his destination in a matter of minutes. His heart hammered in his ears, more from adrenaline than exertion. This could turn out very well for him ... or not. Either way, he had no choice but to go, and he didn't dare be late. He was in too far to back out now, and he wasn't even sure he wanted to if he could. If all went well, he might finally find his place in life. It was obvious he didn't fit in with his family's Christian lifestyle; he had long since given up believing that any of the many Bible stories he had heard growing up could possibly be true. And though he loved his family and didn't want to hurt them, he had to make his own way in life. To have the respect of his home-boys was the desire that drove him, as he rounded the corner and his destination came into view. Thank goodness there was no school tomorrow, because he doubted he was going to get much sleep before the sun came up in the morning.

When Kareem returned home at the end of the day, he scarcely remembered anything his father had said to him as they walked together along the way. Kareem could never understand why his father insisted on walking to and from their factory or the mosque when the family had two perfectly good cars. But Ahmed was a practical man and saw no reason for driving such short distances.

Kareem paid little attention to anything his father said, as he was still fuming about catching Farah and Nura together, whispering about things that he knew they shouldn't be discussing. It infuriated him that he hadn't been able to hear their words, but he was determined that the very next time the two girls got together, he would find a way to listen in on their conversation. Whatever they were up to, he would expose it, and at last his father would see Farah for what she really was.

As it turned out, he didn't have to wait long. The family had no sooner sat down to eat their evening meal than his mother said to her husband, "I just spoke with Sakeena, and Nura is feeling much better. She and Sakeena would like to meet me and the girls for some shopping tonight." She raised her eyebrows questioningly. "Do you have any objections? Would you prefer that we stay home?"

Kareem nearly snorted with contempt, but he managed to control himself. Why did his mother even bother to ask? Her request was only a formality. When had his father denied his mother or sisters anything? It would certainly not be that way when Kareem had his own family. His wife and daughters would obey him unquestioningly or pay the price.

Kareem listened as his father answered, his words as predictable as Kareem had imagined. "Of course not," Ahmed said, smiling as he spoke. "Why should I object? And why should you stay home? You and the girls go, and have a good time. Kareem and I will be fine right here, especially after such a delicious meal." He patted his ample stomach and turned to Kareem. "Isn't that right, my son?"

Kareem forced a smile and nodded. "Absolutely," he said. "I think it's a great idea." A great idea that Kareem was building upon, even as he spoke.

Zarah and Nura, their head
coverings back in place, quickly
and silently made their way
to the facilities.

## Chapter 14

THE PREDAWN DARKNESS SHOWED LITTLE PROMISE OF GIVING way to the sunrise anytime soon, and Emir relaxed only slightly in the knowledge that he would make it home before his family woke up. It was a special school holiday, some sort of in-service day for the teachers, so Sara would sleep in. Even his parents wouldn't be up for an hour or two yet, so he doubted he'd have any trouble slipping back inside his window undetected.

Had it really been only a few hours since he'd raced to his meeting, terrified yet excited at what might transpire? All the hours of waiting and wondering, and now he knew. He had his answer, and it was easily as bad as he had feared, and worse. The faint memory of the little old lady who often walked the neighborhood with her ancient Chihuahua flashed through his mind, but he hardened his heart and reminded himself of what would happen to him if he didn't follow through. Besides, it wasn't like she was going to get hurt or anything... unless something went terribly wrong.

The dim outline of the stately apple tree that waited beside the house to escort him back inside now beckoned him to quicken his steps. His feet longed to obey, but his heart resisted. Why had he ever thought he wanted to be a part of this? Why had it seemed so important to prove himself to his peers, to belong to something so dangerous and deadly? What had begun as a mere curiosity had now taken over his life, and he nearly retched at the thought of where it might lead him. Why hadn't he been content to pursue his studies and sports, as his family assumed he was doing?

His parents—and Sara. They would be horrified if they knew. How could he even consider shaming them so? But it was too late. To back out now would be worse than to take his chances and follow through. He had to admit, however, that the plan sounded foolish, and his chances at pulling off his part without a hitch were nearly slim and none. But if it didn't work... He couldn't even let himself consider the possible outcomes.

Discouraged and fighting depression, Emir arrived at the foot of the apple tree and looked up into its fruit-laden branches. The delicious Rome apples would soon be ready to harvest. Where would he be and what would have happened to him by the time this year's crop of apples was gone?

৯৯৯ ৯৯৯ ৯৯৯

The *suqs* were more crowded than the last time Farah and her mother and sister had browsed them afterhours. Farah imagined it had a lot to do with the fact that the day had been a few degrees cooler than normal, and people were determined to get outside and make the best of it now that the sun had been down for a while. Instead of heading straight for the air-conditioned comfort of inside restaurants and cafés, shoppers seemed content to spend at least a little more time outside.

All three of the women had donned the coolest *abayas* they owned, as they always did when going out during the hottest times of the year. When Nadia complained to her mother that she was still uncomfortable, she was quieted and reminded of the need for good Muslim women to be modest when in public. For the first time in her life, as Farah listened to her mother's admonitions, she found herself questioning the requirement, though she quickly scolded herself and dismissed the thought.

*Why would my dreams about Isa or my discussion with Nura make me think differently about my religious practices? Of course I should remain modest in public; all women should! My body must be completely reserved for my future husband—whoever he might be.*

She knew enough from her studies and her Internet browsing, as well as from reading books and talking with others, that not all women lived as they did in the Saudi Kingdom, not even all Muslim women. Farah had always thought that a great tragedy, as she was certain the restrictions imposed upon them in the kingdom were for their own protection. For the first time in her life, she was beginning to question those certainties.

After nearly an hour of walking and shopping, the women arrived at the restaurant where they had planned to meet Sakeena and Nura. Farah's heart rate escalated when she realized the two weren't there, but by the time Farah and her mother and sister had been inside for a couple of minutes, their companions arrived.

The five were soon seated in a booth with curtains drawn and were able to remove their head coverings so they could sip their coffee and enjoy their pastries while they talked. Once again the conversation centered around shopping and clothes, with the two older women carrying the majority of the discussion and Nadia jumping in when she got the chance. Farah and Nura sat nearly silent, pretending to be absorbed in munching on their sweets while desperately trying to telegraph messages to one another with their eyes. At last Farah excused herself to go to the restroom, hoping that Nura would join her but that Nadia and the others would stay behind. Much to her relief, it happened exactly that way.

Farah and Nura, their head coverings back in place, quickly and silently made their way to the facilities. Once inside, they remained silent while the room's only other occupant washed her hands before exiting. And then they were alone.

"I thought she'd never leave," Nura whispered, removing her head covering as Farah did the same. "Thank you for thinking of this. I was so anxious to talk with you!"

"So was I," Farah agreed. "But this is not a good time or place, do you think? Others will be coming and going, and we just can't take the chance. Maybe you can talk your parents into coming over again tomorrow night, or to invite my family to your house, which might be even better. Kareem is a lot less likely to be snooping around at your place."

Nura nodded. "You're right. I'm worried about what he might have heard. He's always frightened me a little, even though my friends are jealous that I'm his cousin. They all think he's so handsome, which I suppose he is. But..." She paused before continuing, her expression troubled. "Has he said anything?"

"Nothing," Farah assured her. "Not yet anyway. But I catch him glaring at me all the time. We'll have to be really careful not to let him hear us."

"Not to let who hear you?"

The question seemed to come out of nowhere, and both Farah and Nura spun toward the sound at the exact same moment they realized they were no longer alone. Though the intruder was dressed in a full *abaya* and head covering, her familiarity made it apparent that the one who had walked in on them was Nadia. The wording of Nadia's question led Farah to believe her sister hadn't heard any of the previous conversation, but that small consolation didn't help her heart rate slow down any.

"Nadia," she said, "I didn't hear you come in."

"That's because I just got here—and because you were too busy worrying about someone else hearing you. Who were you talking about? Kareem?"

Farah swallowed. How much could she trust Nadia? Very little, she was sure. Taking her into their confidence was not an option. But what choice did she have? And then one very faint hope surfaced in the flurry of her mind.

"Yes, Nura and I were just talking about Kareem," Farah ventured, sensing her cousin grow tense beside her. "We were saying how we'd like to surprise him sometime by making his favorite food when he least expects it. What do you think? Would that be a good idea?"

Nadia took off her head covering, revealing a puzzled expression. "I didn't think you even liked Kareem," she said, directing her words at Farah. "Why would you want to do something special for him?"

Farah wished she had left her own head covering in place to hide her flaming cheeks. "Of course I like him," she said. "He's my brother."

"He's mine too," Nadia answered. "That doesn't mean I think he's very nice." She paused, and a smile lit up her eyes. "Because he's not, you know."

Nadia laughed then, and the others joined in, though Farah noticed Nura's laughter sounded as nervous as her own. But if Nadia had believed their story, then they would be all right—at least for now. It was obvious, though, that they would have to be more discreet in the future.

∗ ∗ ∗

It had been a long and frustrating night for Kareem, as his father insisted on their spending time together, thus preventing Kareem's attempt to follow the women and try to find a way to listen in on any conversations between Farah and Nura. But at last Ahmed had gone to bed, and Kareem was free to leave.

But where would he go? It was after midnight, and it would be difficult to know when and where the women had decided to meet. He knew some of their favorite places, but there was no guarantee they would be at any of them if he went there now. He could call his mother on her mobile phone, he supposed, but if he asked where they were, Farah and Nura would suspect that he was trying to track them down and they'd be watching for him. It would have been difficult enough to find a way to listen in on them if they weren't expecting him to try, but calling ahead would ruin any chance he might have.

He was fuming in his room when he heard the women return. Would it do any good to confront Farah? No. He had nothing specific to ask her, and she would certainly not offer any information, so it would be a wasted effort. But as he heard the chattering voices outside his room, Nadia's voice rose above the others, and he realized he just might have a chance to glean something from the otherwise wasted night after all.

❧❦ ❧❦ ❧❦

It was shortly after noon by the time Sara heard any noises coming from her brother's room. Though she had slept late herself, taking full advantage of the holiday from school, she had begun to wonder if Emir was ever going to get up. She had considered peeking in to be sure he was even there, but scolded herself for being so nosy. Both Emir and Joni had given her an explanation for her brother's strange behavior, and until or unless she found out otherwise, she would simply have to accept it.

Now, as she sat at her desk in the early hours of the afternoon and checked her emails, she heard the unmistakable sounds of a teenaged boy starting his day. What Emir called music but Sara considered noise drifted through the wall that separated their rooms, and she knew for certain that Emir was where he was supposed to be. *Physically, at least,* she thought. *But spiritually? Lord, I know that's his problem. He's been brought up in the church, and he knows all the facts about Christianity...but he doesn't know You. Please, Lord, do something in Emir's life to open the eyes of his heart to see You!*

Since Sara herself had come to the place of making a wholehearted commitment to Christ a few years earlier, it grieved her to realize that her brother wasn't there yet. She had prayed for him, certainly, but now she wondered if her prayers had lacked the passion they needed. Maybe it was because she hadn't sensed that Emir was flirting with trouble or danger until now. But was he... really? Or was it just her imagination? Her mother hadn't seemed in the least concerned that her teenaged son was still sleeping when it was almost lunchtime, so maybe Emir's behavior wasn't so strange after all. Maybe Sara was imagining a problem where there was none.

It was the not knowing that bothered her most. Maybe she should talk to her parents and let them know of her suspicions—and why she had them. Enlisting their prayer support, particularly since she knew they were already praying for Emir, couldn't be anything but positive. Why hadn't she done it before? Her mother and father had a right to know if there was a problem with one of their children. Yet to explain it to them, Sara would have to betray Emir's confidence about Joni.

Turning from her computer, she closed her eyes and rested her head in her folded hands, her elbows leaning on the desk. "I don't know what's going on with Emir," she whispered, "but You do, Lord. Help me to know what to do. And please, please bring him to You before he gets into serious trouble, Father."

"I want nothing from either of
you — except the truth.
And that I will get on my own."

## Chapter 15

D ESPITE HER EXHAUSTION FROM NOT HAVING SLEPT THE
previous night, Farah had been concerned that she would
be unable to do so when they returned from their evening out
with Nura and her mother. When Farah and her mother and
sister had returned home, Nadia was still chattering excitedly,
but Farah had excused herself and gone straight to her room,
as had her mother soon after. Later Farah heard Nadia talking
with Kareem, but the conversation was brief and seemed to have
faded into the distance. Relieved to be alone at last, Farah had
lain down on her bed and closed her eyes, thinking she could at
least rest if she was unable to sleep. She hadn't even bothered to
turn out the light.

Some time later she felt herself jerked back into reality as she
sensed she was being watched. Surprised to realize that she must
have been sleeping after all, she opened her eyes to see Kareem
standing over her. His face was expressionless, and somehow
that frightened her more than his usual malevolent glare.

"What are you doing here?" she asked, sitting upright at the realization that perhaps her brother had come to tell her that something had happened to Nadia or one of their parents. "Is everything all right? Has something happened?"

Kareem lifted his eyebrows. "I don't know, dear sister. Why don't you tell me? You seem to be the one with all the secrets these days."

A stab of fear pierced Farah's heart, but she told herself he couldn't possibly know anything. He was just fishing, looking for something to report to her father. She had always suspected that Kareem hated her and would like nothing better than to discredit her in her family's eyes, but now she was certain of it. Worse yet, she was dangerously close to giving him what he was looking for.

"I don't know what you're talking about," she said, her voice trembling only slightly.

Kareem sneered. "I think you do. And I promise you that I'm going to find out what it is. And when I do..."

The threat hung in the air between them, as Farah fought for control, determined not to let him see how successful he had been at frightening her, for surely that was his intent. Holding her gaze steady, she watched as he turned and stalked to the door before stopping to look back at her.

"By the way," he said, "you and Nura don't need to bother trying to surprise me by fixing me something special. I want nothing from either of you—except the truth. And that I will get on my own."

The door had scarcely closed behind him before Farah dissolved into tears.

≈≈ ≈≈ ≈≈

Nura did not make it a practice to go outside at night by herself, but this was an exception. The slightly cooler temperatures, coupled with the fragrance of roses from the garden, had drawn her out into the enclosed patio where she could enjoy the flowers bathed in moonlight while still remaining secluded from the outside world. Nura knew that even her mother occasionally came out here after dark, to sit and think, and perhaps to pray.

The thought snagged her attention, as she rested on a stone bench beside a small waterfall. The bubbling sounds of the water eased her restlessness as she wondered about her mother's prayer habits. Did she ever talk to Allah when she was alone like this, or did she reserve her prayers for the formal times that were required of her as a faithful Muslim? Nura had always considered her relationship with her mother a close one, but now she realized how little below the surface she knew about the woman who had birthed and raised her. How much less did she know about her own father!

Nura closed her eyes and pictured her father's face. She had adored him for as long as she could remember. He was her provider and protector—a strict one, yes, but loving and fair, or so it seemed to her. She also knew that not all her friends enjoyed such a safe relationship with their father. She and her cousins, Farah and Nadia, were fortunate indeed.

She snapped her eyes open, her head lifted as she stared into the moonlight. *Just how safe will that relationship be if Kareem—or anyone else, for that matter—exposes our secrets? Will our fathers understand? Will they support us, or at least, overlook our transgressions? Or will we, like so many other wives and daughters and sisters in the kingdom, pay a lethal price for what would surely be considered a betrayal of Islam?*

Despite the still-warm temperatures, a chill passed over Nura as once again the vision of a young girl, struggling against her captors and being held underwater until her flailing ceased, teased her memory and tortured her heart. A young teenager. The child had not lived to grow up, and her transgression had been no worse than Nura's.

The realization robbed her of the garden's beauty, and she rose from the bench and returned to the seclusion of her room.

∽∾ ∽∾ ∽∾

Emir had been awake for nearly an hour, playing his music to make sure his sister knew he was there and everything was normal in his world. But, of course, it wasn't. The very thought caused beads of sweat to break out on his forehead, as he considered what would happen when he crawled out of his window tonight. The last couple of times he'd sneaked out for preparation meetings only; tonight would be the real thing. Tomorrow morning he would either wake up in his own bed, a lazy Saturday in front of him, or —

No. He couldn't let himself think of the alternatives. Snatching up his cell phone, he cranked up his music another notch. He wasn't about to risk anyone overhearing what he had to say.

❧ ❧ ❧

Kareem smiled to himself as he padded back to his room. He had accomplished exactly what he'd set out to do. Farah was squirming, frightened even, and it was all the confirmation he needed to reassure him that she was up to something. Now she knew that he was on to her, even if he hadn't yet discovered what she was hiding. But he would know soon enough. He would not relent until he had exposed Farah for what she was. And if he had to use Nadia to make that happen, the victory would be all the sweeter.

*So my sister and cousin want to do something special for me,* he mused as he stood at his bedroom window gazing out into the moonlit courtyard. *As if I would believe that! Even Nadia doubted it, and it didn't take more than five minutes to get that information out of her. Now, with two of us watching Farah, it will be easier to catch her at something. Nadia can go where I can't, and she knows better than to keep things from me.* He smiled. Yes, it was just a matter of time, and at last he would have complete triumph over the sister who had never accepted her true position in a world of men. And if he could take his female cousin down in the process, why not? Neither of them meant a thing to him. Eliminating them would be no different than swatting a couple of annoying flies. And he would gain a stronger position with his father in the process.

❧ ❧ ❧

As the earliest rays of dawn began to light the skies over Riyadh on this last Saturday before Ramadan's Night of Power and even

Farah and Nura had managed to drift off to sleep, the darkness of night was just beginning to envelop the little town of River Crest. A light drizzle had fallen earlier, but now the clouds had broken up and nearly disappeared as a smattering of stars began to twinkle in the vast Pacific Northwest heavens.

Emir, his stomach tense and palms sweating, had scarcely been able to get through dinner. But he had forced himself to eat, not wanting to draw any attention to himself. He had been greatly relieved to learn that Sara was going over to a friend's house to study and spend the night. At least he wouldn't have to worry about her coming into his room and finding him gone again. And as long as he didn't leave until after he was certain his parents had gone to bed, he wouldn't have to be concerned about being caught.

At least not by his family, he reminded himself as he stood in front of the mirror over his dresser, staring at the one who looked back at him as if he were a stranger. The thought darted through his mind that if anything went wrong he could end up in jail—or worse—before the night was over, but he dismissed it as quickly as it had come. They had told him to concentrate on what he had to do, rather than worrying about what could go wrong. If all went as planned and he didn't slip up, he would no longer be treated as an initiate but would be considered a full-fledged member. But if he failed....

No, he couldn't let himself think about that. They had already warned him what would happen if he didn't stick exactly to the plan. It was too late to back out now. Though at times he wished he'd never allowed his curiosity or desire for acceptance to drive him to such a precarious spot, he now had no choice but to follow through.

He nodded at his image in the mirror as if sealing an agreement. He would follow the plan as ordered. He would not slip up. And by tomorrow he would be one of them.

He heard a car door slam outside, and he knew his mother was taking Sara to her friend's house. It wouldn't be long now. Once his mother returned, she and Emir's father would watch a little TV or read before heading upstairs to bed. They would both stop by his room to say good night, and then he would give them an hour or so to be sure they were asleep. After that, it would be time, and his life would change forever—one way or the other.

❧ ❧ ❧

By the time Emir arrived at his destination, his heart was pounding so hard and fast he was sure everyone within a mile could hear it. He had dressed in black, as instructed, carrying only a six-inch switchblade for protection. Would he need it? He hoped not. It was one thing to take something that wasn't his; it was something else entirely to hurt someone in the process. Though it had been several years since he'd prayed, he found himself doing so as he slid open the window to the old woman's house. He'd been assured that she was always in bed early and slept without her hearing aids and that her dog was as deaf as she was, so there was no way either one would hear him. He knew the layout of the house and exactly where to go to find the valuables, so what could go wrong?

Yet there had to be some element of danger involved, or this wouldn't count as an initiation. So what was it? What hadn't anyone told him? He was trusting that he had all the information he needed to pull this off, but what if those whose instructions he blindly followed weren't trustworthy after all? What if he was being set up?

The questions rolled through his mind and churned in his gut as he slid one leg into the now open window, his silent prayers intensifying with each shallow breath. Would God even listen to him at such a time and after such a long absence? He doubted it, but he wasn't about to stop begging for His protection until he was out of this place and back, had reported in as instructed, and was home, safe and sound, in his own room once again.

By the time she reached twenty-five,
Emir's heart was racing so fast he
could scarcely breathe.

## Chapter 16

Farah had managed to doze off only sporadically after Kareem's visit, and now the first call to prayer was ringing out from the minarets. During the long hours of the night, Farah had come to a conclusion: She must reject what was most certainly an imaginary call from the prophet Isa and rededicate herself to Allah and the true religion of Islam. For certainly her dreams had been only that—the results of an overactive imagination combined with her desire to be more faithful and devout. No doubt the dreams had come to test her, and she had nearly fallen prey to the temptation, particularly when Nura told her of her own dabbling with the false religion of the infidels. But now Farah was determined to reject such talk and focus only on the truth. She would also make it a point to pray for and encourage Nura to come to the same decision.

As she nearly fell to her knees in gratitude at having come to such a conclusion, the familiarity of her prayer rug beneath her comforted her aching heart. She wouldn't even allow herself to consider that she might have made her decision based on fear, for what did the reason matter? The important thing was that she had finally done what was right, and even if Kareem didn't believe or accept it, at least he would have no further grounds for suspecting or reporting her behavior to her father or anyone else.

With the final week of Ramadan now underway, Farah rejoiced at her personal triumph, even as she prayed that Allah would reward her with a deeper faith and appreciation for her religion. She also prayed that her new commitment would be evident to all who saw her.

∽∾∽ ∽∾∽ ∽∾∽

Emir was no sooner standing inside the house, the kitchen window still open beside him, than the yapping began. The sounds came from a room at the opposite side of the little house, a room that Emir knew from the planning meeting was the bedroom where the old woman slept. But they'd told him the dog was deaf, just like the old woman! Had they lied on purpose, or did they just not know? Either way, if the dog had heard him and kept on barking, the woman would no doubt get up to check things out.

He reminded himself of the knife, but took little comfort in its presence as he considered what he would have to do with it if the woman truly did come in and catch him. *What do I do?* Should he try to grab the valuables before the woman came in—or were there any? Had that been a lie too? Emir felt beads of sweat pop out on his forehead. He wiped his already clammy hands on his pants. The smart thing would be to scramble right back out the window and race into the darkness before the old woman came in and saw him, but what would his homies say about that? The instructions had been to carry out the plan, no matter what. So what was he supposed to do with the old woman when she confronted him?

He didn't have long to consider his options because the sounds of barking were quickly drawing closer. And then the kitchen light flipped on, flooding the room and nearly blinding him in the process. He blinked in disbelief at the woman who stood in the doorway, her hand still on the light switch. She was

112

wrapped in an old blue robe and wearing scruffy slippers and some sort of pink plastic curlers in her white hair. Her over-fed brown Chihuahua stood in front of her, barking as if its life depended on being heard in the next county. The only thing Emir could find to be grateful for at that moment was that the woman liked small dogs. If the barker had been a German shepherd or a Doberman, he would have been in serious trouble.

And yet, in the few seconds it took to process the unbelievable scene, he knew he was in trouble anyway. What was he supposed to do? Threaten the woman and her dog with his knife? Force them back into the bedroom so he could finish what he'd come for? He didn't even want to think of what would be required of him if they didn't cooperate. If only he'd worn something to cover his face! But he'd been assured it wouldn't be necessary because the house's only residents would never even know he was there. He'd be able to take whatever valuables she might have and get out without anyone being the wiser.

Obviously that wasn't the case—and perhaps had never been. It suddenly occurred to him that he'd been set up—not to steal from the old woman but to kill her. They knew she would confront him, and they wanted to know if he had the guts to finish her off. Emir knew he didn't but hoped the old woman didn't know it as well. His best option now seemed a bluff, so he decided to go for it.

"Get back in your room," he ordered, quickly brandishing his switchblade and praying the woman would obey. "Now!"

The flash in her eyes told Emir his plan was not going to work. "Young man," she said, drawing herself up to her full five feet while the Chihuahua's barking became more frantic, "I most certainly will not. This is my home, and God is my protector. It is you who needs to leave, and I will give you exactly thirty seconds to do so before I call the police."

She moved her hand from the light switch to the old-fashioned yellow phone that hung on the wall just inches from the doorway. "One… two… three…" she counted slowly, her eyes never moving from Emir's face.

By the time she reached twenty-five, Emir's heart was rac-ing so fast he could scarcely breathe. Dismissing the jumble of thoughts in his mind, he threw a leg back over the transom and hopped outside before she could reach thirty. Dropping his knife in the process, he didn't even turn back to try to retrieve it. Instead he ran as fast as he could into the night, praying he would reach the safety of the apple tree below his window before any of his homies caught sight of him. And he had no doubt that at least one of them had been assigned to watch him and report back to the others. When they found out he had run from the woman's home to his own house, rather than coming to them as ordered, they'd know he'd failed. Worse yet, they'd know he was a coward and wouldn't trust him not to snitch. The results would not be pretty.

He knew all that, and yet he kept running toward his house. He just couldn't seem to get himself to turn around and go the other way.

❧❧❧ ❧❧❧ ❧❧❧

Nura's heart was heavy as she lay in bed, having been awakened after a restless sleep by the call to prayer, which she ignored. She had given up trying to force herself to her prayer rug in the morning, though she would certainly observe the required fast throughout the day, as she was too upset to even think of eating anything. She hoped to avoid her parents as much as possible, and she was seriously considering calling Farah to see if she would come over. It would be a bit more difficult than usual to reach her cousin during Ramadan, since it was expected that Nura as well as Farah would observe the required prayer times through-out the day, but she would make it a point to call between those times. Even then she hoped that Farah would answer, rather than her mother. The less people involved in the communication, the better. True, Farah and Nura were cousins, and there was no reason they shouldn't talk to one another on the family phone, even though their parents had opted not to give them mobile phones of their own. But they had never made a practice of calling one another before, and Nura knew it wouldn't be wise to bring too much attention to the cousins' suddenly deepening friendship—

particularly with Kareem already watching them with a suspicious and vindictive eye.

As Nura lay in bed, knowing she should at least get up and make a pretense at observing the first prayer time, her eyes wandered to the blank computer screen on her desk. She would so like to be able to talk to Sara and to let her know what she was feeling, but the girl was undoubtedly sound asleep by now. How Nura envied her American friend and what was no doubt an easy life with few, if any, cares! Even the pressures and added responsibilities that went with the freedoms Sara enjoyed sounded like a welcome alternative to the oppressive fear that had plagued Nura throughout the night. If only she were free to more openly pursue the claims of the prophet Isa and make her decision about Him without fear of repercussions! If she could, she might ultimately reject those claims and return to her Muslim faith, but at least it would be by choice and not out of terror.

The thought reinforced her decision. She would find a way to speak with Farah today, and then tonight she would connect with Sara online and tell her everything that was going on in her heart, in her mind, and in her life. It was time to make a commitment, regardless of the outcome. She could not go on any longer without doing so.

⌘ ⌘ ⌘

The yard and the tree were in sight, and Emir allowed himself to think that he just might make it. What would happen after that he had no idea, but at least he would be safe and sound in his own home. Could his parents protect him from the punishment he would most certainly receive for failing his assignment? Probably not, even if he locked himself inside the house and never left again. Sooner or later he would have to face the wrath of those who demanded strict obedience and showed no mercy—and who had ordered him to come straight to them after leaving the old woman's house. But what else could he have done? The woman had confronted him, refusing to do what he told her even when he threatened her with a knife. Why had he been so foolish as to believe their story that both the woman and her dog were deaf?

115

Kathi Macias

And why did his intended victim have to be a woman of faith who wasn't afraid of death? Even then, he knew he should have gone to the assigned meeting place anyway. It would have been bad, but if they caught him now, it would be worse.

His foot landed on the relative safety of his lawn, but he hadn't even had time to take a second or third running step before he heard the screech of tires rounding the block and racing in his direction. He knew without looking back that the speeding vehicle was coming for him—and he wasn't going to make it. Racing blindly toward the tree, his arms outstretched as if to reach it sooner, he felt the burning explosion in his back almost instantaneously with the first sounds of the automatic rounds. The impact knocked him to the ground as the sound of shots continued before the car raced away, leaving Emir facedown in the grass, just inches from the tree.

"Help me," he whispered. "Help . . ."

But the darkness closed in before he could say another word.

It was as if her entire life was at
a crossroads, and she was compelled
to make a choice.

## Chapter 17

SARA AWOKE AS IF SHE'D BEEN SNAGGED BY AN ELECTRIC WIRE. The jolt sat her up in bed and set her heart pounding in her ears. Had she just imagined she'd heard gunfire and squealing tires? Surely it was just a nightmare, launching her back into reality.

But then she heard her father, Yusef, calling to her mother to dial 911. The front door opened then, and Sara knew her father had gone outside. No! If someone was out there shooting, he should remain inside where it was safe.

And then she heard her mother's frantic voice, telling someone to send the police and an ambulance quickly. *Oh, Father God, what's happening?*

Throwing on her robe, Sara didn't even bother with slippers as she raced out her bedroom door, nearly colliding with her mother in the already-lit hallway.

"What is it?" she cried. "Mom, what happened?"

Her mother still held the phone in her hand, her wide eyes glistening with tears.

"I don't know," she said. "We heard guns—and a car. Your father insisted on going out to see if anyone was hurt and needed help. The police are coming."

Layla glanced then at the closed door to Emir's room. "Go to your brother," she instructed. "You two wait there together. I'll watch at the front door in case your father needs me, but I'll come and tell you as soon as we know something."

Sara wanted to protest, to insist on waiting with her mother, but she realized this was no time for arguments. Someone should wait with Emir, and she was the obvious one to do it. Thank God she'd decided not to stay overnight at her friend's house as she'd originally planned! She needed to be here with her family.

As her mother hurried downstairs, Sara turned to her brother's door, even as the realization that he had not come out of his room struck her in the chest. Why? How could anyone not hear what happened, and who wouldn't immediately try to find out what was going on? Perhaps he was watching out of his window....

Her hand trembling, Sara turned the knob and pushed open the door. "Emir?" she called. When he didn't answer, she flipped on the light. Once again, she found his room empty, and this time she knew he was not out with Joni. Her heart nearly stopped at the implications, as she turned and raced down the stairs, screaming her brother's name.

∽✼∽ ∽✼∽ ∽✼∽

The first prayer time of the day was completed, and Nura couldn't wait any longer. She dialed her cousin's number and prayed Farah would answer. When Kareem's voice came on the line, she quickly clicked off, her heart racing as she realized what she'd done. She had assumed Kareem would have been at the mosque, but apparently he had observed the first call to prayer at home. Since he'd answered the phone, he had no doubt seen her number come up before he answered, so now he knew she was avoiding him. She had made the problem worse without meaning to, when she could so easily have simply greeted him and asked for Farah. Was there anything wrong with cousins calling one another? Of course not, though admittedly it was a bit early in the day for such a thing. But her fear of Kareem had overcome her good judgment, and she had reacted without thinking.

What now? Should she wait awhile and then call back, acting as if nothing had happened? If anyone asked why she'd called earlier and hung up, she could always say she had dialed and then decided it was too early and she should call back later. Surely Kareem and his father would be gone soon...wouldn't they? Oh, how she despised this second-guessing and sneaking around, as if she were doing something terrible! She wanted only to know the truth about Isa, one of Islam's own prophets. Was that so terrible?

A shiver passed over her as she placed her phone back in the stand on her dresser and looked at herself in the mirror. Who was she fooling? Certainly not herself—and certainly not Kareem, even if he didn't know the details about what was going on with her or Farah. He somehow sensed that they were moving beyond the accepted boundaries for women in the Saudi Kingdom, and he wasn't going to stand for it. Nura had always suspected Kareem had a mean streak, and something told her she was in danger of finding out just how mean her cousin could actually be.

And yet she knew she could no longer deny her quest or put off her decision. Soon—very soon—she was going to have to make some very serious choices, and there was little doubt in her mind that she could pay equally serious consequences. That she and Farah had at last connected in the midst of their mutual seeking for truth made the experience bittersweet.

⁓⁓⁓ ⁓⁓⁓ ⁓⁓⁓

By the time Sara descended the stairs and reached the open front door where her mother stood, they could hear their father's cries.

"Emir! Oh, Emir, my son," he wailed, "what has happened to you? Emir, answer me! Emir!"

Sara and Layla exchanged terrified glances, then together raced out the door and toward the base of the apple tree, where Yusef cradled his motionless son in his arms, crying and praying as he rocked him back and forth.

"Emir!" Layla screamed, as the women came close enough to make out the face of the young boy in Yusef's embrace. The terrified mother fell to her knees beside her husband and joined him in his weeping and praying, while Sara stood motionless, her eyes wide and her mind frozen in time. What had happened? Emir wasn't moving, her parents were crying, and she'd heard gunshots and squealing tires. Surely someone hadn't shot her brother! Why would anyone do such a thing? Sara knew Emir had been secretive lately, and though she shoved aside the thought that she might have been an accomplice in whatever he was involved in, the stab of guilt brought her back from the numbness of disbelief.

"Emir!" she screamed. "Emir, what happened?"

But her voice was drowned out in the sound of approaching sirens.

⚉⚉⚉

Though Nura was nearly certain that Sara would not be online at this hour, she needed to think of something besides her foolish act of hanging up on Kareem. Logging in to the chat room, she held her breath and prayed that perhaps the American was having trouble sleeping and might be sitting at her computer after all. But no one named Sara greeted her, and she didn't know any of the others well enough to join in the conversations. She decided she would lurk in the background for a while and try to forget about Kareem.

It was pointless. Even when she left the chat room and tried to find something else of interest on the Internet, her mind would not focus. It was as if her entire life was at a crossroads, and she was compelled to make a choice. One way would lead her down a safe and comfortable path toward a prearranged marriage, children, a home, and continued worship of Allah and observation of her Muslim religion. The other road...

A chill snaked up her spine at the thought. The other road beckoned with an almost irresistible call to a depth of truth and love that she had never even imagined could exist, let alone be hers. But oh, the price that could be exacted for taking that road!

She turned off her computer and once again picked up her phone. Surely Kareem and Uncle Ahmed had left for the day, and either her aunt or one of her female cousins would answer. All she wanted was to arrange something with Farah so they could talk. Maybe just a few words on the phone, if they were sure no one would pick up and overhear them. She'd been thinking that she'd like to show Farah the chat room and get her opinion of what she thought about it. Until now Nura had only told her about it. Why not introduce her directly to Sara?

The thought encouraged her. With trembling fingers, she dialed the number and waited.

❧❧❧ ❧❧❧ ❧❧❧

As the attendants loaded Emir into the ambulance and closed the door, allowing Layla to ride inside with him, Sara stood with her hands over her mouth, staring straight ahead. When Yusef spoke to her, she didn't respond. Then he touched her arm.

"Sara," he said, "we must hurry and get dressed and go to the hospital. Help me get clothes for your mother as well. Come on. We haven't much time."

Sara turned toward her father, feeling her eyes widen when she saw the lines of grief in his face. Could someone age that quickly? The one who had always seemed the strongest man on earth now stood before her, seeming shorter and much more frail than she remembered.

"Sara," he said, his dark brows drawing together, "do you hear me? We have to get dressed and go to the hospital—now!"

"Hospital?" Sara finally managed to squeak out the word. Taking a deep breath, she spoke again. "You mean Emir isn't dead? He's going to be all right?"

Yusef looked puzzled. "Didn't you hear the ambulance attendants? Yes, he's still alive, but his condition is serious. We need to be there with him and your mother. And we need to call everyone we know to pray." He leaned close and peered into her eyes. "Do you understand, Sara? Are you hearing me?"

Slowly, Sara nodded. Yes, she understood. She heard his words. Emir was still alive—for now. But what if God didn't answer their prayers? If her brother died, it would certainly be her fault.

She swallowed. "Yes, Daddy," she said, not realizing she had reverted to her childhood name for her father. "I hear you. Let's go."

Nura sat stunned in her room.

## Chapter 18

Farah sat at her desk, so focused on reading her Quran that she didn't even hear the knock on her door. It was her mother's voice that finally penetrated her concentration and caused her to lift her head.

"Farah," Sultana repeated as she stood in the open doorway, holding a phone in her hands, "it's Nura. She's called a couple of times now and wants to speak with you. Didn't you hear the phone?"

Farah raised her eyebrows. Actually, she had heard it but assumed it was for her mother. Even if she'd known it was for her, she probably would have ignored it anyway, particularly if she'd known it was Nura.

"I'm sorry, Mom," she said, smiling. "Did Nura say what she wanted? Is it urgent, or can I call her back?"

The look of disapproval on Sultana's face was evident as she held out the phone in front of her, covering the receiver with her other hand. "Why don't you ask her yourself?" she whispered.

With a sigh Farah nodded and took the phone from her, offering a brief thanks as she did so. When Sultana had gone and closed the door behind her, Farah put the phone to her ear, extending a somewhat hesitant greeting to her no-doubt confused cousin. But Farah would just have to make it clear to Nura what she had decided.

"Are you all right?" Nura asked, her voice hesitant.

"I'm fine," Farah assured her. "But I have something to tell you. I've made a decision about Isa, and I hope you will understand."

⁓ ⁓ ⁓

The sterile atmosphere of the hospital was nearly lost in the chaos and clutter of the emergency room. Sara was stunned to realize so many people frequented this place at such an hour. Small children ran in circles and played with toys, while others slept on plastic chairs and still others cried or whimpered as concerned parents watched anxiously each time the double doors opened and a nurse called someone to come to an examination room.

Emir had been given priority over those with stomachaches and sore throats, ankle sprains and abrasions. He had been immediately wheeled in through the ambulance-only entrance, as doctors and nurses surrounded the unconscious teenager and began running necessary tests to prepare him for surgery. Sara and Yusef had arrived just moments behind the ambulance, and now did their best to calm a frantic Layla, who had refused to leave Emir's side until her husband had nearly carried her out to the waiting room. Even now, as she sat in her robe and slippers, refusing even to acknowledge Sara's offer to go with her to the restroom to help her get dressed, her eyes were fixed on the doors that separated her from her son.

*Oh, God,* Sara prayed, *please let my brother live! Please, Lord! Not for me; I was wrong. I should have told my parents that something was going on with Emir, but I didn't. And now... Please, Lord, don't punish them for my sin! And above all, don't let Emir die, because he doesn't know You. He isn't a true believer, Father! Please, please let him live so he can accept Jesus as his Savior!*

She sobbed at the thought that her brother's life hung by the slimmest of threads and that he had never committed his life to

Christ. Could there be anything worse than to lose a loved one in that condition?

Her father, who sat on the other side of Sara's mother, reached across behind Layla's back and patted his daughter's shoulder. Sara turned and met his eyes, wondering if he too was thinking and praying about Emir's spiritual condition.

A commotion at the doors leading inside from the parking lot caught her attention, and she broke away from her father's gaze and turned her eyes toward the group who had just entered. She gasped. Their pastor and his wife had apparently spotted them and were headed their way, followed by a group of about ten or twelve people, all from their church. Even Layla turned from her silent vigil toward the approaching group, and for the first time that evening Sara saw a flicker of relief and hope on her mother's face as she nearly jumped to her feet.

Jackie, the pastor's wife, scooped Layla into an embrace and held her close, as the terrified mother sobbed on her shoulder. The rest of the group greeted them with hugs and words of support and encouragement, and Sara soon found herself relaxing a bit as well, as the sounds of prayer began to fill the room. Surely God would hear them, and Emir would be all right!

ళ్ళ ళ్ళ ళ్ళ

Nura sat stunned in her room. Her conversation with Farah had been anything but what she had expected. The bright spot in her current turmoil had been her deeper connection with her cousin, but now they seemed more distant than ever before. Farah had made it quite clear that she was dismissing her questions about Isa and was accepting the limitations and claims of Islam that He was nothing more than one of the prophets, and certainly not as great as Muhammad himself. She had even told Nura that she wished never again to discuss the subject and that she hoped Nura would make the same decision and recommit herself to being a faithful Muslim.

How could things have changed so quickly? Had Nura only imagined that Farah too was searching and questioning, that the dreams Farah had spoken of had caused her to consider Isa in a new light? Nura had trusted Farah, confiding in her about the chat room and her conversations with the American named Sara, a girl who would be considered an infidel by faithful Muslims. An icy fear clutched Nura's chest at the realization that Farah knew something that could mean life or death to Nura, particularly if Kareem got hold of the information.

What should she do? Would Farah betray her? If Farah told her brother, Kareem would certainly tell Nura's parents. Would her father's affection for her be enough to protect her from what would surely infuriate him?

The vision of the young girl struggling in the swimming pool while her father and brother held her head under the water and her mother looked on, helpless and weeping, rose up in her mind with terrifying clarity. Was she next? Was that how her life would end?

As the questions rolled through her mind, an inexplicable peace flowed down upon her, coming as if from somewhere above her and making its way down over her head and shoulders until it covered her and the fear was gone.

"Isa," Nura whispered, knowing without reason that it was He who had covered her with a peace she could not understand, "I want to know You. I want to understand who You really are. Help me. Send Sara, or someone. Please, Isa."

≈≈≈ ≈≈≈ ≈≈≈

As minutes turned to hours, Sara and her parents waited, surrounded by supporters who prayed for them and for Emir. Sara sat by quietly while Yusef talked with the police and hovered over them to protect them from overzealous news reporters. Sara was unclear how much time had passed, but the next time she looked toward the doors that led outside, the first streaks of light were beginning to pierce the darkness of the skies. And with the light came another visitor, anxious and weeping.

Joni burst through the doors and hurried straight to Sara. "You should have called me," she sobbed. "I would have come! I didn't know. My mom didn't tell me until this morning. I don't know how I slept through it. I'm so sorry! I should have heard the noise—should have been here. How is he? What's happening?

130

Oh, I can't believe any of this!" She sobbed again and fell into the empty chair beside Sara, burying her head in her hands as she continued to cry.

Sara reached her arm out to surround the young girl's shaking shoulders. At that moment she realized that though Emir had been lying about his feelings for Joni, the girl had been quite sincere about hers for him. No wonder she had been willing to cover for him! The entire scenario was beginning to fall into place now, and at last Sara understood.

"You really do care for him, don't you?" she whispered, leaning over to speak into Joni's ear.

Joni nodded, though she didn't look up. "Yes, even though I don't think he really cares about me. But that's OK. It doesn't matter." She raised her head then and looked at Sara through puffy red eyes, as tears continued to drip down her blotchy cheeks. "It really doesn't matter. I just want him to be OK." Her voice turned to a whimper then, and her chin quivered as she said, "Please tell me this isn't because I lied for him. Please, Sara! He didn't tell me what was going on in his life, and I still don't know, but I shouldn't have lied to you, even though he asked me to. I'll never forgive myself if, if..." Her voice broke off, and her face crumpled. "Oh, Sara, is he going to be OK? Please tell me he is!"

Sara swallowed. She desperately wanted to be able to reassure her friend, but how could she? No one knew at this point. They all waited, watching each time the doors to the waiting rooms opened and a doctor or nurse came out. But each time they spoke to someone else. No word yet about Emir.

"I don't know," she said at last. "I'm sorry, Joni. I just don't know. But we're all praying."

Joni nodded. "So am I," she said. "I've been praying ever since I heard." A fresh crop of tears erupted from her eyes. "Oh, Sara, you don't think God will let him die, do you?"

Sara's own composure failed then, and she pulled Joni close, unable to answer except to cry with her. Would God let Emir die? It was a question Sara had been asking herself for the last several hours, even as she begged and bargained with God for a miracle.

*He would never tolerate being
mocked by females.*

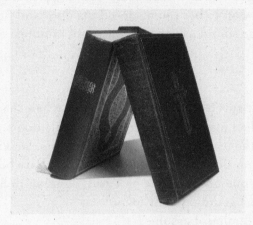

## Chapter 19

Farah told herself the day had been successful. She had spent it in prayer and studying her Quran, and had even explained her decision to Nura over the phone, encouraging her cousin to make the same choice and to forget the foolishness about Isa being more than a prophet of Islam. Admittedly Nura had sounded confused and hadn't reacted as positively as Farah had hoped, but maybe Nura had spent the day considering Farah's words. If those words helped Nura to wholeheartedly return to the true faith, then Farah would have performed a very good deed. With Ramadan winding down in the next few days, maybe such a response from Nura would be the answer to Farah's prayers throughout the holiday for a deeper and more meaningful faith. Surely Allah would be pleased, as would her family, though Farah hadn't yet decided if she would tell them about the incident. She particularly didn't want to tell Kareem, and yet it might be just the thing to improve his opinion of her.

*Still, I don't want to get Nura in trouble. I'll wait to see what Nura decides.*

Meanwhile, she had enjoyed the *Iftar* meal and was looking forward to getting some much needed sleep. She was relieved that her mother and sister hadn't suggested going anywhere tonight, as the thought of her comfortable bed beckoned her. Heeding the call, she went to her room, closed the door and turned out the light, and was sound asleep in a matter of minutes.

⁓⁓⁓ ⁓⁓⁓ ⁓⁓⁓

Sara thought surely her heart would stop when she realized the doctor who had just emerged from the double doors was heading straight for them. Yusef stood up to greet him, shaking his hand but offering no smile as he waited. Layla and Sara had also stood to their feet, one on each side of Yusef, clinging to his arms as if they could not stand on their own.

"Mr. Al Tamimi, I assume?"

When Yusef nodded, the man continued. "I'm Dr. Hunter. Your son has made it through the surgery, but he's lost a lot of blood. The next few hours, possibly even days, will be critical."

The man's voice turned to a faint buzz, as Sara tried to process his words. Emir was still alive! He had made it through the surgery, but he was still in danger. *Oh, God, please!* Sara shut her eyes. *Please, Lord, help him! Don't let him die, Father! Don't let him die!*

The sound of someone weeping at her side brought her back from her thoughts, and she turned to see Joni standing beside her. The girl's pain seemed almost worse than her own, and Sara took her in her arms and once again allowed her to sob on her shoulder. She realized the doctor and her parents were still talking in hushed voices, but she could no longer make out the words because of Joni's distress. She would just have to wait and get the details from her parents later. For now she knew the most important thing: Emir was alive, but who knew for how long? He could die at any moment—without Christ.

No! A loving God would surely not allow such a thing. She must continue to pray, as must everyone else who had gathered together to support them. They absolutely could not allow Emir to die under any circumstances, but definitely not in his unrepentant state.

134

Sara's sobs mingled with Joni's now, as she prayed silently. She'd always been told that nothing was too hard for God and that he was a God of miracles. If ever they needed one, it was now.

∽≈∾ ∽≈∾ ∽≈∾

Kareem sat under the stars in the enclosed patio, looking forward to the cooler temperatures that would soon be upon them. Tonight it was still hot, but he felt better being outside for a few moments, away from the rest of the family, as he tried to analyze Farah's behavior.

Something had been different tonight. As they all sat around the table, breaking the fast and speaking of their day, Farah had seemed more humble, more compliant, more...

What was it? Kareem couldn't quite identify it. Had he seen it in any other woman, he might have admired it. But in Farah? No. There was something not believable about it. She was putting on a front; he was sure of it. He trusted nothing about the older of his two sisters, and he would not be easily fooled. Maybe he would enlist Nadia's help to see if she could discover something. So far she had been of no use to him except to report to him about the conversation she had overheard between Farah and Nura in the women's restroom at the restaurant, and she had only given him that information because he'd forced her. He knew Nadia didn't like him any more than Farah did, but he didn't care. He was the brother, and both of his sisters had to obey him. If they didn't like him, what was that to him? One day soon Kareem would marry, and he didn't care if his wife liked him or not. She would do as she was told or suffer the consequences.

Until then, he would exercise such control over his sisters — and possibly his cousin Nura as well. For all he knew, Farah and Nura ridiculed him behind his back when they got together for their secret conversations. It didn't bother him at all that they might not like him, but he would never tolerate being mocked by females.

∽≈∾ ∽≈∾ ∽≈∾

The sun was up by the time Sara and her parents returned home, dropping off Joni along the way. Members of their church who had not come to the hospital to pray and wait with them had instead stayed home to cook and bring meals to their house. The kitchen was full by the time the Al Tamimis made their way back inside, but no one felt up to eating anything.

"How did they get inside to leave all this food?" Layla asked, her bleary eyes fixed on the casserole and dessert-laden table.

Yusef laid a hand on his wife's shoulder as he spoke. "John Lingle still has the backdoor key from when he house-sat for us last summer, remember?"

Layla nodded. "Oh. Yes, I'd forgotten." She sighed. "This is very nice of them, isn't it?"

"Very nice," Yusef agreed, though neither of them moved or showed any real interest in the food.

"I'm going upstairs to try and get some sleep," Sara said at last.

Her parents turned to her as one. Layla forced a smile, and Yusef nodded as he spoke. "Good. That's good, Sara. Yes, get some rest. You've been up all night."

"So have you," Sara reminded them.

When they didn't answer, she turned and walked toward the stairway. She doubted she'd be able to sleep, but she had to try. Staying awake to think was just too painful.

⤡⤢ ⤡⤢ ⤡⤢

The hours and minutes of the night ticked by, and still Nura lay awake, staring at the ceiling. Why had Farah changed her mind so rapidly? It had to be fear. It was the only thing that made sense. But what would happen now?

The questions with answers she did not want to consider rolled through her mind, as she pondered the many times she and Sara had talked about Isa. How often had she come to the point of nearly making a decision to accept Sara's claims about Isa, including that He was the Son of God and had died for her sins, and then shied away at the last minute? Why couldn't she simply dismiss the entire issue, as Farah apparently had? Nura knew her life would be so much simpler if she could do that, but she also knew she had long since passed the point where that was possible. She had to be sure, one way or the other. Once she was, she would follow that way, whatever the cost.

With that in mind, she booted up her computer and immediately checked in to the chat room. Oh, if only Sara would surface! What could her American friend be doing that kept her from their usual visits?

᷈᷈᷈ ᷈᷈᷈ ᷈᷈᷈

Sara had tossed and turned for nearly an hour, frustrated that despite her exhaustion she just couldn't seem to dismiss her thoughts. She'd prayed, counted sheep, and listened to music, but nothing had helped. All she could think of was the sight of her father, holding her lifeless brother in his arms, and weeping as he begged God for mercy. Surely God would answer... wouldn't He?

The possibility that He might answer with a no was not a thought she was willing to consider. Emir was only fifteen — and he wasn't a born-again believer. If he died in the state he was in....

Sara nearly cried aloud, putting her pillow over her face to drown herself out. She desperately wanted to talk to someone, but not her parents. Sara had heard them go to their room a few minutes earlier, and she wasn't about to disturb their rest, though she doubted they'd do any better sleeping than she had. Joni crossed her mind, but the girl was an emotional basket case, so she'd be no help at all.

All her other friends were in school, and the people from church who had waited up with them during the long night had also gone home to get some rest. Surely there was someone.

*Nura.* The name came to her in a flash, and she somehow knew that her Saudi friend would be online waiting for her. Though the girl wasn't a Christian and therefore wouldn't understand Sara's concern for her brother's spiritual state, she was a compassionate young woman who could also be objective since she was not emotionally involved in the situation. She was exactly the one Sara needed at this moment.

Firing up her computer, she wasn't in the least surprised when she found Nura already online and waiting in the chat room.

Isa, are You there?
Can You hear me?

## Chapter 20

Nura's heart soared when she received the greeting from Sara. At last, her friend was back! She had missed her even more than she realized, but now that they had connected, Nura wondered where to start. There was so much she wanted to say, but she reminded herself that she needed to be polite and ask how Sara was doing before jumping into her own concerns.

*How are you?* Nura wrote. *I've missed talking with you.*

*I'm sorry,* came the reply. *We've had a lot going on here — not good, I'm afraid.*

Nura frowned. What did that mean? Was someone sick or injured? *I'm sorry to hear that,* she wrote. *Is it something you'd like to talk about?*

*Yes. It's about my brother, Emir. I think I've told you about him, haven't I?*

*You mentioned him, yes. Has something happened to him? Is he sick?*

*Not sick, no. But he's in the hospital.*

Nura's hands paused over the keyboard. Hospital? If he wasn't sick, he must have been in some sort of accident. She hoped it wasn't anything too serious.

*What happened?* Nura asked. *Was he in an accident?*

For a moment Nura thought Sara had broken the connection, but at last she received an answer.

*I wish it was just an accident,* Sara wrote. *But it's worse. He was shot. The police suggested it was gang-related, but Emir has never been involved with gangs, so that doesn't make sense. Still, the police are stationing a guard outside Emir's door . . . just in case.*

Nura felt her eyes widen. Shot? Gangs? Police? She had heard about the excessive violence on the streets of America, but she had no idea it was that bad. Maybe things weren't quite as easy for Sara as Nura had imagined.

*I'm so sorry to hear this, my friend,* Nura wrote, her hands trembling as she typed. *What do the doctors say? Will Emir be all right?*

*It's too soon to tell. He came through the surgery OK, but he lost a lot of blood. He's still in critical condition.*

Nura felt hot tears sting her eyes, and she was amazed that she would take something like this so personally when she didn't even know Sara or her family. Yet she realized that this girl who lived so many miles and cultures away had willingly spent many hours of her time talking with her, and until this moment Nura hadn't appreciated it. Now she did, and she wanted to help in some way. But how?

*I will pray for you and your brother,* Nura ventured, not sure how Sara would take such a statement because of the difference in their faiths. And yet it seemed to be all she had to offer.

*Thank you,* came the reply. *I appreciate that very much. Many people from our church are praying for a miracle. I know you don't believe in Isa the same way I do, but will you do something for me?*

*Of course.*

*When you pray for us, will you ask Him to show you that He is real and that He loves you very much? That would mean more to me than anything right now.*

The tears that had been pooling in Nura's eyes now spilled over onto her cheeks. *Yes,* she answered. *I will do that. I promise.*

*Then maybe I'll finally be able to get some sleep,* Sara wrote. *We were up all night at the hospital and I'm exhausted, but I couldn't sleep when we got home. That's why I signed in to the chat room. I'm glad you were here.*

*I'm glad too.*

*Was there anything else you wanted to talk about?* Sara asked.

Nura hesitated. Should she tell her what had been on her mind when she came to the chat room, as well as what was going on with Farah and Kareem? No, not now. Not with all Sara was going through with her brother. She'd wait to see how that was resolved. In the meantime she would pray as Sara had requested.

*No, nothing else,* she wrote. *Go get some sleep. I'll check in with you later.*

*Thank you, my friend. And please remember that I am praying for you too!*

Nura signed off, her heart heavy for her American friend. It was time to pray, keeping in mind her promise regarding the prophet Isa.

⁂ ⁂ ⁂

Nura's throat tightened each time she attempted to fulfill her promise to Sara. Though she prayed silently, afraid to speak the words aloud, it was difficult for her to address Isa directly. Always she had been taught to pray only to Allah, though she had never felt as if she'd had a direct response from him. Now she struggled to readjust her thinking and address her silent words to a prophet who lived and died centuries before. She knew that Sara believed He was so much more—that He still lived and was God as well as man—but it wasn't a fact Nura had yet accepted without question.

She had to admit, however, that just hours earlier she had imagined a peaceful sensation and had reacted with a direct request to Isa. What had she asked? Yes, that's right! She had asked that He would send someone—possibly Sara—to help her, to answer her questions, to steer her in the right direction. And what had happened? She had found Sara in the chat room, and without even telling Sara why she had hoped to talk with her, Sara had sent her back to Isa.

Amazing! And now she had promised her friend that she would ask Isa to make Himself real to her and to show her how much He loved her. She felt torn between the need to keep her promise to Sara and the fear that Allah would be displeased by her actions. Would something terrible happen to her if she prayed to Isa, rather than to Allah? And without meaning to, hadn't she already done that? Would it really even be a prayer if she spoke to Him again, asking Him to show her that He was real and that He loved her? She imagined that it would, but it might also be just what she needed to clear up her confusion over Sara's claims about Isa once and for all. Because Nura doubted that anything would come of her request, she reasoned that she would then be free to drop her pursuit of the truth of Isa, for she would already have her answer. If Isa did not respond—and why would He, even if He could?—then Nura would be certain that He was indeed no more than one of the lesser prophets of Islam.

The thought brought a tinge of relief to the otherwise tense young woman, as she sat at her desk in front of her now blank computer screen and closed her eyes. She had decided it might be sacrilegious to kneel on her prayer rug and pray to anyone other than Allah, so she would pray right where she sat when she broke her online connection with Sara.

Sara. The reminder of what her American friend was going through shot like a jagged arrow through her heart. How could she have been so naïve as to think Sara had no problems simply because she lived somewhere other than the Saudi Kingdom? Nura had tended to believe that though she was privileged to live where she did, other women in other cultures had a much easier life. Now she wasn't so sure.

Squeezing her eyes more tightly shut, she took a deep breath and silently uttered the words that terrified her even as she thought them: *Isa, are You there? Can You hear me? I know You are a prophet, but Sara says You are also the very Son of God. I don't understand how that's possible, but if it's so—if You're really who Sara claims You are—will You please show me…somehow?*

Nura hesitated. Did she dare continue? She must; she had promised.

*And can You also show me that You love me? I know it's a lot to ask and I have no right to do so, but if You are who Sara claims You are, then You already know that I made a promise I must keep. And so I have asked You these two questions. I will wait now to see if You answer.*

~ ~ ~

Sara was still surprised that she had been able to speak to Nura about Jesus with such confidence. Right now her faith felt shaky at best, and yet she'd had no doubts when asking Nura to make those two requests of Jesus. Why was it so much easier to believe for others than for herself?

She lay on her bed, staring up at the ceiling. It was midmorning, and still she hadn't been able to sleep, though she was glad she'd taken the time to go online and talk with her Saudi friend. How strange that she would find comfort in sharing what was on her heart with someone who didn't even have the same faith! Yet she somehow knew that even in the midst of her own pain, she was being used to minister to a girl far away who needed to know the truth about Jesus.

*Maybe it's easier to believe for Nura and others because I don't live in their skin,* she mused. *I know me. I live with me every day. And I know how much I fail at being the strong witness I truly want to be. Is that it, Lord? Is that why I have so much doubt when I pray about my own situations?*

A picture of Emir, lying in a bed in the intensive care unit, with tubes and monitors surrounding his bed and a uniformed police officer standing watch outside his door, flashed in her mind. They'd only been allowed in one at a time to see him for a couple of minutes before they were each ushered out of the room and encouraged to go home and get some rest. She knew someone from the hospital would call them if there was any news, but it had been so hard to leave her brother lying there, helpless and without the assurance that he would go to be with Jesus if he died.

*Oh, why didn't I try harder to witness to him, to pray for him, to convince him to accept Jesus as his Savior? And why didn't I tell Mom and Dad about my suspicions that something was going on with Emir, even if I didn't know what it was?*

She thought then of Joni and how the girl had sobbed and wept and prayed aloud, over and over again, for God to heal Emir. As she had come to realize while waiting at the hospital with her friend, Joni most surely had deep feelings for Emir, though Sara had no idea if Emir felt anything at all for Joni.

*How do we think we know people—especially those in our very own families—when we really don't know them at all? I have no idea what was running through Emir's heart or mind during these last weeks or months. What could have been going on with him that he would get involved in whatever this is?*

She closed her eyes. *What is it, Lord? Are the police right that the whole thing is gang-related? Mom and Dad were adamant that Emir wasn't involved with gangs, but I'm not so sure. The way he's been acting lately...*

A tear trickled from her eye, and she wondered what her parents would say if they found out that Emir truly was involved with a gang, though she herself wasn't ready to accept such an idea. But her parents still thought of Emir as the good student who loved sports and never gave them any problems. Had they all missed the changes in him lately? Apparently so, though Sara of all people should at least have had an idea. Why didn't she follow up when she found him climbing inside his window that evening? She'd known in her heart that his story of going to meet Joni was a lie, and yet she'd tried to believe it simply so she wouldn't have to find out otherwise.

And now her brother was in the hospital, fighting for his life. How could she ever forgive herself if he didn't make it?

Help me, Allah, she whispered,
her face to the floor.

## Chapter 21

NEARLY AN HOUR HAD PASSED SINCE NURA HAD PRESENTED HER silent petition to Isa. She had waited patiently in her chair, but her back and neck were beginning to ache. How much longer should she wait? Would Isa answer if she gave in to her desire to go lie down on her comfortable bed? Would He even answer at all, even if she stayed right there in her seat?

Islam was a religion of self-disciplines, and Nura had always practiced those required of her. But speaking to Isa was not a teaching of Islam, so maybe it would be all right to leave her chair for the comfort of her bed. After all, if Isa was who Sara claimed He was, He could certainly answer her anywhere.

Doubts multiplied in her heart as she rose from her position and walked the few steps to her bed, where she lay back on the soft pillows and mattress. *What has happened to me since meeting Sara that I now take such foolish chances?* In all fairness, though, she had to admit that even before meeting Sara, she had been dabbling with danger just logging in to a chat room inhabited by infidels. The very thought terrified her, and the realization that she was indeed the one who had instigated such behavior was nearly incomprehensible. Nura had never thought of herself as brave or adventurous, and yet here she was doing things that few in her position would even consider. Why? Life would be so much simpler if she could just let go of this ridiculous quest of hers—because that was exactly what it seemed to her now.

*A quest,* she thought. *Yes, a quest for truth. Isn't that what this is really about? And if Isa doesn't answer me soon, then I will know what the truth is. Isa is a prophet of Islam, period. Nothing more, nothing less. And I can go back to being a good and obedient Muslim girl without all these worries. It would be such a relief—*

She had scarcely completed the thought when a sense of peace flowed over her, reminding her of warm honey. Much like the sensation she had experienced earlier, the peace that covered her now drove out all lingering fear.

"Is it You, Isa?" she whispered, as joy flooded her heart and she thought she might burst with the exquisite pain of it. "Are You truly who Sara says You are?"

Wordlessly the assurance came, and Nura's doubts melted away. As impossible as it seemed, she knew that Isa was truly the Son of God. And she knew without asking again that He loved her beyond reason or limits.

"I love You," she whispered in response. "I love You, Isa!"

With tears of happiness flowing from her eyes, she lifted her hands toward the heavens, wanting only to touch the One who had reached down to touch her. Soon she would go to her computer and try to reconnect with Sara so she could tell her of this wonderful encounter. She had so many questions to ask of her American friend, though she would have to be considerate of Sara's situation with her brother.

But for now, she just wanted to bask in the joy and peace of knowing that Isa was so much more than a prophet—and that He loved her. Could there be any greater Truth anywhere?

⤋⤋⤋ ⤋⤋⤋ ⤋⤋⤋

When the first call to prayer pulled Farah from her sound sleep, she was surprised that she hadn't awakened sooner—and that she didn't feel more refreshed. After several hours of such sound sleep, she shouldn't feel so sluggish. Yet she did, and somehow she sensed that it wasn't a physical problem.

Dragging herself from her bed, she mechanically went about her morning routine, reciting her prayers by rote and fighting the feeling of depression that hung over her. She had flipped on the bedside lamp, and yet she still felt as if she were shrouded in darkness. *What is wrong with me? Of all times, after making my decision to faithfully follow and practice my religion and reject all thoughts of my dreams of Isa, I should be feeling better than ever. My questions have been answered and my doubts resolved. I am a Muslim, and I have no desire to do or be anything else. It's the last week of Ramadan, with the Night of Power nearly upon us. I should be rejoicing and anticipating what might happen on that wonderful night. Instead I'm restless, tired, depressed—and more confused than ever.*

"Help me, Allah," she whispered, her face to the floor. "Help me, please! I don't want to be unfaithful to you! I don't want to be deceived."

But even as her voice trailed off, the feeling of darkness increased, and Farah shivered at the thoughts that swirled and danced around her.

⤜⤙ ⤜⤙ ⤜⤙

Sara was surprised to realize she'd dozed off at last, only to be awakened by her mother, who sat beside her on the bed.

"Sara, wake up, honey. Do you want to go back to the hospital with us?"

Struggling to focus, Sara squinted at her mother. Usually so neat and composed, she appeared ragged and disheveled, her eyes red-rimmed and puffy. Was something wrong? Why would she be asking about going to the hospital? And why was it still light outside? The last rays of sunshine filtering through her window told her it was evening. Why was she in bed?

Then she remembered. While vivid sights and sounds flooded her mind like painful shards of broken glass, it was her heart that felt the pain.

Gunshots. Squealing tires. Emir.

151

The tears she thought she had long since exhausted filled her eyes, as her mother reached out to touch her cheek. "Poor Sara," she crooned. "Did you get much sleep?"

"I don't know," she admitted. "Some, I suppose. What about you and Dad?"

Layla smiled, though it seemed a message of sadness. "A little. Your father thought we should let you sleep, but I knew you'd want to go with us to check on Emir."

"No one has called?"

Her mother shook her head. "No. Your father says that's a good sign. If Emir was worse, they would have called."

*Or if he was better*, Sara thought, though she said nothing. At last she returned her mother's weak smile. "You're right, Mom. I definitely want to go with you. I want to see Emir, to pray for him."

The words nearly stuck in her throat, and the tears that she'd managed to keep in her eyes spilled over onto her cheeks. "Oh, Mom," she cried, wishing she could stop the words even as they flowed from her lips, "what if... what if Emir dies without...?"

Layla moved her hand from Sara's cheek to her mouth, stopping the question midsentence. "I know," she said, her own voice cracking with emotion. "I know, Sara. I have asked myself the same thing all night, as has your father. We've prayed and prayed, and I know you have too."

"But, Mom, what if—"

Layla shook her head, once again interrupting her daughter's anguish.

"I have no answer for you but this, Sara. It is the same answer your father gave me after wrestling with it most of the night. God is good. He is faithful. And He is always, always right. I wish I could tell you that God will not allow this horrible thing to happen, that our own Emir..." She caught her breath and paused before continuing. "That God would not allow Emir to die without first receiving Christ as his Savior. But I cannot guarantee you that, Sara. I want to, but I can't. I'm not God, and I'm not omniscient. God's ways are so far above ours, and we are unable to understand how He works all things together for good to those who love Him and are called according to His purpose.

But He does. And we can—and must—trust Him. No matter what happens."

"But..." Sara swallowed. "But we must keep praying that it won't happen, right? That God will heal him, and even if He doesn't, that somehow He will reach Emir in time."

Layla nodded. "Of course we must. That is exactly how we must pray." She stroked a loose strand of hair from Sara's forehead. "And we must never lose sight of the truth that God will do the right thing, for His very nature would not allow Him to do anything else."

Sara knew her mother's words were true, but her heart rebelled at the thought that God could answer in any way other than to heal Emir and to bring him to a personal relationship with Jesus. How would she ever bear it if that wasn't the case?

*Everything else could be found on the Internet; why not a Bible?*

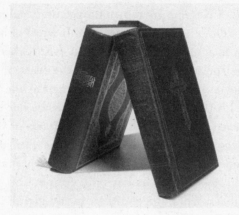

## Chapter 22

NURA HAD ALREADY BEEN AWAKE WHEN THE FIRST CALL TO prayer rang out. She ignored it. Still wrapped in her smooth sheets and a light blanket, she'd been praying since she first opened her eyes.

At least, she assumed that's what she was doing. Did talking to someone count as prayer? She felt as if she'd been having a conversation with Isa all morning, though admittedly she'd never heard Him speak back to her. It had all been her, whispering or thinking words of happiness and love and directing them to Him. It seemed the most pure form of prayer imaginable, and so much more heartfelt than anything she had uttered from rote through the years.

Oh, if only Farah hadn't acted so strangely when she spoke with her the previous day! Nura would love to be able to call her or go to her home and discuss with her all that she had been experiencing since the previous evening. But now she wouldn't dare. Farah had seemingly rejected all thoughts and considerations of Isa beyond the Islamic belief that He was a prophet on a lesser plane than Muhammad, and had returned to her worship of Allah with renewed fervor. And yet, Nura couldn't help but wonder how much of that fervor was inspired by fear of discovery and retribution from Kareem.

The thought of Kareem stirred an unwelcome feeling of concern in her own stomach, but Nura dismissed it. If word of her newfound belief that Isa was actually the Son of God ever leaked out beyond the walls of this room, Kareem would be the least of her worries. Her vivid memories of the dying girl, drowned at the hands of her own father and brother, were enough to convince her of that.

But what was she to do about it? If the basis of the truth and joy she had discovered was that Isa was the Son of God, then she must somehow learn more about the faith that went with that truth. Right now Sara was her only connection, and she was determined to learn what she could from the girl. But how could she do that until Sara's own tragedy was resolved?

"Isa," she whispered, "I don't know the right way to pray, but I know now that You love me, so I believe too that You love Sara and her family. Please do something to help them. I don't know what else to ask, but You must know what they need. Please give it to them, and please show me how to be a help to them as well. I am so grateful to Sara for telling me about You." She smiled as the morning light began to penetrate the windows of her room.

"Thank You, Isa." She sighed. "Whatever happens, thank You for loving me. It's enough."

❧ ❧ ❧

Emir could have only one visitor at a time, and then only for a few minutes. Even then the police guard kept a close watch.

Sara waited while her parents each took their turn with their son, and she watched their faces as they returned to the waiting room where she sat. The sadness tore at her heart. She knew what her mother had said was true, but how would any of them ever live with the outcome if Emir died without regaining consciousness and receiving Jesus as his Savior? It would be bad enough to lose him in this life, but to be separated from him for all eternity would be too much to bear.

The sight of her father's slumped shoulders bothered her most. She had always thought her tall, handsome dad was the strongest, best-looking man anywhere. But suddenly he looked old and tired. Though he continued in prayer and did what he could to encourage Sara and her mother, it was obvious that the grueling wait was taking its toll.

It was just as her mother was returning from her visit with Emir that their pastor arrived, and Sara breathed a sigh of relief. Somehow it was easier for her to leave her parents behind in the waiting room and go in to see Emir if she knew that someone was there with them. She could already hear the pastor's comforting words as he gathered her parents together and she stepped through the double doors into the immaculate hallway that led to the sterile room where Emir waited, silent except for the beeping monitors that surrounded him.

Ignoring the policeman at the door and the lone metal chair by the wall, Sara stood at her brother's bedside, trying to convince herself it was all right to take his hand. A needle was taped to it, and she saw a plastic bottle of blood and another bottle of a clear liquid hanging on a stand at the head of Emir's bed. The bottles dripped into tubes that in turn fed into the boy's seemingly lifeless body.

"Oh, Emir," Sara whispered, her heart breaking at the sight of what her brother had become in less than twenty-four hours. He had always appeared so strong and healthy, and now he clung to this world by a frail thread. Would it break, allowing him to slip away, falling into the darkness of eternity without a safety net beneath him? *Oh, Lord, no,* she begged silently. *Please don't let that happen!*

She remembered then that she had once heard that those in comas could sometimes hear people talking to them, even if they couldn't respond. She had no idea if that was true, but she leaned down near her brother's ear and once again spoke his name.

"Emir," she said, "it's me, Sara. I came to see you, to pray for you. Emir, I don't know if you can hear me, but if you can, you have to listen. Pay attention, please! This is so important. Your life is hanging between heaven and hell right now, and if you die without receiving Jesus as your Savior, you'll spend eternity in hell. Oh, Emir, please don't let that happen!"

She sobbed, and then composed herself, determined to deliver the message of salvation to her brother before they came to tell her it was time to leave. "You need Jesus," she said, ignoring the lump in her throat. "There's no other way, Emir. Listen to me, please. I'm going to pray the sinner's prayer. If you can hear me, even if you can't speak, you can repeat it in your mind. God will hear you, I promise! He's just waiting for you to do it. He loves you so much, Emir—and so do I!"

Her voice cracked then, even as tears flowed down her cheeks. But she knew her time was nearly spent, and so she began to pray, hoping Emir was praying with her. It seemed to be the only hope either of them had.

≈≈≈ ≈≈≈ ≈≈≈

Farah continued to struggle throughout the day, though she faithfully prayed, read her Quran, and fasted. At one point while she was facedown on her prayer rug, she heard her bedroom door open, but no one came in or said a word. Farah pretended to be so caught up in praying that she didn't notice the momentary intrusion. She told herself it was her mother, checking on her, but the thought that it might be Kareem only reinforced her need to remain in prayer.

*What will it take for Kareem to get over his suspicions?* she agonized. Farah had no idea, particularly since the two of them hadn't even been close before. But if she remained faithful to Allah, she reasoned, then even if Kareem maintained his attitude toward her, at least he would never find anything to prove his suspicions. And Farah was determined to make it so. Kareem could dig and hunt and sneak around all he wanted, but he would find nothing because Farah would live such an exemplary life as a devout Muslim girl that she would be faultless before Kareem's scrutiny—and, she hoped, before Allah as well.

*Is that possible?* she wondered, the thought popping into her mind unbidden and unwelcome. *Can anyone ever accomplish such a thing, to live faultless before Allah?* No, she decided. It was impossible. But she would pour out every ounce of her strength and energy to get as close to that ideal as possible. Surely then she

158

would at last discover what she'd been seeking throughout the Ramadan season, and before.

∾∾∾  ∾∾∾  ∾∾∾

Nura wanted desperately to talk with Sara, but she wasn't signed in to the chat room. Nura hoped nothing had happened to Emir, and she breathed a quick prayer for his safety and healing. Would Isa listen to her? She wasn't sure. She knew now that He loved her, so it was certainly possible.

That very question continued to nag at her, along with so many others. She couldn't talk to Farah about it, even if her cousin hadn't already severed their communication on the subject. Farah knew no more about the real truth of Isa than did Nura; Sara was her only connection, and who knew when she would surface again?

As Nura sat in front of her computer, staring at the chat room screen that did not include Sara's name that morning, her eyes flicked to the side of the computer where her Quran sat waiting on her desk. *The holy book of Islam,* she thought, *given to us by the Prophet Muhammad. If only it contained the answers I'm looking for!*

A picture of another book took shape in her mind, and her heart began to race when she realized it was the Bible, the book that Muslims claimed had been perverted by those who read and believed it. Would it help her learn more about Isa? If so, how could she get one?

Her gaze returned to her computer monitor. Of course! Everything else could be found on the Internet; why not a Bible? Typing in *Bible* and clicking on SEARCH, she waited, a sense of excitement dispelling the fear that fought for dominion within her. As the results of her search popped up on the screen, she was stunned at the many choices in front of her.

"Help me, Isa," she whispered, almost without realizing she had spoken. "Show me which site to go to and what to read when I get there."

An assurance that He was indeed guiding her gave her the courage to proceed.

*Sultana had been concerned for days.*

## Chapter 23

Sara had scarcely breathed a heartbroken "Amen" when a nurse arrived to tell her she had to leave. Nodding, she wiped away the tears from her face, bent down and kissed Emir on his cheek, and then turned without a word and made her way back to the waiting room, where she found her parents sitting with their pastor. She forced a smile and greeted them with the news that there was no change, and then excused herself to go out into the garden. She just couldn't bear the thought of sitting in the stuffy, sterile room while they all waited and wondered and prayed.

Once outside, she felt her shoulders relax as the slightly damp evening air bade her a familiar welcome. It was cooler today than it had been in a couple of months, a sure sign that though they might yet enjoy a few nice days of Indian summer, autumn was just around the corner—meaning that the long, cold, wet winter of the Pacific Northwest wasn't far behind.

The memory of a familiar slogan teased her, and she smiled at the words: "Celebrate the Seattle Rain Festival, September–June." It wasn't quite that bad, she told herself, but close.

And then she realized she was smiling, and a stab of guilt pierced her heart. How could she smile at anything when her only brother lay in a hospital bed, somewhere between life and death—and heaven and hell? The tears came again then, and she angrily brushed them away as she opted to put some distance between herself and the door that led back inside.

Setting a fast pace, she took off down the path that led through the still blooming roses toward the far end of the garden. She set her sights on an empty stone bench beneath a grape trellis and headed straight for it. At least there she could enjoy the fresh air without having to stare at the building that housed her unconscious brother and her grieving parents.

By the time she reached the bench, she had warmed up a bit from the brisk walk, but the cool stone beneath her quickly cut through her jeans and started her shivering. She wrapped her arms around herself. Why hadn't she thought to bring a sweater or light jacket? The short-sleeved shirt she'd tossed on before leaving the house was hardly enough to keep the dampness of the encroaching night from making its way right into her bones.

Cold or not, she told herself, it was better to be alone outside in the brisk air than inside that stifling waiting room, where death hovered just inches away from those who sat in the uncomfortable, stiff chairs. How long would her parents stay there? Why not go home to wait? It was only a fifteen-minute drive if they got a call and had to return in a hurry.

But she knew why they stayed. It was the same reason she was there, shivering and waiting. How could they do anything but stand watch, praying and hoping for a miracle? The reminder that their pastor was there, waiting and praying with her parents, offered her a bit of encouragement. She wondered then if her parents had prayed with Emir as she had. She imagined so. And then she wondered if there was any chance at all that he had heard—and responded.

*Oh, please, God*, she prayed silently. *Please don't let him die—especially without knowing You! Please, Father.*

This time she didn't even try to stop the tears or wipe them away. Unmoving, she allowed them to drip down her face and into her lap, as the faint, mournful cry of a loon called to her from the nearby river.

⚜ ⚜ ⚜

Sultana had been concerned for days. As she sat at the kitchen table during the late morning hours, trying to decide what to fix for their *Iftar* meal that evening, she knew something wasn't right. Kareem was simmering, seething, restless. Though that described his personality much of the time, his apparent anger and discontent were worse than usual. She was sure of it, though he'd never admit it. She loved her only son—adored him, actually—and she was certain he loved her, in his own limited way. But they'd never been close as Sultana had hoped. They'd never shared intimate, meaningful conversations, even when Kareem was young. Stoic and stubborn, he'd seldom even come to her to bandage his minor cuts and scrapes. Sultana felt as if she'd been forced to watch her son grow up at a distance, though they spent countless hours together in the same house.

To be fair, Kareem appeared no less distant with his father, though it was obvious he sought the older man's approval. Yet even Ahmed had confided in his wife that he felt as if he really didn't know their son. But for some time now, at least since the beginning of Ramadan, Sultana had noticed an accelerated agitation in Kareem that concerned her, particularly since it seemed directed primarily at Farah. She wondered sometimes if her son's restlessness might be curtailed if he were married. Perhaps it was time to begin making the arrangements.

She sighed at the thought, tracing with her fingertip the extended nick in the middle of the old table. The family never ate their meals here, preferring the beauty and elegance of their cherry wood dining table and chairs, but the little spot in the kitchen felt comfortable to Sultana. She had spent many hours here, cooking for her beloved family. Her husband and children were everything to her. She couldn't imagine her life without any one of them, and she was grateful to Allah that she had never suffered the loss of her husband or one of her children, as had some of her friends. No one in their family had even been seriously ill, and she felt very blessed at the thought.

The only dark cloud on Sultana's otherwise sunny horizon was Kareem's animosity toward Farah—a sentiment Sultana was sure Farah did not share. The breach between the two was completely of Kareem's making, and Sultana had no idea how to remedy it. She only hoped it would never grow worse or bring about a tragedy within their family. Lately the sense that something like that just might happen had caused Sultana to lose many hours of sleep.

*Perhaps if I am more faithful in my observance of Ramadan, Allah will do something wonderful on the Night of Power and effect a healing between my children.*

Smiling at the thought, Sultana decided to spend some time in prayer before beginning the preparation of their evening meal.

It was nearly midnight by the time Sara and her parents left the hospital. Their pastor had gone home several hours earlier, and Sara had forced herself to stay, only because the thought of leaving seemed more painful. Joni's mother had dropped off her daughter for a little while, and the poor girl had been nearly overwhelmed with gratitude when she was allowed to see Emir. Within minutes, however, she had returned to the waiting room in tears. Sara felt sorry for her friend but seemed unable to offer any meaningful words of comfort. She knew she should pray with her, but Sara wasn't certain her own faith was strong enough now to attempt to encourage someone else. And so Joni had sat beside them in silence until her mother came to pick her up less than an hour later.

Now Sara was home, back in her own room, sitting on the edge of her bed and wondering if she would ever be able to sleep. Her body screamed for rest, but her mind still buzzed with the unbelievable events of the last couple of days. How had their lives come to this? Everything had seemed so normal and predictable until gunshots and squealing tires had changed it all.

But was that really where it had all begun? Sara buried her face in her hands, as hot tears of guilt once again began to flow. She knew full well that the situation had not developed in that moment of time in the middle of the night, but rather it had been developing for weeks or months—perhaps longer.

*I could have stopped it—tried anyway. All I had to do was tell my parents, and they would have watched Emir more closely, talked to him, convinced him not to—*

She stopped herself. Convinced him not to do what? They still didn't know what Emir had actually done, or why. The police had a theory, but it was not one that Sara or her parents wanted to accept. Would they ever know what really happened? Unless Emir recovered and decided to tell them, she imagined they wouldn't. And once again, it all came back to rest on her shoulders.

But at her age, she was used to
sleepless nights.

## Chapter 24

EMILY THOMPSON KNEW SHE HAD TO DO SOMETHING, THOUGH she didn't want to make a move until she had clear direction from the Lord. After all, He had protected her from certain injury, or even death. Because of His faithfulness, she hadn't lost even one single valuable—not that she had that many to lose, of course. But now a young man's life was at stake, and a family anguished over the not-knowing.

Would the knowing be worse? That was what stopped her, even now. Only God saw the answer to that one; therefore, only God could make the correct choice. Emily would just have to wait and listen until He told her what to do. She did hope it wouldn't be long, though, as she imagined she should have reported the incident to the police when it first happened.

Had there been any injury or theft, she would have. But the only injury had been to the young man who had come into her home, obviously terrified, only to be confronted by an old Chihuahua and an even older woman. She had hoped the incident had scared some sense into him and he would change his ways, and she had prayed fervently to that end. But then she'd read the newspaper and realized the teenaged boy who had been shot in what the police suspected was a gang-related incident was the same one she had confronted in her kitchen.

That's when she began to second-guess her decision not to report the incident to the police. If the boy truly was involved with a gang, would the others break into her home to finish what he had started? She imagined the thought should strike fear into her heart, but it didn't. She had led a long and happy life, and had served the Lord for nearly seven decades, since she was a young girl. God had protected her before, and He could do it again. And if it was her time to go home, then she was more than ready and eager to do so.

Logic, on the other hand, had told her from the beginning that she should have reported the break-in the moment it happened, but her spirit had cautioned her to wait. And so she had, having learned from experience that it was wise to listen to that part of her that communed with God.

*Deep calls to deep.* Emily smiled at the words from the Scriptures as she lay in her bed, her faithful dog, Pepe, snoring peacefully beside her. A glance at the clock on the bedside table told her it was nearly one o'clock in the morning. Another hour had passed as she watched and prayed. But at her age, she was used to sleepless nights.

*Deep calls to deep. Call to me, Lord. Let me know in my spirit what is the right thing to do—and when. Whatever it is, Father, I'll do it. I want only to please You. Until then, I'll pray for that young man, and also for his family. What an awful ordeal for all of them!*

⊱❧ ⊱❧ ⊱❧

The sun had not yet risen when Sara was awakened from a dream-filled sleep, this time by her father.

"Sara, wake up," he called, his voice sounding so very far away, though she knew immediately that he held her hand in his so he had to be close. Confused, she blinked her eyes open and frowned, staring at the outline of her father in the semi-darkness.

"Dad? What is it?" Her heart jumped as the memories came together and she struggled to push herself to a sitting position. "Is it Emir? Has something happened? Is he—?"

Yusef laid his hand on her shoulder and shushed her. "It's all right, sweetheart. Don't worry. Yes, it's about Emir, but he's fine—well, not fine, but not worse. In fact, the hospital just called and said he's showing signs of regaining consciousness. They thought we'd want to be there in case he does. We're going right away. Do you want to come with us?"

Sara's eyes widened, and for the first time in days she felt a spark of hope leap within her. Was it possible? Had God heard their prayers? Was Emir going to be all right after all?

"Yes, of course I want to come," Sara exclaimed. "Give me five minutes, and I'll be ready. I promise!"

For the first time since before the shooting, Sara saw her father smile, though it was tentative and his eyes didn't light up as they usually did. "Take ten," he said. "We'll leave as soon as you're ready. Your mother is already getting dressed."

Her heart nearly bursting, Sara bounded from bed as soon as her father left the room. He may have given her ten minutes, but she'd be ready in five, just as she'd said. She wouldn't miss her brother's return to consciousness for anything! And she was certain they would witness it before another day passed them by.

≈≈ ≈≈ ≈≈

Nura had never read such amazing stories. True, the Quran had taught her much over the years, but nothing like this. Isa was different from any man who ever lived. More than a good man or a prophet or a teacher, He truly had to have been the Son of God to do what was recorded in this Gospel of Luke.

She had been so grateful when she found the Bible in its entirety online and remembered that Sara had once told her that if she ever had the chance she should read that particular Gospel. Looking through the contents, she had found it immediately and began reading without a moment's hesitation. At times she went back and reread a chapter or two, but always she pressed on, wanting to finish this wonderful story of Isa's life. By the time she reached the story of the Crucifixion, she was crying and had trouble seeing the words through her tears. But then she came to the most wondrous scene imaginable—the women, arriving at the tomb to find the stone rolled away and Isa gone! Oh, it was all Nura could do not to cry out with joy! Not even the tomb could hold Him! Surely He was the Son of God, for no mortal man could ever achieve such a miracle.

By the end of the Gospel, she was convinced. Without a doubt, Isa was the Son of God. And somehow she knew that with that as her foundation, the rest would begin to fall into place, whether she had someone to guide and teach her or not. For now she had the Bible itself, the book that so many claimed was God's Word but which Muslims said was a perversion of the truth. It mattered not what anyone said to her at this point; Nura knew the truth in her heart, and she knew too that every word found in this book was part of that truth. Before she began reading it from front to back, she would go back one more time and reread the Gospel she had just finished, this time more slowly to see if there was anything she had missed.

She had no idea of the time or that it would soon be the hour for the family to gather together to break the fast, nor did she care. She cared only for this wonderful Isa, who was real, who was the Son of God, and who loved even her. The joy of those truths was enough to sustain her and to push her forward to learn more.

∽∂ℰ∾ ∽∂ℰ∾ ∽∂ℰ∾

For the first time in their brief visits to Emir's bedside, Sara and her parents were hopeful. Layla had gone to see him first and came out insisting that she was certain he could hear her now, though she couldn't say why she felt that way. Yusef seemed a little less enthusiastic than his wife after he returned from Emir's room, but Sara refused to be deterred. Surely God had heard their prayers, and Emir would emerge from his unconscious state, awake and alert and well on his way to recovery—though she tried not to think of what might be involved on the legal front as the case unraveled.

For some reason she was surprised when she arrived at Emir's room and nothing appeared different. A police guard still stood stoically at his position, unsmiling and seemingly not in the least excited about the possible change in Emir's condition. The monitors still beeped and flashed, and the fluids still dripped through the tubes. Worst of all, Emir still seemed as pale and lifeless as when Sara had last seen him the night before.

She stepped up to his bedside. "Emir?"

Nothing.

She laid her hand on his arm, careful not to disturb the tubes or needles. "Emir, can you hear me?"

Not even his eyes fluttered. She had thought surely...

She pulled up the chair and sat down beside him, taking his hand in hers. "Please, Emir," she said, "if you can hear me, please squeeze my hand. Just a little. Try, please!"

The beeping monitors were her only answer. Burying her face in the thin white blanket, she sobbed. *Oh, God, where are You? Why don't You do something?*

*A chill swept over Nura's mother,*
*even as a jagged knife of fear*
*pierced her heart.*

## Chapter 25

SAKEENA KNOCKED SEVERAL TIMES BEFORE SHE MADE THE decision to open the door and peer inside. She had always tried to give her daughter the respect of not entering her room without first being invited, but she was beginning to get concerned. She hadn't heard a sound from Nura all day, and it wasn't like her not to come out and join the family on her own.

Gently she pushed the door until she was able to see inside. Nura sat quietly at her computer, her back to her mother.

Sakeena cleared her throat. When Nura still didn't respond, Sakeena stepped into the room. "Nura?" She took another step and raised her voice. "Nura, are you all right? Didn't you hear me knocking?"

Slowly her daughter seemed to return from somewhere very far away, as she slowly swiveled in her chair and fixed her eyes on her mother. The look of surprise on her face went beyond that of being startled or surprised; the girl seemed almost confused, as if she didn't recognize Sakeena.

"Are you all right?" Sakeena asked again, moving toward her daughter. "What's wrong? Has something happened?"

As quickly as the recognition lit Nura's face, the girl spun back to her computer and clicked her mouse, turning her monitor dark—but not before Sakeena saw the name Isa amidst the lines of text.

A chill swept over Nura's mother, even as a jagged knife of fear pierced her heart. "What are you doing?" she said, her voice scarcely above a whisper. "Nura, answer me. What are you doing in here?"

Nura turned back to her mother, her eyebrows raised as if in surprise. "What do you mean, Mom? I'm just browsing the Internet. I do that sometimes, you know."

Sakeena narrowed her eyes. Nura had never been a deceitful child. Both Sakeena and Ahmed had always trusted her. Sakeena had no desire to do otherwise, but...

Nura flashed a smile, though Sakeena was certain it was a nervous one. "Is it time to break the fast?" she asked. "Do you want me to come and help you prepare our *Iftar* meal?"

The girl's dark eyes were as lovely as ever, and though Sakeena knew her daughter was not considered an exceptional beauty, she had always been so in her eyes. Her mother's heart melted at the thought, and she returned her daughter's smile. "I would like that very much," she said, holding out her hand.

Nura immediately stood to her feet and took her mother's hand, her smile widening. "So would I," she said, and she planted a kiss on Sakeena's cheek.

∽≁ ∽≁ ∽≁

Despite having slept only fitfully, Emily was up with the morning sun. After feeding Pepe—more than she should have, she knew, but she just couldn't resist his pitiful look—she decided that today was the day she would have to go to the police department and tell them everything she knew. Admittedly, that wasn't much, but perhaps she could shed some light on their investigation. She only hoped there was good news about the boy in the hospital, whom the newspaper had identified as Emir Al Tamimi.

*I wonder if he's Muslim*, she thought. *He certainly has the name for it—the looks too.* She thought back to that night and pictured the face of her young intruder. She'd never had any children of her own, but she imagined the boy named Emir couldn't have been more than fifteen or sixteen at most. How did such a young man get so sidetracked in life that he would break into someone's home in the middle of the night? Was it a crime of opportunity, with her house being one of convenience and ease to get into, or had it been planned? Was it indeed gang-related as the news seemed to indicate? Could the boy have been looking for drugs? If so, he certainly picked the wrong house! In fact, if he was looking for money or jewelry, he wouldn't have found much of that either.

She shook her head as she rummaged through her small closet, looking for something appropriate to wear to the police station. None of it made sense. Why had the boy come to her home, and why had he then been shot in what the authorities seemed to believe was a gang-related shooting? Emir had not looked the part of a gang member or even a drug user. He had looked more like a scared kid who wanted to be nearly anywhere but where she'd found him, in her kitchen.

Emily sighed. Perhaps between her information and what the police already knew, the truth might eventually come to light. If there was one thing Emily had learned in her life, most of which had been spent serving the Lord, it was that truth and light always seemed to show up together somewhere along the line.

❧ ❧ ❧

Sara and her mother had resisted Yusef's suggestion that they go to the hospital cafeteria for a little breakfast, arguing that at least one of them should be with Emir when he regained consciousness. One of the nurses, a stocky, middle-aged woman with premature gray hair and a kind smile, had finally convinced them that if that did indeed occur, she would personally call them immediately so they could return. Armed with their cell numbers, the helpful nurse had shooed them down the hall toward the smell of fresh-brewed coffee and otherwise tasteless but filling hospital fare.

Sara eyed her parents, who sat across from her at the table. Though her father had been the one to suggest getting breakfast, she couldn't help but notice that he wasn't eating much of his eggs or toast. Her mother too spent most of her time pushing her fruit chunks around the bowl, while Sara sipped a glass of orange juice and didn't even make a pretense of eating her bagel.

"I guess we're not very hungry," she said at last, evoking almost identical reactions from her parents. Jerking their heads up, they raised their eyebrows as if surprised by her observation, though she doubted they were.

"I suppose not," Yusef said after a moment. "But thank you for bringing it to our attention. We all must take care of ourselves—for Emir's sake. When he recovers, we will need to take him home and care for him. It will take a lot of time and energy, so we need to keep up our strength." He nodded toward Sara's bagel. "Eat," he said, an obviously forced smile accompanying his words.

Sara returned his smile, though her heart still felt heavy. "I will if you will," she said, looking from one parent to the other. At last her mother laid her hand on her father's arm and said, "She's right, my love. I will if you will—and so will she."

Yusef nodded and used his toast to push his eggs onto his fork. Soon they were all eating their meals, though none of them spoke. Sara imagined their thoughts were similar to her own, as concern for Emir wrestled with hope for his recovery. But at least her parents didn't have to deal with guilt on top of everything else.

A jingling phone interrupted their meal. Sara knew it was her father's cell, as he was the only one who had opted for a simple ring rather than a favorite song. Yusef dropped his fork onto his plate and snatched his phone from his pocket, flipping it open and pressing it to his ear as he muttered a quick hello.

Sara and Layla watched him closely as he listened. Within seconds he flipped the phone shut and nearly exploded from his chair. "It was the nurse," he said, "calling about Emir. We need to get there right away."

Sara knew it wasn't good news when the three of them tried to burst into ICU, only to be stopped by the nurse who had sent them to breakfast, then called them to return.

"You can't come in here right now," she said, holding up her hand as she confronted them just inside the door to the unit. Sara was surprised that the woman who had appeared so kind and gentle when she'd insisted they leave earlier now exhibited a strong sense of no-nonsense authority. It was obvious she was not about to break the rules and let them all in at once.

"I understand," Yusef said, darting a glance toward his wife and daughter who stood on either side of him. "They will wait while I see him, and then come in later."

The nurse, who Sara noticed for the first time was identified on her nametag as Julie Something, shook her head. "I'm afraid none of you can go in right now," she repeated. "When I called you to come up here, I should have been clearer. The doctor asked me to call you because he wanted to speak to you. But in the few moments since I called, something has happened—"

She glanced nervously over her shoulder in the direction of Emir's room before returning her gaze and completing her sentence. "Now you need to wait. The doctor is with your son, and..."

Sara's eyes grew wide as she realized even the usually unmoving police guard that stood outside Emir's room appeared agitated. There also seemed to be several people inside the room, gathered around his bed. What was going on?

Apparently her father had just come to the same realization because he pushed past the nurse and strode purposefully toward Emir's room.

"Mr. Al Tamimi," Julie called. "Wait, please!"

But Yusef was not about to wait, nor was Sara or her mother. It wasn't until the policeman at the door physically blocked the entrance that Sara realized why everyone was acting so strangely. Emir was not better, and he would never be. In fact, she knew in that moment that he had already died. Even as her parents pushed and pleaded to get to their son, Sara turned away and wept. There was nothing left to hope for. Her prayers had not been answered.

Now she sat in front of her
computer screen, watching and hoping
for Sara to sign on.

## Chapter 26

THE LATE SUMMER SUN WAS JUST BEGINNING TO TEASE THE morning air with a promise of warmth, but Sara didn't feel it. She had raced from the building virtually unnoticed, even by her parents, who were still focused on breaking through the human barrier to reach their son. But Sara had no desire to see Emir now that she was certain he was dead. What was the point? She could no longer speak to him, no longer hope for a miracle or pray for mercy. Her brother was gone, and for all she knew, already experiencing the first agonies of eternal separation from the God he had rejected.

*Maybe he was right,* she thought, as she slowed her pace once she reached the riverbank less than a mile from the hospital. A few early morning walkers and joggers were already working their way in one direction or another along the paved pathway. At any other time Sara would have enjoyed the stroll, as she followed the route of the peaceful little waterway that eventually joined the Columbia and then flowed out into the mighty Pacific. This particular spot was especially beautiful in the early morning on those rare days when sunshine kissed the evergreen landscape. But none of that registered as she passed her fellow walkers without even a glance. If any of them noticed her tears, she didn't care. The pain was just too great to think of anything but the fact that Emir had died without first receiving Jesus. And the majority of the blame fell squarely on her shoulders.

⤮  ⤮  ⤮

As hard as Farah had tried, the joy of breaking the fast and sharing the *Iftar* meal with her family had somehow eluded her. Kareem's probing glances hadn't helped, but it was more than that. Even the excellent stewed lamb with saffron her mother had prepared hadn't tempted her. What was it? Why did she feel as if a great sadness had overtaken her, a weight or darkness that she just couldn't shake? This should be a time of rejoicing, as Ramadan drew to a close and the Night of Power was nearly upon them. But even her redoubled efforts at concentrating on her prayers and the reading of the Quran hadn't helped. Farah's heart was heavy, and she didn't know what to do about it.

When she had finished helping her mother clean up after the meal, she excused herself and returned to her room. Thankfully no one had mentioned going anywhere that night, as she really didn't feel up to prowling the *suqs* or meeting anyone for a late snack—especially her aunt or cousin. Farah lay down on her bed, staring at the ceiling, and thought of how recently Nura had lain in this very place, and how the two of them had talked about the prophet Isa—

No! She shut her eyes tightly, but Nura's face remained in her vision. Why couldn't she block it out? Why couldn't she forget the words they had shared? Farah wanted no part of this discussion about the One who had come to her in a dream and called her to His heart. Why couldn't He leave her alone? Couldn't He see that she was already a good Muslim girl with a strong faith in Allah? Why must Isa try to woo her away into something that would only bring her trouble?

Tears began to drip from her still-closed eyes, as she realized it was no longer Nura's image that haunted her, but rather the hooded figure of Isa in the garden. Part of her longed to scream at Him to leave her and never return, while another part cried out for Him to remove the hood so she could at last see His face.

∽⬧∽ ∽⬧∽ ∽⬧∽

Nura had returned to her room after a pleasant meal with her parents, though she'd found herself wishing she could tell them of all she'd discovered about Isa. She couldn't, of course, and that was the only negative spot on an otherwise pleasant evening.

Now she sat in front of her computer screen, watching and hoping for Sara to sign on. Nura wanted to tell her of her recent experiences, but she also wanted to know how Sara's brother was doing. It troubled Nura that she didn't really know how to pray to this Isa who had revealed Himself to her in such a new and startling way, but she had begged Him to help Emir and his family. She couldn't imagine being in her friend's place, worrying and wondering about the fate of her only sibling.

Nura had never had any brothers or sisters. That had bothered her when she was little, since none of her closest friends were only children. But she had grown used to it over the years, asking her mother only once about why there were no other children in the family.

Sakeena's dark eyes had filled with tears that day, as she and then ten-year-old Nura sat together in the garden one cool evening. "I wanted more children," her mother had confessed. "Lots of them. And of course your father wanted sons. But..." Her voice trailed off, and she had stopped to dab her eyes and blink back the tears. She sighed. "I had many problems when you were born. It was a miracle you arrived safely. But the doctor told me I should never get pregnant again, or I wouldn't live through it. I was so afraid your father would reject me and find another wife who could give him the sons he wanted." She had smiled then, and Nura had been glad that the story was going to end happily. "But my beloved Faisel, your wonderful father, told me that you and I were enough for him. He said all he wanted was for you and me to be healthy and happy, and he has done everything in his power to ensure that." She laid her hand on Nura's knee. "Your father is a very good man. Never forget that."

As Nura watched in vain for Sara's name to pop up on the screen, she knew she would always remember that conversation with her mother, just as she would always remember that her father was a very good man. But would he still think that she and her mother were enough for him if he knew what his only child now believed about the prophet Isa? Somehow she doubted that, and despite her joy at the eternal truth she had recently discovered, she felt a cold chill of fear pass over her.

∽≈∾ ∽≈∾ ∽≈∾

Emily Thompson eased herself down the bus steps and onto the sidewalk. She had long since given up driving and kept her travels as simple as possible, either riding the bus or calling for a reduced-rate ride on the seniors' van that made its rounds through town. She was grateful for both and glad she no longer had to fight the traffic or worry about her slowing reflexes.

Her eyesight was still good, though, despite the glasses she'd worn for reading for years. She didn't doubt that the police would want to be aware of that fact, since she was even now marching up the walkway to the front entrance of the police station, ready to tell them what had happened just before young Emir Al Tamimi had been shot. Perhaps her story would help them put together the pieces in an otherwise vague puzzle.

Stepping inside the building, she stopped and blinked a time or two, giving her eyes time to get used to the inside lighting. She had removed her sunglasses and put them back into their case in her purse, and now stood in front of a large counter with several windows. Where should she start?

She was just about to read the signs in front of each window in an attempt to get some direction when she heard a voice call to her, "Can I help you, ma'am?"

Turning toward the voice, she smiled. The young woman peering at her through the window above the counter looked warm and welcoming. Perhaps this wasn't going to be so difficult after all.

Or God, she thought. The
realization nearly drowned her in grief.

## Chapter 27

Sara walked until she felt as if she couldn't take another step. Even the nearest bench looked too far away, so she slumped down onto the grass under a towering pine tree and leaned back against the rough trunk. Maybe no one would notice her there, and if she pressed herself hard enough against the bark, she might blend right in and disappear.

Disappear. That's what she'd really like to do, but life wasn't going to let her off the hook that easily. Sooner or later she knew she was going to have to go back and face her family. And eventually, she'd have to tell them what she'd suspected about Emir and kept to herself. Would they ever forgive her? Why should they? She doubted she'd ever be able to forgive herself.

*Or God*, she thought. The realization nearly drowned her in grief. No matter what else had gone on in her life, she always knew she had God's unchanging love as a sure anchor. Now that anchor had disappeared, and she was adrift in an ocean of confusion and pain. How could God leave her here this way? Didn't He care about her at all? Had it all been just one big cruel joke?

For a brief moment she transferred her thoughts from losing Emir to her discussions with Nura. What would she ever say to the Saudi girl now? How would she tell her that Jesus was real and that He loved her when she was no longer sure she believed that herself?

"Sara?"

The deep, soft voice seemed to come from very far away, and Sara was determined to ignore it. There was no one she wanted to see or speak with, at least not for a while.

She sat very still, willing the owner of the voice to go away. He didn't. In less than a minute, Sara's father dropped to the damp grass beside her and took her hand in his own. When she still didn't respond, Yusef lifted her hand to his lips and kissed it, so softly Sara scarcely felt it. Tears began to pour from her eyes then, as her father waited silently at her side, holding her hand and staring out at the water while she cried.

∞ ∞ ∞

Once Emily had explained to the pleasant young woman at the window why she was there, she had quickly been escorted into the office of a middle-aged man with a slight paunch, a receding dark hairline, and a no-nonsense demeanor. Detective Worley immediately indicated the only extra seat in the tiny room and then offered her a cup of what smelled like yesterday's coffee. Emily took the chair and declined the drink.

"So," Detective Worley began, sipping at his own steaming cup of caffeine, "you think you have some information that might tie in with the shooting of Emir Al Tamimi. Tell me about it."

*No preliminaries*, Emily thought. *Just jump right in with both feet. All right, here goes.*

Scarcely taking a breath, Emily related the events of the night she'd been awakened by her dog, growling and barking and refusing to settle down. She continued right up to the part where Emir had threatened her with a knife and then, when she refused to comply, exited her home the same way he'd entered, dropping his knife in the process.

186

Mention of the dropped knife brought the first visible reaction from the detective. Plunking his cup of coffee down on his cluttered desk, he raised his dark eyebrows and exclaimed, "Not only was this boy in your house, threatening you, but he left a weapon behind—and you're just now coming in to tell us about it? Do you have the knife with you?"

Emily frowned. She had expected the police would mention that she should have come to them sooner, but it did seem the man was overreacting a bit. She shrugged. "No, I do not have the knife with me. I am not in the habit of carrying weapons around in my purse or pocket. But don't worry; it's in a safe place at home. And I didn't contact you sooner because I didn't know at first who the boy was or what else had transpired once he left my house. Then the next afternoon I read in the paper about the shooting and saw the picture of the young man, and I knew it was the same boy. I suppose I should have come right away, but it isn't easy for me to get around, you know. And besides, I needed to think and pray about it first. But by last night I knew I should get in and tell you about it first thing this morning." She took a deep breath. "So here I am."

Detective Worley, his cheeks flushed and brown eyes bulging, leaned forward. "Why didn't you at least call us last night? Why wait until this morning?"

Emily shrugged again. "I was already in my nightgown, and I don't like company when I'm not dressed. It made perfectly good sense to me to wait until this morning. And I caught the very first bus I could—as soon as I'd fed Pepe, of course."

The detective continued to stare for a moment, then let out a long puff of air. "Of course," he muttered. "You had to feed Pepe first. And Pepe would be . . . ?"

"My Chihuahua. The one that woke me up when he heard someone in the house."

"I see." He took a deep breath, and Emily had the distinct impression that he was struggling for control, though she couldn't imagine why. Was it really such a big deal that she had waited until this morning to tell them what happened?

Detective Worley smiled, though it seemed tight and, Emily thought, forced. She smiled back, ready to help in any way she could. She only hoped the young man who'd climbed in her window and later been shot was recovering, though she decided to wait a bit before asking about him.

⤬ ⤬ ⤬

Sara had no idea how much time had passed, as she leaned gratefully against her father's strong shoulder. Somehow his compassion for her in the midst of his own pain made her guilt so much worse, but she doubted she could survive without his support at that moment. She clung to his hand as if it were one of the tubes that had carried life-giving liquid to Emir for the past couple of days.

*But he doesn't need the tubes anymore*, she thought. *The fluids and machines aren't keeping him alive now. Nothing is. He's gone. Dead. I'll never see him again—not in this life and not in the next.*

She sobbed, and her father reached around her shoulders and pulled her close, holding her while she cried on his chest. At last, exhausted, she looked up at him, her eyes feeling as if they'd been rubbed with sandpaper.

"Where's Mom?" was all she could manage to say.

As tears shimmered in his own dark eyes, Yusef answered, "She stayed with Emir. She couldn't bear to leave him, so the doctor advised me to let her have some final moments with him." His voice cracked but he went on. "I told her I was going to leave and look for you, but I'm not sure she heard me."

Sara's heart squeezed. Could she be any more selfish? Not only was she guilty for not telling her parents about what she suspected was going on with Emir, but she had run out on them when they needed her most, forcing her father to leave her mother behind while he come looking for her.

"I'm sorry, Dad," she whispered.

He shushed her and stroked her hair. "You have nothing to be sorry for, sweetheart. Nothing. We are all brokenhearted right now. Even the Father cries with us in our grief."

Sara bit her tongue. She did not want to hear about God's unfailing love or His compassion for those who sorrowed. Where was He when they needed Him, when they begged and implored

Him for a miracle? Couldn't He at least have let Emir live long enough to come out of the coma and receive Christ before slipping into eternity? But she wasn't about to say any of that to her father, at least not now. This was going to be the hardest thing any of them had ever had to endure, and she wasn't going to do anything to make it worse. Whether or not to confess her part in the tragedy was something she would have to consider long and hard before coming to a decision.

She smiled as she stood at her window and watched the first thin streaks of morning tease the skyline.

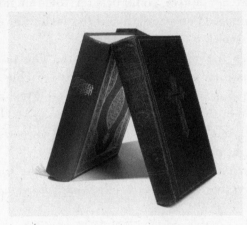

## Chapter 28

The night passed slowly for Farah. She tossed and turned and even got up out of bed more than once to pace the floor. A couple of times she thought she heard or sensed someone outside her door. Kareem? Undoubtedly. But why?

She shivered, pulling the covers higher around her neck, though the room certainly wasn't cold. The thought that her brother was stalking her, watching her, waiting for her to make a mistake, to somehow reveal to him something—anything—that he could use against her, unnerved her, despite her resolution to make sure that everything she did was completely in line with being a good Muslim girl.

Which is exactly what she was, she reminded herself. Surely she couldn't be faulted for having a dream! It wasn't like she went online to a chat room like Nura had done....

The reminder of her cousin stirred up feelings in her heart that Farah did not want to acknowledge. But even as she attempted to push them away, the thought came to her that if Nura really was into something she shouldn't be and Farah knew about it, would she too be in trouble if she didn't report it?

The question was almost more than Farah could bear to consider. To betray her cousin would be a terrible thing; yet wouldn't it be much worse to betray Allah and the Islam faith by concealing Nura's actions?

No. It was too much to contemplate. The possibilities of what might happen to Nura if her parents discovered that she was spending time online with infidels and Muslims who had betrayed their faith were too horrible to imagine. Farah determined to block out all thoughts of Nura and to focus only on the upcoming Night of Power.

*Surely something wonderful will happen then*, she thought, *and I will no longer feel this torment inside. Oh, please, please, may it be so!*

∽◦⊱ ∽◦⊱ ∽◦⊱

The sun was high overhead by the time Sara and her parents returned home. Their pastor accompanied them and offered to stay a while, but Yusef had insisted they all needed some rest. The pastor promised to come back later, and assured them that members of the congregation would stop by later as well, bringing food and support.

Sara didn't care about any of it. She just wanted to be alone in her room, locked away from everything and everyone. The very idea that Emir's empty room was on the other side of her wall nearly crushed the air from her lungs. Oh, what she would give to hear his music pounding through that wall, assuring her that all was well!

But all was not well, and Sara wondered if it ever would be again. How did life continue when someone you loved so much was suddenly ripped away, leaving a bloody, gaping wound with nothing to heal it? Would it always hurt this much? Would she ever smile again? Somehow she doubted it, though she knew well-meaning people would tell her otherwise.

Restless, she felt unable to lie down on her bed for any length of time, and she knew for certain she wouldn't be able to sleep. Her gaze landed on her computer screen, and she decided she might as well check her emails to see if the temporary distraction would ease the ache inside her. After deleting most of them, she checked those that remained and decided there was nothing that needed an immediate answer. She supposed she could visit the chat room, but then she risked being confronted by Nura, who would undoubtedly ask about Emir. Nura would also expect Sara to be steadfast in her faith, despite what had taken place since they last talked, and Sara knew she would never be able to do that.

She flipped off the computer and decided to give sleep a try, though she wasn't optimistic. The minute she lay down, her mind returned to the night she had discovered Emir's bed empty and her brother missing from his room. Why, oh why, hadn't she gone to her parents immediately? And why had she even pretended to believe Emir's story about Joni?

*Joni!* The realization hit her like a stone dropped on her chest. Someone had to tell Joni about Emir. And there was no doubt that she was that somebody. It would be one of most difficult messages she had ever delivered to anyone. The familiar urge to pray for wisdom and strength before calling touched her thoughts, but she dismissed it and picked up her phone. What was the point of praying when God didn't even listen, let alone answer? She would just have to handle this on her own.

ക്രික ക്രിക ക്രിക

Emily once again stepped off the bus, this time just a block from her home. The police had offered her a ride, but she declined, explaining that she was used to riding the bus and saw no reason to change her routine now. When they told her they'd be sending extra patrols through her neighborhood, as they were concerned about her safety, she had thanked them but assured them she'd be fine. She had so hoped to return from the police station with a sense of relief, having unburdened herself of the secret she had kept for the last few days. But now, sadly, her heart was heavier even than when she'd left home.

Carefully placing one foot in front of the other in her practiced avoidance of a fall, she carried herself homeward, realizing she would arrive just in time for lunch. But food was the last thing on her mind, though she knew Pepe would be waiting expectantly beside his empty bowl. The thought of her faithful four-legged friend encouraged her to keep walking and to hold back the tears.

*Oh, Father,* she prayed silently as she continued on, *only You could bring tears to my eyes over the death of one who so recently broke into my home and threatened me with a knife. Without Your unconditional love inside me, I'd probably be thinking that the young man got exactly what he deserved. But I know, Lord, that if You delighted in giving us what we deserve, we would all end up in hell—and rightfully so! It is only by Your mercies that we are not consumed.*

Stepping up onto her porch and fitting her key into the lock, she heard Pepe's yaps of welcome. Usually that was enough to cheer her heart, but not this time. With the exception of a promised visit from a police officer to pick up the knife, the remainder of the day would be dedicated to prayer and intercession, for surely there was a family suffering great pain.

❧❧ ❧❧ ❧❧

The first call to prayer echoed out from the minarets, filling the skies over Riyadh with the reminder that tonight was the most holy night of the entire Ramadan celebration. Tonight was the Night of Power, and faithful Muslims rose from bed that morning with a sense of excitement and anticipation.

Except for Kareem. Though he welcomed the morning more than any others during Ramadan, it was not because he expected anything great to happen in the way of a miracle. It was simply because he was glad to see the month nearly at an end. He hated the extra prayer times, the fasting, the attention to good deeds and reading of the Quran. It was all so much wasted time, in his opinion. Yes, he considered himself a Muslim, but he saw no reason to become a fanatic about it. His only concern was the one female in their household who did not line up with what he believed was required of a faithful Muslim woman, and he would not rest until he found a way to resolve it.

With that thought driving him, he rose from his bed to begin the day that would culminate in the Night of Power. He could only hope that would include the miracle of his discovering and exposing what was going on in Farah's life, once and for all.

∽✵∾  ∽✵∾  ∽✵∾

The Night of Power. Nura stood up from her bed with the realization that tonight was the most holy time in all of Ramadan, a time that had once filled her with excitement, though she never actually witnessed anything miraculous as a result of it.

She smiled as she stood at her window and watched the first thin streaks of morning tease the skyline. As far as she was concerned, she already had her miracle, and it had come when she realized that Isa was more than a prophet. He was truly the Son of God, as those the Muslims sometimes referred to as the "people of the Book" claimed He was. Of course, the Jews were also called people of the Book, and they certainly didn't believe the Christians' claims about Isa, but now Nura did. And that changed everything.

Rather than bow on her prayer rug, Nura opted to fire up her computer and return to the Bible she had found online. How wonderful to have at her fingertips the entire book of writings that told of Isa! Though it would take many, many hours of reading and study even to begin to understand the complete message of the book, it was thrilling to be able to press a button and click a mouse and have the words pop up on the screen in front of her. Though she longed for someone to help her understand, to teach her more about this wonderful Isa, for now she was more than content to have His story to read—and she vowed to do so every chance she got.

Sara felt her eyes widen,
and she swallowed.

## Chapter 29

S ARA STILL COULDN'T IMAGINE HOW THEY'D MADE IT THROUGH that first day. She hadn't been able to sleep at all, and she doubted her parents had either. Now they were all in the family room, along with a couple of women from their church who had stopped by to drop off another casserole and a dessert.

While her parents smiled vacantly and did their best to keep the conversation going, Sara didn't even make a pretense of participating. All she could think about was how in the world they were supposed to eat all the food that had arrived at their home in the past few hours. Her mother told her they needed to be gracious and appreciative, and Sara supposed she was right, but why did people feel they had to feed you when the last thing in the world you were interested in was eating?

With the freezer and refrigerator now full to overflowing, slow cookers and cake pans covered the kitchen counter, each filled with something that no doubt would have been delicious under normal circumstances. But these circumstances were anything but normal.

Sara sat, unmoving, in the rocker near the empty fireplace. How many evenings had their family sat in this very room and not appreciated how wonderful it was just to be together? This was the room where they had always put their Christmas tree. When Sara closed her eyes, she found her mind replaying the many Christmas mornings when she and Emir had raced down the stairs and stood in the doorway, staring in awe at all the colorful presents that had appeared under the tree during the night. Sara had never completely bought into the Santa story, and her parents hadn't really pushed it, preferring instead to focus on the true meaning of Christmas, which was something Sara didn't want to think about at the moment. The memory that tore at her heart was of the day Emir had come home from school crying because his friends had told him there was no Santa. It was as if he had stopped believing in the baby Jesus at the very same time.

She squeezed her eyes tightly, trying to stop the tears. Could there really be more of them? It seemed she had cried herself dry more than once throughout the course of the day, and now here they came again! And all at the reminder of the Baby Jesus.

*Why, God? If You sent Your Son to die for our sins, why couldn't You have healed Emir, or at least kept him alive long enough to receive Jesus as his Savior?*

The words came as a silent whisper, but they jolted her upright in her chair and snapped her eyes open at the thought: *What makes you think I didn't?*

She looked around the room, certain someone had spoken to her. But her parents and the women from the church hadn't moved. They still sat in the same spots, murmuring comforting words to one another and occasionally stopping to pray together, seemingly oblivious to her presence.

Before Sara could even begin to consider the words she'd heard, the doorbell jangled, and Yusef excused himself to answer it. When he returned a moment later, he gazed down with concern at Sara.

"It's Joni," he said. "I don't think she knows yet. She just got home after being at school and then gone with her mother this afternoon. She got your phone message and decided to come over instead of calling back. She..." He paused and took a deep breath. "She somehow thinks we have good news about Emir."

Sara felt her eyes widen, and she swallowed. She'd been disappointed when she'd called Joni and she didn't answer, but she'd decided not to leave the entire message on voice mail. She'd asked only that Joni call her back as soon as possible. This news was something no one should hear in a recording, and she certainly didn't want to risk having Joni hear it at school the next day—and certainly by then it would be common knowledge there.

"Can you handle it?" Yusef asked. "Or would you rather I—"

Sara held up her hand and shook her head, interrupting his offer. "No. Thanks, Dad, but I'll do it. I think it would be better that way."

Her father hesitated, and then nodded. "All right," he said. "But we're here if you need us."

⁓⁓⁓ ⁓⁓⁓ ⁓⁓⁓

Emily had spent the majority of the afternoon and evening in prayer, though she'd broken it up a bit by taking Pepe for a walk. Later, Detective Worley had stopped by to pick up the knife, and she'd shown him around and answered a few more questions. Before he left, he had assured her again that they had stepped up patrols in the neighborhood and were only a phone call away if she needed them.

Emily sighed. The detective was a nice man, she supposed, and she appreciated his concern, but he just didn't seem to understand that she knew God was protecting her, just as He had the night Emir broke into her home—and all the nights throughout her long life.

The sun had set now, and bedtime was nearly upon them again. Her feet ached as she closed up the house and slowly made her way to her room.

"It's tough getting old, isn't it, boy?" she observed as the Chihuahua seemed to hesitate before jumping up on the bed and settling into his familiar spot. Emily had noticed he'd been having a little trouble getting up that high lately. Maybe she should put a stool or bench on the far side of the bed to make it a little easier for him.

"You know, Pepe," she said, removing her robe and slippers and sitting down on the edge of the bed, "I just have this feeling that Emir Al Tamimi did not pick our house at random. I think God sent him here so I could pray for him and his family. He's gone now and it's too late for him, though I pray he asked Jesus into his heart before he died. But it's his family I'm concerned with now. I wish I knew if they were Christians."

She sighed and lay down, pulling the covers up to her shoulders. "I suppose, unless I find out otherwise, I'll just assume they're not and pray accordingly. Besides, even if they are, they're still going through a very bad time right now." She glanced over at her faithful companion. "We know what that's like, don't we, boy?"

Pepe whimpered, and Emily reached up and turned off the light.

∽◊∾ ∽◊∾ ∽◊∾

Sara and Joni sat on the floor, slumped against the side of Sara's bed. By the time the girls had reached the top of the stairs and headed into Sara's room, Joni had realized the news about Emir wasn't good and had burst into tears. That was nearly two hours earlier, and they still took turns sniffling and sobbing periodically. Though they'd been slightly more than casual friends for years, having grown up in such close proximity, Sara had never felt nearer to Joni than at this moment. Somehow she sensed that their shared grief would bind them together for many years to come.

"I still can't believe it," Joni mumbled, staring down at the crumpled tissue in her clasped hands. "He was only fifteen, the same age as me."

Sara nodded, though she knew Joni couldn't see her. "I know. I feel the same way. I just want to wake up and find out this is all an ugly dream. I want to hear Emir's music pounding through my wall from his room, just so I can go over there and tell him to

200

turn it down." She swallowed a sob. "But I don't think I would now. I'd let him play it as loud as he wanted."

The sob Sara had swallowed burst forth from Joni's throat and she whimpered for a moment as she dabbed at her eyes with her tissue. "He'll never play that music again," she whispered.

Sara nodded one more time. So many things Emir would never do again. How different it would be if only they knew he was with the Lord!

"I'm glad I at least had a chance to pray with him," Joni said, her voice soft but the impact of the statement startling Sara.

"What?" Sara demanded. "What do you mean? When did you pray with him?"

Joni lifted her head, fixing her puffy eyes on Sara's face. "The last time I visited him at the hospital. I held his hand and told him I wanted to make sure that if he died, he'd be waiting for me in heaven when I got there. I told him it was OK that he couldn't talk. All he had to do was agree with my prayer in his heart." She took a deep breath. "Even though I miss him, I feel better knowing that I had a chance to do that."

Sara felt her shoulders slump. She had so hoped that Joni was going to tell her that somehow, miraculously, she'd had a chance to pray with Emir and lead him to Christ before the shooting. Obviously that wasn't the case.

Joni ducked her head. "You probably think it's strange that I did that. I haven't exactly been a very strong Christian in the past. But lately I've been wanting to get closer to God. Seeing Emir in the hospital like that just changed me somehow."

Joni lifted her head, and Sara knew from her friend's questioning look that she was seeking affirmation. Sara nodded and forced a smile. Only a few days earlier she would have been thrilled at Joni's change of heart, but right now it only added to the pain in her own.

Sara was about to sign off when
she saw Nura's name pop up
on the screen.

## Chapter 30

THE FIRST TWENTY-SIX DAYS OF RAMADAN HAD COME AND gone, and at last the Night of Power was upon them. Farah approached it with a sense of anticipation that bordered on desperation. If nothing special happened to her tonight, she somehow sensed it never would. All she wanted was a deeper call to faith, a more meaningful understanding of Allah and Islam and what that meant to her. She wanted to come away from this night with a clearer direction of what she was supposed to do as a faithful Muslim girl. Perhaps her parents would soon arrange a marriage for her, and then her only real purpose would be to become the best wife and mother possible. If so, that would be enough. But was that truly all there was? Would being a good Muslim daughter or wife or mother — or sister — erase the longing that still stirred in her chest when the unbidden images of the hooded Man in the garden called to her?

Oh, how she prayed it would be! For if it wasn't, how would she continue on as she was? How could she live without pursuing the nagging in her heart? How could she continue to ignore or avoid her cousin, who at least was more honest in her own search for the truth about Isa?

Farah knew that if she opened her window she would be able to hear the distant chants of the men at the mosque, praying more intently and longer than at any other time during Ramadan. Most Muslims believed that on the Night of Power, Allah was more likely to answer their prayers, and she so hoped they were right. Though as a woman she couldn't go to the mosque and pray with her father and brother, she had every intention of staying awake to pray until dawn. If she had no miracle by then, she'd resign herself to the fact that it would never come.

⊱✿⊰ ⊱✿⊰ ⊱✿⊰

Joni had asked if she could stay overnight, and both Sara's parents and Joni's mother had readily agreed. The girls had lain awake long into the night, occasionally reminiscing about Emir and more often than not, continuing their marathon of tears. Somewhere in the early morning hours they had finally fallen asleep. Now, with the sun beginning to infiltrate the curtained windows, Sara stirred.

She opened her eyes slowly. Why did they feel so swollen and dry? Memories jumbled in her mind but didn't come into focus until she heard the soft breathing beside her. Turning her head on the pillow, she spotted Joni, and the entire nightmare of the last few days came flooding back.

*No!* she thought. *No more tears. At least not yet. Please!*

Easing herself from the bed, she slipped on a light robe and padded to her desk, where she sat down and pressed the computer's ON button. Though she knew she might regret it, for some reason she simply couldn't resist the urge to try to connect with Nura. Perhaps it was because their communication had been so important to her before —

She shook her head. *Don't go there. No thoughts of Emir right now. Not yet anyway. Not until you're ready to start crying nonstop again.* She took a deep breath and concentrated. At last she was in the chat room. But where was Nura?

204

And then she remembered. It was Ramadan. With the time difference, faithful Muslims in Riyadh were no doubt beginning their observation of the Night of Power. There was little chance she'd hear from Nura any time soon.

꩜ ꩜ ꩜

The Night of Power. Nura felt a twinge of guilt at the way she'd taken advantage of her mother's assumption that she was going to her room to pray to Allah when, in reality, she fully intended to spend the long hours of the night reading about Isa. Her father had already gone to the mosque to pray with the other men and might very well remain there until morning, while her mother would no doubt pray for a short time and then go to bed for some much needed rest.

Nura wasn't tired at all, though she'd slept little in the past few days. It seemed the more she read from the Book, the stronger her love became for Isa. How was that possible? And yet she knew it was.

Pulling up the life-giving words on her monitor, she sighed. Oh, how she wished she had someone to talk to about this wonderful new life she was just beginning to experience!

*If only Farah hadn't withdrawn from me! Will it ever be safe to mention Isa to her again? But who else is there? Who can I possibly talk to about all this? Sara claims there are a few others in the Kingdom who believe as I do about Isa, but they certainly don't say so publicly. How can I connect with anyone who shares my views and can help me understand them better?*

She smiled. Sara. Would her American friend at last be back online? And would she have good news about her brother, Emir? Nura hoped so, as she so wanted to rejoice with her friend—and then talk with her about the many questions and feelings she had in her heart.

꩜ ꩜ ꩜

Sara was about to sign off when she saw Nura's name pop up on the screen. A mixture of relief and apprehension swept over her as she immediately established the connection. She wasn't look-ing forward to giving Nura the news, but she had to get used to telling people about this, as much as it hurt.

*Sara, I'm so glad to hear from you! I've been worried. How is Emir?*

*Right to the point,* Sara thought. *OK, I guess I'll just get right to the point too. Maybe it'll be easier once I get the words out.*

Her fingers trembling slightly, she typed, *Emir died yesterday. I still can't believe it.*

There was a pause before the response came. *Oh, Sara, I'm so sorry! I had so hoped he was doing better.*

Sara nodded, suddenly wishing Nura weren't so far away. How she would love to bury her head in the girl's shoulder and sob. They had never even met face-to-face, and yet Sara sensed a closeness between them that hadn't been there before.

*We had hoped so too,* Sara typed. *But it just didn't happen that way.*

After another brief pause, the statement came, *I'm glad you at least know your brother is safe with Isa now, and that you will see him again one day.*

Sara gasped. Where had that come from? What had hap-pened in Nura's life since they last talked? She would have to be careful. If Nura truly had come to faith in Christ, Sara didn't dare damage the girl's new beliefs by venting her own doubts and pain. Nor did she dare even mention the fact that as far as she knew, Emir had not received Jesus as his Savior before he died.

*Thank you,* Sara answered. *That is very kind of you. But I'm a bit surprised that you would say that. Has something happened that I'm not aware of?*

*Yes,* came the answer. *Do you have time for me to tell you about it? Or would you rather I wait awhile?*

Sara's heart felt like lead, but she nodded at the screen. Why not? This was as good a time as any. What else would she do today except cry—and maybe help her parents plan Emir's funeral?

*Sure,* she wrote. *I'd love to hear about it. Please tell me.*

❧❧❧ ❧❧❧ ❧❧❧

206

Emily awoke a bit later than her usual "getting up with the chickens," as she often called it—though she hadn't had chickens or gotten up in the dark to feed them in many years.

The thought brought a poignant smile to her lips, as she remembered her many years on the missions field with Hank. They'd traveled to so many countries and led such an exciting and rewarding life, though they'd never amassed much in the way of worldly goods. But who needed them? They'd always had a roof over their heads and food in their stomachs, and God had blessed them to be able to minister to people around the globe, even though they'd never had children of their own.

*Spiritual children*, she thought as she eased herself to a sitting position and heard Pepe stir as well. The dog was definitely sleeping more these days. She didn't even want to think about losing her beloved companion, though the loss certainly wouldn't begin to compare to losing Hank, and both she and Pepe had somehow survived that.

*Not without Your help, Lord*, she thought, sliding her feet into her slippers and reaching for her robe. *I would never have made it without You. As always, You were faithful.* Absently she patted Pepe's head, as he nudged his way under her arm. *Fifty-four years of marriage. What a blessing! I wouldn't have traded a day of it, Lord. Thank You!*

Pepe's nudging was growing more pronounced, and Emily stopped her musings to look down into his large brown eyes. "Hungry, fella?" she asked. "Silly question. Of course you are! You're always hungry."

She stood to her feet. "All right, boy. Let's go start another day, shall we?"

The voice came from without, and
yet from within, pulsating in the air
while echoing in her heart.

## Chapter 31

FARAH PRAYED LONG INTO THE NIGHT, CONTINUING ON HER prayer rug even when her back hurt and her legs and feet felt numb. When she could stand it no longer, she convinced herself she would lie on her bed and pray there, maybe even study the Quran for a while. So long as she was concentrating on Allah, that was all that mattered.

She'd scarcely been on her bed for more than a few minutes when she drifted off and found herself once again in the garden that flooded her senses with the most vibrant colors and heady aromas imaginable. Oh, why had she stayed away so long? She wanted to run barefoot through the lush green grass, or sit beside the gurgling waterfall and breathe the clean air. Was this paradise? *Is this where the righteous went when they died?*

"Farah."

The voice came from without, and yet from within, pulsating in the air while echoing in her heart. Tears of joy filled her eyes as she realized she would at last see the face that had been hidden from her by the hood, yet she ducked her head, afraid to look.

Kathi Macias

"I told you I had come to call you to My heart," said the voice. "Are you ready to come now, Farah?"

Slowly she lifted her head, terrified yet overjoyed at what was sure to happen. And then she saw Him. He stood only a few feet from her, draped in the same robe she'd seen Him in before. His hands were outstretched, and she shuddered at the wounds she saw there. Then she raised her eyes, yearning to see the One who called to her. The hood was gone, and though she saw etchings of pain in His face, His eyes shone with love for her. Could it be? Certainly He loved everyone equally, but somehow she knew this was personal.

"I did it for you," He said.

She frowned, confused. Did what?

Behind Him a light began to glow, slowly taking the shape of a cross. She gasped. She knew the people of the Book, the ones who called themselves Christians, preached that Isa had died on a cross for the sins of the world, but Muslims rejected the need for such a thing. Now, at this very moment, Farah realized it was true. But Isa hadn't simply died on the cross for the sins of the world; He had died for her—for *her* sins! He had taken the punishment that she deserved because He loved her.

Falling to her knees, she cried out in anguish and in joy, trying to absorb the impact of the price this Isa had paid for her, even as she thrilled at His willingness to do so. How could she not follow such a loving and merciful God?

For surely that was exactly who He was.

❧❧❧

Joni had gone home midmorning, leaving Sara to ponder her conversation with Nura. The Saudi girl had experienced some amazing transformations since they last spoke. How had it happened so quickly? While Sara grieved the loss of her brother, Nura was falling in love with Jesus—Isa, as she called Him. There was simply no other way to describe the relationship Nura was developing with the Savior who had so obviously invaded her life. And Sara couldn't help but feel more than a bit envious.

210

Once again lying sleepless on her bed and staring at the ceiling as she listened to her parents downstairs, talking with yet more visitors from the church, Sara scolded herself for being so petty. But the feelings of envy only grew stronger. She'd been in love with Jesus once. He'd been everything to her, and she'd trusted Him implicitly. But He'd let her down. When she needed Him most, He hadn't been there. Of course her love for Him had cooled!

But was that truly when it started? A twinge of guilt pierced her heart as she realized that though she had continued to read her Bible and pray and attend church regularly, she had allowed her closeness to God to fade into the background of all the other activities that crowded her life. Even her online witnessing to Nura had been effective only because God had spoken through her, not because Sara's passion was evident.

Hot tears stung her eyes again, but this time they were tears of shame. "I'm so sorry, Lord," she whispered. "I didn't mean to drift away, but I did. I realize it now, but what do I do about it? I'm still so heartbroken about Emir. If only You'd kept him alive long enough to receive Jesus as his Savior—"

*What makes you think I didn't?*

The words she'd heard earlier but forgotten in her grief now came flooding back to reverberate in her heart. Was it possible? Had Emir somehow heard Sara's words—or his mother's or father's or Joni's—and been born again before he passed from this earth into eternity?

Sara wanted desperately to believe it, but how could she be sure?

❧❧❧ ❧❧❧ ❧❧❧

Nura's heart was torn. She was thrilled that she had reconnected online with Sara, who had so graciously listened to Nura's story and answered some of her questions about certain verses and chapters in the Bible. But she was also grieved that her friend had lost her brother. Fifteen! So young—and to have been shot! America must indeed be as dangerous a country as she had heard. And yet, as Nura had said to Sara earlier, at least they could rejoice to know that Emir was now with Isa. What better future could there be for any of them? And one day they would all be reunited in that wonderful place. Nura was certain of that now. After talking with Sara, she no longer had any doubts that she was God's child and that Isa was her Savior. If she died before the night was over, she could do so with joy, knowing where she would be after her last heartbeat on earth.

But what about her parents? How could she ever tell them about Isa? And yet...if she didn't, how would they ever know the truth?

*I must pray for them,* she thought, switching off her computer at last as the words from the Bible had begun to blur before her weary eyes. *And for Farah. She said Isa had appeared to her in a dream and told her He had come to call her to His heart. She must answer Him! Oh, Isa, please continue to call to my cousin until she hears and answers! I would so love to share this joy with her!*

⤙⤚ ⤙⤚ ⤙⤚

When Farah awoke the next morning, she felt completely refreshed and at peace, though everything within her screamed that she was now in more trouble than she'd ever imagined. If Kareem found out—

But why should he? She certainly wasn't going to tell him, and no one else knew.

Nura's face swam into view, and Farah winced. How could she hide this from her cousin? Nura had a right to know. They had trusted one another, shared their most intimate secrets, and then Farah had turned her back on her. She owed it to her cousin to make it right and to tell her of the miracle that had taken place during the Night of Power. Surely Nura would keep the news to herself, and so long as neither of them ever told anyone else, they would be safe.

Farah smiled. Yes, they would be safe and they could share their discoveries about Isa with one another. She would call Nura today and arrange a meeting. They would have to be careful that Kareem was nowhere near, but that shouldn't be a problem. Farah knew her brother's routine, and she and Nura should be able to get together privately very soon. The thought warmed her heart, and she nearly leapt out of bed with anticipation.

The most difficult thing for Emily
to accept was that her days of
usefulness were nearly over.

## Chapter 32

THE DAY HAD PASSED SLOWLY, AND NOW SARA SAT ON ONE side of the dining room table with her parents at each end, while the empty chair across from her nearly screamed with accusations of guilt. *Emir.* His name echoed in her hollow heart as she used her fork to push the nameless serving of chicken casserole around on her dinner plate. She knew her parents weren't any more interested in eating than she was, but she had overheard her father telling her mother that they needed to try to get back to some sort of routine "for Sara's sake."

*For my sake? Why should they do anything for my sake? It's my fault we're sitting here like this, trying to eat when we're not hungry and staring at an empty chair and—*

"Sara? Did you hear me?"

Her father's voice penetrated the darkness of her pain, and she lifted her head to glance from one parent to the other. Both stared at her with obvious concern, adding to her already over-whelming layers of guilt.

She swallowed. "I'm sorry, Dad. I didn't. What did you say?"

Her father's dark eyes softened, and he reached toward her and laid his hand on hers. "I said that we need to plan for the funeral on Saturday. That's only two days away. A lot of people will be there."

When he paused, Sara wondered if he expected some sort of response from her, so she nodded and waited. After what seemed like several minutes but was probably only a matter of seconds, during which Sara realized her father was struggling to maintain his composure, he spoke again. "Your mother and I have made all the arrangements. I hope you don't mind, but it seemed you were just too caught up in your grief to get involved. And the one time we did mention it to you, it didn't seem to register. So we went ahead without you. Are you OK with that, sweetheart?"

OK with that? The words started a buzzing in Sara's ears. Why wouldn't she be OK with it? What right did she have to complain about anything, or even to expect to be included, for that matter? If her parents knew her part in this tragedy, they wouldn't even want her at the service.

She nodded again. "Sure," she managed to say. "I'm fine."

Yusef raised his eyebrows. "Positive?"

Sara forced a smile, but the crack in her voice when she spoke belied her assurance. "Absolutely."

Her father paused again and then squeezed her hand before releasing it. "Good," he said. "Then we must start thinking about details. Will we share our memories of Emir at the service? The pastor asked me that today, and I told him I wasn't sure. How do you feel about it, Sara?"

The thought horrified Sara, as the lump in her throat grew and fresh tears pushed against her eyes. Speak about Emir in front of what would no doubt be a very large gathering? Never! How could she? What would she say? That she knew Emir was sneaking out of his bedroom window at night and was probably involved in something he shouldn't be, but she had chosen to ignore it rather than help him?

No. She would have a hard enough time just getting through the ordeal of a funeral and graveside service, but recounting one of her memories of the brother she had betrayed was out of the question.

᠀᠊᠊ ᠊᠊᠊ ᠊᠊᠊

As another day drew to a close, Emily and Pepe sat together on the front porch. The faithful Chihuahua was curled up at Emily's feet, as she rocked slowly and watched the last fading rays of sunlight disappear below the mountains that ran behind the small river not far from her home. She loved this old place, and the older she got herself, the more she felt it was perfectly designed for her in her last years of life on earth. She and Hank had bought it when they retired from the missions field, thinking they would spend their last years together in the little cottage in the Pacific Northwest, where the two had grown up, met, and married when they were young and full of energy and dreams. So many of those dreams had been fulfilled during their many trips abroad; now they were mere memories—joyful ones, to be sure, but memories nonetheless. The most difficult thing for Emily to accept was that her days of usefulness were nearly over. Surely God had something more for her, even in her final stage of transition to heaven, and she consoled herself with the fact that it was about praying for others. Still, she sensed something more.

A cool breeze interrupted her thoughts, reminding her that summer was truly over and fall was settling in. There would be few evenings warm enough to sit outside, and she'd have to get a cord of firewood ordered and delivered for the long, gray, wet winter that lay ahead.

*One more thing that Hank used to do for me,* she thought. *Now I'm on my own—except for You, of course. I know You're my Husband now, Lord, but I must admit that I do grow weary at times with all the details I need to attend to.*

Pepe stirred, and a whisper of a yap escaped as he slept. Immediately Emily felt chastised. "Forgive me, Father," she whispered. "I have no right to complain. You have been faithful through all my years, and so very good to me. Thank You, Lord! Though I know I don't deserve all the blessings You've given me, I truly do appreciate them."

217

The thought that there were more yet to come brought a smile to her wrinkled face, and Emily rose to her feet to escort Pepe inside, where they would once again get ready for bed.

❧ ❧ ❧

Nura was excited but confused. Farah had called to ask if she could come by for a visit, though she hadn't indicated why. Her mother was coming, though Nadia would not join them until later as she already had plans with a friend. This meant Sakeena and Sultana would be free to visit while the cousins did the same. After Nadia arrived, they would all pitch in to prepare the evening meal, and the men would join them to eat it at the end of the day.

Farah and her mother were due any moment, and Nura's stomach churned at the possibilities. Was there are a specific reason the women were coming early in the day, rather than waiting until evening when the family could come together as they most often did? Was the visit Farah's idea, or her mother's? Either way, what would Farah and Nura talk about when they were alone? Their last conversation on the phone had left Nura feeling rejected and even a bit frightened. What would be the result of this visit? Did Farah plan to try to convince Nura to discard her interest in Isa? Nura shivered at the thought. It would be more difficult to keep her secret from her cousin than from others because Farah already knew of Nura's visits to the chat room.

The front door chime interrupted her thoughts. Farah and Aunt Sultana had arrived, and Nura's questions would soon be answered. She took a deep breath and exited her room to greet their visitors.

❧ ❧ ❧

Emily had been sleeping soundly when she was awakened by the feeling that she and Pepe had a visitor. But the dog snoozed on, not disturbed in the slightest.

She glanced at the clock. Just a little after midnight. Emily listened. The only sounds she heard were an occasional car driving past and the wind in the cherry tree outside her window.

She smiled, realizing the familiar presence she felt was not human. "Father," she whispered. "Forgive me for not recognizing You sooner. You've come to tell me something, haven't You?"

The answer came as a peaceful assurance in her heart, as she closed her eyes and determined to listen with her spirit, the way she had trained herself to do over the years.

The thought that Emir's funeral would surely be taking place soon became a surety in her mind. Did God want her to pray for the family in regard to that event... or was there something more?

"Do you want me to go, Lord?" Emily asked, her voice scarcely rising above the sound of her pounding heart. "Is that what You're telling me?" She waited until a quiet peace flooded her soul, and she smiled.

"All right, Lord," she said, as Pepe stirred beside her. "I'll do it. But You'll have to show me the details of how and when." She chuckled then, and her dog came to full attention. "I know You will, Father. You always do."

Pulling the Chihuahua close, she shut her eyes and drifted back to sleep.

Zarah and Nura at last stemmed
their tears and quieted their anxiety
by turning to the computer.

## Chapter 33

FARAH WAS SO EXCITED SHE COULD SCARCELY KEEP HERSELF under control as she struggled through the exchange of hugs and greetings. Once she'd contributed what she considered the bare minimum of acceptable conversation, she managed to catch Nura's eye and tried to telegraph to her that she wanted to talk to her privately. Had she understood?

Nura's expression was puzzled, but at last she shifted her confused gaze from her cousin to her mother. "Excuse us, Mom. Farah and I are going to my room for a little while—unless you need us to help with something."

Sakeena smiled. "You two go ahead. We'll call you when we need you."

Nearly bursting with relief at escaping her mother and aunt while at the same time eagerly anticipating the conversation to come, Farah had to restrain herself from squealing as she hurriedly followed Nura to her room. Once inside, Farah almost slammed the door behind her, startling her cousin in the process.

Kathi Macias

Farah grinned, watching Nura's obvious confusion. Confident that no one was listening and it was safe to talk, Farah stepped closer to her skittish cousin and whispered, "I met Him. Face-to-face, Nura. I met Him!"

She waited, watching Nura's eyes grow wide as understanding slowly displaced the confusion. "Isa?" she whispered. "Are you talking about Isa?"

Swallowing the laughter that begged to escape, Farah nodded. "Yes. Last night. The Night of Power. He came to me again in a dream, and this time..." She paused for effect, and then continued. "This time He let me see His face, and I knew that He loved me. Me, Nura! He loves me!" She leaned closer. "And He loves you too."

Eyes still wide, Nura nodded. "Yes," she said, her voice scarcely audible. "I know. He has shown me the same thing, through the reading of the Bible."

Farah gasped and stepped backward. "You have a Bible? Here? In your room?"

Nura's eyes darted nervously toward the door, and then back to Farah, even as she shook her head. "No, no, of course not. I don't have the book—not really. But I found it online. The entire thing, Farah. All of it! The entire story of Isa, and it's amazing! I've been talking to my American friend, Sara. She helped me understand, and..."

Before Farah could respond, Nura's eyes widened and filled with tears. After only a brief hesitation, she launched into an account of Sara's loss. Farah's eyes burned with tears as she listened, but again, before she could respond, Nura switched gears.

"Wait a minute. I thought you didn't want to talk about Isa any longer, that you were rededicating yourself to Allah and to Islam."

Farah hung her head and took a deep breath before lifting her gaze to resettle on Nura. "I'm sorry," she said. "That was wrong of me. But I was scared. Of Kareem, of what could happen if he or someone else finds out. I truly meant to turn my back on my interest in Isa and to focus only on being a good Muslim girl. But when I fell asleep last night, I was right back in the garden with Isa."

Tears resurfaced, and impulsively she pulled her cousin into an embrace. "Oh, Nura, what will become of us? We mustn't let anyone find out about this—ever!"

Nura didn't answer, but Farah knew the girl's tears fell equally with her own.

∽∾ ∽∾ ∽∾

The Night of Power had come and gone, Ramadan was nearly over, and Kareem was not pleased. His anger toward Farah had grown to a near hatred, and her seeming compliance and faithfulness to her religion and her obedience and submissions to her family only fueled his rage.

"What is wrong, my son?" his father had asked as they left home for the mosque that morning. "You seem irritated about something."

Kareem had swallowed his retort, his irritation elevated because he resented that his father always seemed able to read his thoughts and moods, no matter how hard Kareem tried to hide them.

"Nothing is wrong," Kareem had answered, trying to force a note of cheerfulness into his voice. "Everything is fine."

But he knew his father hadn't believed him. And yet Farah could fool him so easily. The man believed everything she said, trusted her implicitly, doted on her unseemly. Kareem vowed to stop at nothing to change that.

∽∾ ∽∾ ∽∾

Farah and Nura at last stemmed their tears and quieted their anxiety by turning to the computer. Nura introduced Farah to the chat room, though she knew Sara wouldn't be there, as it was the middle of the night in America. Then she showed Farah how to pull up the Bible, the book that told of Isa from beginning to end, both in what was called the Old Testament and also the New.

"I haven't read as much in the Old Testament yet," Nura explained, thrilled to have someone who shared her new passion and interests. "Sara told me it might be best for me to concentrate on the New Testament first, since it would help me understand about Isa's life when He was on earth, and about His first followers. But she said the Old Testament is good too because it tells of the promises of Isa's coming."

Farah frowned. "You do realize what would happen if anyone found out you were studying this book, don't you? The Old Testament is what our hated enemies, the Jews, call their Scriptures. And the Christians accept both the Old and New." She lowered her voice. "And even though the Quran says we can go to the Old Testament for answers if we can't find them in our own book, we've been taught that we should have nothing to do with the infidels' Scriptures."

Nura nodded. She had thought of this many times and was well aware of the danger. "I know. But what else can we do? Now that we both know Isa is real, that He is the Son of God as the Christians claim, how else are we to learn about Him unless we read and study this book?"

Farah took a deep breath. "You're right. I can't depend only on dreams when Isa has provided such a book for us. Now that I know it is available on my own computer, I too will begin to read it."

Nura smiled, encouraged. "Let's exchange email addresses so we can talk to each other about what we're reading, and when Sara is back online, we can talk to her too." She dropped her eyes for a moment, the reminder of Sara's loss stabbing at her heart. "Of course, she may not be online a lot for a while. I used to talk to her nearly every day, but since she lost her brother..."

Farah thought of her own brother, and though she imagined Sara and Emir had been much closer than she and Kareem, she could still understand what a difficult time this must be for Nura's American friend. "You're right," she said. "While Sara is dealing with her grief, you and I will be able to study the book and talk online every day without worrying about Kareem or anyone else picking up the phone and overhearing us. It's a miracle, don't you think?"

Nura smiled. It was indeed. That both she and her cousin had discovered this life-changing truth about Isa and now had the means to learn more about Him was the most amazing miracle imaginable! God had surely answered their prayers, and despite her fear, she was hopeful about where this might lead them.

∽✶∾ ∽✶∾ ∽✶∾

The girls' temporary excitement was nearly derailed as the two families gathered around the table that evening. Though their parents and Nadia seemed animated and enjoyed the conversation and the deliciously prepared stewed chicken and rice, Kareem had arrived with a scowl and had continually glowered at both his younger sister and cousin.

*What is wrong with him?* Farah wondered, as she did her best to avoid eye contact and to pretend interest in the meal and the company. She assured herself there was no possible way her brother could know about her dream or what she and Nura had discussed earlier, or even the time they spent on the computer reading the Bible and visiting the chat room. They had stopped all that activity immediately upon Nadia's arrival, wanting to be certain that the younger girl didn't catch them and be persuaded by Kareem to betray them.

*Would she?* Farah looked at her younger sister, her beauty accentuated by her glowing face. Because they were all immediate family, the women didn't have to wear their *abayas* in the house and were able to talk and eat with ease. As a result, they could study each other's expressions, and Farah took full advantage of the opportunity.

It was obvious that her parents, as well as Nura's, had little or no idea of the extent of the undercurrent between Farah and Kareem—or if they did, they ignored it as unimportant. Farah sensed that it was much more important than even she had previously realized, and somehow, sometime, she was going to have to deal with it. What did that mean? And how would she do so? She was a woman, and an unmarried one at that. She was completely at her father's mercy, and though she knew he loved her, she also knew that Kareem exerted great influence upon him. Her safety was guaranteed only so far as she stayed within the acceptable boundaries established by the family's faith and customs.

Avoiding looking at Kareem, she dared a glance at Nura. Their eyes met, and a flicker of fear on her cousin's face told her the girl's thoughts were similar to her own. This was an exciting and joyous new life they had discovered, but a dangerous one as well.

Farah dropped her eyes and gazed down at her plate of nearly untouched food. What was to become of her and Nura? Would Isa protect them? She certainly hoped so, for she sensed that no one else would.

*Oh, Father,* Emily prayed silently, *how our actions impact others!*

## Chapter 34

SATURDAY HAD WOKEN TO A FAMILIAR PACIFIC NORTHWEST gray dawn and an ache in her heart that Sara was beginning to think would never end. Today they would bury her brother, and she wondered how any of them would survive the next few hours.

She knew they would, of course. And though she still heard her mother weeping and saw her father brush away tears more than once, she also heard them speak words of faith in God's goodness and mercy that she struggled to believe. Maybe it was true for them, since it wasn't their fault Emir was dead. But for her? She couldn't even let herself think about it or she'd never make it through the day.

What little extended family they had, including her father's parents, had flown in the day before. Sara scarcely knew her grandparents, as they lived on the East Coast and seldom visited. Layla had told Sara it was because they were still upset with their son and his family for converting to Christianity, while they continued to practice their Muslim faith. But at least they had come. Layla's family had refused even to do that, and Sara knew that was an ongoing pain in her mother's heart.

Now all the family members were loaded into two black limousines, one behind the other, as they snaked along the preplanned route to the funeral home where the service would be held. Yusef had explained to Sara that after the service they would all go to the cemetery, where their pastor would perform a brief graveside ceremony before Emir was lowered into the ground. The very thought brought a lump to Sara's throat that she thought surely would choke her if she tried to swallow.

The limos stopped, and Sara realized they had arrived at the funeral home. An icy fear clutched at her heart as she forced herself to follow her parents out of the car and into the building, where they were escorted to the front couple of rows. She couldn't help but notice that her grandparents and a handful of other relatives sat a row behind them, as if showing their support at a distance while not condoning the treason of Emir's immediate family. Sara even wondered if they might somehow think it was the family's conversion to Christianity that had caused Emir's death.

As the pastor spoke and then invited others to share their memories of Emir, Sara shut out the voices. She had no desire to hear what any of them would say, and she had made it clear to her parents that she was not going to say anything herself. Let the others reminisce; she would stay stuck in grief and guilt, for there seemed to be nothing she could do about it.

෴ ෴ ෴

Emily sat quietly on one of the back rows, listening and thanking God as she listened to the pastor and quickly came to the conclusion that the family really did know the Lord. But what of Emir? If he had been raised in a Christian home, what had happened to send him so far astray? She could only pray that he'd had time to repent in his last minutes of life, even if while in a coma.

She smiled. Few people knew better than she how that could happen. The thought encouraged her that perhaps Emir was even now rejoicing in the Father's presence.

For a moment her gaze wandered and fell on a teenaged girl sitting in the front row between what were no doubt Emir's parents. Emily had read in the obituary that the boy had an older sister, and there she was, her head bowed and her shoulder-length dark hair falling forward. From the occasional shaking of her shoulders it was obvious that she was crying.

*Oh, Father,* Emily prayed silently, *how our actions impact others! Emir was so young, and undoubtedly thought himself invincible. But how wrong he was! Now he's dead, and his family must endure such terrible pain.*

She wiped a stray tear from her cheek and sighed. It had been bad enough when Hank died, though she knew she would soon see him again. She hoped the Al Tamimi family had the same assurance about Emir, though even that couldn't obliterate the agony of losing someone so young.

*Why did You call me here, Lord? Was it just to see the family so I could know better how to pray for them? I will do that, of course. But somehow I think it's something more. Show me, please, if I should go to the cemetery for the graveside service. I'm not family or a close friend, but I'll go if You want me to—though You'll have to provide a ride for me. I can't get there from here on the bus on time, but You can certainly lay it on someone's heart to take me there if that's Your purpose.*

She smiled as she thought of the many times God had intervened for her over the years, providing food, housing, transportation—everything imaginable, even when there seemed to be no possible way for those things to materialize. She knew from experience that a ride to the cemetery was certainly no difficult thing for the God of the impossible to arrange.

The funeral service was over and nearly everyone had exited the building to wait outside as the family made their way to the limos. Sara moved, stiff and unthinking, toward the back door, following her parents without a word. She was grateful that the first part of the day's ordeal had ended; now she would move on to the next. If all went well, she would hold it together until she could return to her room and collapse on her bed in tears. Right now that was the only place she wanted to be.

As they emerged into the subdued daylight, a couple of stray raindrops teased her face, and she wondered if there would be a Northwest deluge by the time they arrived at the cemetery. She didn't care so much for herself, but she hated for her parents and grandparents to be caught in the rain. Had her father thought to bring an umbrella? He was always so organized and usually remembered everything, but today was certainly not normal circumstances.

Apparently they didn't need to worry because as they moved toward the limo that awaited them, the driver approached her parents with an open umbrella and walked them the rest of the way. The driver of the other limo did the same for her grandparents. Before either could return for her, Sara found herself walking beside an elderly woman who held an umbrella over the two of them and said, "Let me walk you to the car, dear."

Sara complied even as she glanced sideways at the diminutive woman with the white curls and wrinkled skin. Should she know her? She seemed vaguely familiar, though she couldn't place her. Surely she was someone from church whom Sara didn't remember meeting.

"Thank you," Sara said as they neared the open door of the limo. Then, spurred by curiosity, she asked, "Forgive me, but do I know you?"

The woman's smile touched a place in Sara's heart that she'd thought had died with Emir, and she returned it before she realized what she'd done.

"No, you don't," the woman said. "Though I believe we've passed one another on occasion when I've been out walking my Chihuahua in the neighborhood." As the memory teased Sara's consciousness, the elderly lady smiled. "My name is Emily Thompson. I met Emir once."

Sara stopped, and Emily stopped with her. Just feet from the car, they looked at one another. "Where did you meet him?" Sara asked, puzzled as to why it meant so much to her to find out.

Emily dropped her eyes and then raised them again. It was apparent to Sara that she was stalling, trying to decide how to answer. At last she did.

"I met him in my kitchen," she said. "Just before he was shot."

Sara felt her eyes go wide. The police had told her parents about the woman, but the name hadn't registered with her until now. So this was the woman who had caught Emir breaking into her home! Why would she come to Emir's funeral?

Sara opened her mouth to voice her question, but Emily answered before she could. "God told me to come," she said. "I'm not sure why, but I know He wanted me to be here. I've been praying for your family, and perhaps He just wanted me to meet you so I could pray more effectively."

"You're a Christian?"

Emily nodded. "Yes. And I see that you and your family are as well."

"Sara." Yusef's voice beckoned her from the car. "We need to go."

She turned to her father. "This is Emily Thompson," she said. "The woman who..." She stopped. It was evident from the expression on Yusef's face that he recognized the name. "Emily is a Christian," Sara added. "God told her to come to the funeral. She's been praying for us."

Yusef nodded, unsmiling. "Please," he said, speaking to Emily, "will you ride to the cemetery with us? My wife and I would like very much to talk with you."

Sara wondered if that was wise and if the police would be happy about that in the midst of an ongoing investigation, but she too wanted Emily to accompany them. She helped the old woman into the vehicle and climbed in behind her.

Zarah couldn't decide if she was
frightened or just confused.

## Chapter 35

NURA LAY IN BED, STARING AT THE UNSEEN CEILING AND PRAYING to God in Isa's name, as her American friend had told her to do when last they'd talked. Nura couldn't help thinking about Sara. She knew that right now, thousands of miles away, her friend and her family were going through the services that would commit Emir's body to the earth—and his soul to God. Sara hadn't told Nura many details about the shooting that took Emir's life, but perhaps that was because Sara herself didn't know them all. Nura imagined that Emir must have been an innocent bystander, targeted in what was known in America as a drive-by shooting. Surely that was the case, as Sara and her family were Christians, and that must have included Emir. As a result, Nura knew Sara and her parents could look forward to seeing Emir again one day.

*If only I had that assurance about my own family!* Nura grieved to think what would happen if her parents died without first receiving Isa as their Savior. She loved her parents dearly, and it hurt to think that they didn't understand about who Isa truly was and what that meant to them personally when they died. Lately she found herself thinking of that very thing and praying that Isa would appear to them in a dream, the way He had to Farah. For Nura to think that God might require her to speak to them herself and tell them what she had discovered and how it had so changed her heart and life was simply too terrifying to contemplate.

How grateful she was that she now had Farah as well as Sara to talk to online! The thought sparked a longing in Nura's heart, urging her from bed to her computer. Her American friend certainly wouldn't be sitting at her computer right now, but maybe Farah was also having trouble sleeping and might check in. How encouraging it would be to hear from her cousin right now!

❧ ❧ ❧

Farah knew she should be sleeping, but she was too excited to turn off the computer quite yet. She had always been an avid reader, and now that Nura had shown her where to find the Bible online, Farah was determined to read it from start to finish, and then begin reading again. Each word thrilled her soul, as if Isa Himself were standing beside her, speaking directly to her heart. Never had she experienced such life-changing truth when reading the Quran, though she'd tried desperately to find it.

She smiled, reading about one of Isa's many miracles when He walked the earth. Hadn't she prayed and fasted and hoped for a miracle from Allah? Instead she had received it at the hand of Isa, the Son of the true God. It was all she could do not to sing or laugh aloud with joy.

The nearly indistinguishable sound of a bell alerted her to the fact that she had a new message. She finished the chapter she was reading and then checked her inbox.

Nura! Farah smiled again. So she wasn't the only one awake and sitting at her computer in the middle of the night! How glad she was to think that she and her cousin could now have a discussion about Isa without any concern of being discovered.

❧ ❧ ❧

The limo pulled away from the funeral home, leading the procession of mourners toward the cemetery. But Sara nearly forgot for a few moments where she was and why. Ever since hearing from the police that Emir had apparently broken into someone's home just before he was killed, Sara had been reluctant to believe it. If it were true, then Emir had been involved in something even worse than she imagined. But she needed to know. She *wanted* to know—and so did her parents, as they had gently but firmly encouraged Emily Thompson to tell them her story.

And so she had, as brief and unbelievable as it was. Her dog had awakened her with his barking and growling. She had opened the bedroom door and followed him to the kitchen, only to find a young man standing there, looking nearly as scared as she should have felt.

"But I wasn't," she said. "I can't really explain it, but somehow I knew he wasn't going to hurt me, even when he threatened me with the knife."

Layla gasped, and Sara darted a look at her parents, who seemed as stunned as she felt. Yusef laid his hand on his wife's arm and nodded to Emily to continue.

"That's about it," she said. "When I refused to go to the other room when he threatened me, he turned and climbed back out the window. He dropped his knife in the process, and I prayed for him most of the night. I had no idea what had happened to him until I read the paper late the next day. The following morning I told the police what happened, and here I am." She paused and, for the first time, appeared uncomfortable. "I hope you don't mind that I came. I just sensed that God wanted me to be here."

Layla nodded, as Yusef spoke. "I'm sure He did. Though it grieves us to know our son broke into your home and that he threatened you with a knife, we're pleased to know he couldn't bring himself to hurt you. The police think it may have been some sort of gang initiation, and when it didn't go as planned, they killed him." He hung his head. "Of course, unless they catch the ones who did it and they decide to tell the truth, we may never know the whole story. And from what the police say, with no witnesses to the shooting and the near surety that no one in the gang is going to come forward with a confession, the killer or killers may never be caught."

Sara's eyes moved from one to the other of the adults, all of whom seemed in pause mode for a moment. At last Emily Thompson spoke. "God knows what happened," she said. "He knows the entire story, from beginning to end. He knew Emir would come to my home and threaten me; He also knew he wouldn't hurt me. And, as much as I hate to say this, He knew Emir would be shot and that he would die. From what I understand, he never regained consciousness. Is that right?"

Yusef raised his head and, with tears shining in his eyes, nodded. "That's right," he whispered. "We never got to say goodbye, at least not so that he could hear us."

Emily smiled. "Ah, but that's where you may be wrong. Many years ago, not long after my husband, Hank, and I were married, I was in a car accident. Hank had been driving, and I nearly died. I was unconscious for several days, while he sat by my bedside and cried and prayed. He was in agony because he blamed himself for the accident. Of course, he didn't realize I could hear him and that my greatest desire was to comfort him and tell him it wasn't his fault."

The sob that was building inside Sara finally escaped, and her parents and Emily all turned to her at once.

"What is it, sweetheart?" Layla asked, reaching toward her daughter, even as Yusef pulled her into his arms.

Emily covered her mouth with her hands. "Oh, I'm so sorry," she murmured. "I've upset your poor daughter."

Sara shook her head as she cried into her father's shoulder. "It's not your fault," she sobbed. "It's mine! It's all my fault! I knew about Emir, and I didn't tell anyone. Oh, Daddy, I'm so, so sorry!"

As Yusef stroked Sara's hair and tried to comfort her, the limo continued along its route to the cemetery.

❧❧ ❧❧ ❧❧

Nura was thrilled when Farah answered her email. She hadn't really expected a response, but it was good to know they were

both awake and could talk privately. Quickly they began to compare notes, ask questions, make points, and discuss the passages
they'd been reading in the Bible. Never before had Nura known
such exhilaration at sharing with someone else what she'd been
reading in the Quran. Each excited email from one of the girls
spurred an equally excited one in return, and so it continued for
more than an hour.

Nura was so engrossed in the online conversation that she
didn't hear the door to her room open, nor did she notice the
change in the atmosphere that should have told her she was no
longer alone. By the time she became aware that someone was
standing behind her, it was too late.

⁓⁓⁓ ⁓⁓⁓ ⁓⁓⁓

Farah couldn't decide if she was frightened or just confused.
Maybe something had happened to Nura's online connection, or
her computer crashed, or...

Possibilities danced in her mind, but she refused to consider
the one that made the most sense. They'd been sending emails back
and forth for at least an hour, with scarcely a pause in between,
and then suddenly all communication from Nura had stopped. It
wasn't as if they'd completed a thought or she'd hinted that she
was tired and wanted to go back to bed. She just disappeared.

Farah shuddered. *Please, Isa,* she prayed silently, huddled in
bed under the covers and trembling at the thoughts she continued to try to push from her mind, *please let her be all right! Please
don't let anything happen to Nura!*

That was the priority, and
Sakeena would have no peace
until it was accomplished.

## Chapter 36

SAKEENA WAS HORRIFIED. WHAT WAS NURA THINKING? WHAT had happened to make her behave so foolishly? She had never been a rebellious child, never unfaithful to Allah or disobedient to her parents. Sakeena had been so grateful for her sweet, compliant child, particularly knowing she could not give more children to her husband.

Faisel. How would she ever tell him? For surely she must. To keep it from him would only compound the sin. And yet she couldn't burden him with it before he left for work in the morning. She would wait until he returned. Perhaps by then Nura would have had enough time to think things over and to realize the foolishness of what she was doing. Yes, a little time was surely all they needed to work this out. Sakeena would give her daughter that time before talking to Faisel.

As she lay in the darkness beside her still sleeping husband, she was nearly overcome with the way the situation had unfolded. She'd been slightly suspicious of Nura's seemingly secretive behavior when it came to her computer, but Sakeena was more than willing to believe the best about the daughter she loved. But when she'd awakened during the night and been unable to sleep, she'd risen quietly from bed, as she often did, to go to the kitchen to make some tea. On the way she'd seen the light under Nura's door and decided to check on her. When she didn't respond to her mother's light rap on the door, Sakeena had let herself in. Never had she expected her heart to be broken by what she found when she entered there.

That she'd managed to confront Nura and leave her daughter's room with her laptop computer and phone without waking Faisel was as close to a miracle as Sakeena had ever experienced. She'd hidden them both in the back of a cupboard in the kitchen and then slid soundlessly into bed.

Had she done the right thing? Should she have awakened Faisel and told him immediately? Surely he would know what to do to help Nura see how wrong she was and to convince her to turn back to the true faith of Islam before it was too late. But wasn't it better to give Nura one last opportunity to recognize her own error before Sakeena brought Faisel into the picture?

Lying in the darkness, nearly afraid to breathe, Sakeena allowed herself to wonder what good her life would be if her only child truly became an infidel. Surely Nura would think better of her decision and repent of her behavior! And if she didn't do so on her own, Faisel would intervene and turn her back to the truth. Oh, if only she could tell him now of this terrible turn of events! It was almost too much to bear on her own, for she and Faisel had always shared everything, and she trusted him implicitly. If indeed she had to tell him when he returned from work the next day, he would certainly take care of the situation, and everything would be all right once again.

Her thoughts turned back to Nura, her beloved daughter, sequestered in her room, forbidden to come out and no doubt terrified as she waited and wondered what would happen to her. Sakeena hoped that would be enough to frighten her into doing the right thing. At least she couldn't communicate with anyone, since she had no computer or phone. The last thing Sakeena wanted was for anyone, especially Farah, to know what was going on in their household.

Farah. Sakeena felt nauseated at the thought that her own sister's child might also be involved in this blasphemy. It would certainly explain the deepened relationship between the two cousins lately. If it proved to be so, she and Faisel would have to tell Ahmed and Sultana, but not until they'd first resolved the immediate situation with Nura, one way or the other. That was the priority, and Sakeena would have no peace until it was accomplished.

                           ⫷⫸ ⫷⫸ ⫷⫸

By the time the limo pulled into the cemetery and began to wend its way along the curving lanes between the plot-lined fields, Sara had poured out her entire story, sobbing between details. Yusef's arm remained around her shoulders throughout, while Layla held one of Sara's hands and Emily took the other. As she uttered her final words of sorrow, the vehicle slowed to a stop.

"What happened to Emir was not your fault," Yusef said, lifting Sara's chin with his spare hand and waiting until she finally looked up into his eyes. "Do you understand that, Sara?"

Though she desperately wanted to believe him, she certainly didn't understand it. How could it not be her fault? If she'd said something—

"Stop thinking that way," Yusef said, his voice gentle but firm. "If you've asked the Lord to forgive you for your part in what happened, then He has. Now you must forgive yourself. You must also realize that even if you played a small part in this tragedy, it was in no way your fault. If anything, the responsibility falls on my shoulders for not having recognized Emir's problem. I am the head of this household, and I failed to protect him. Therefore I need to ask God's forgiveness as well—and yours too. If I'd been doing my job, I might have been able to stop Emir in time. But whether I could have or not doesn't change the fact that if anyone failed your brother, it was I, not you."

Sara's heart constricted at the pain his words brought, and she shook her head as she cried, "No, Daddy! It wasn't your fault."

"Shh," he said, pressing her against his chest. "We need to go to the graveside now. Everyone will be waiting for us, and it's starting to rain. We can't leave them out there, wondering where we are. Afterward we'll talk about this again. And we will pray together." Gently he pushed her back so he could look into her face. "I promise you we will do that before the day is over. All right?"

Sara swallowed and nodded, unable to speak. First they had to get through the final good-byes to Emir before they lowered him into the ground. How would they ever be able to do that?

"Father, be with us and help us through this," Yusef prayed, and Layla and Emily whispered "Amen," as Sara silently thanked God for the strength and love of her family, despite her confession of guilt.

≈≈≈ ≈≈≈ ≈≈≈

Somehow Sara had made it through the final graveside service, though most of the pastor's words faded into the mist that surrounded them. The one time she had raised her bowed head to look at those gathered around the spot that would be the final resting place for Emir's remains, Sara thought it appropriate somehow that the majority of mourners stood beneath black umbrellas and gazed downward. It was a solemn experience at best, she thought.

Once back in the limo, they sat quietly as they followed Emily's directions to her home, where Yusef escorted her to the front door. Sara watched through a rain-streaked window and found herself wondering why Emir had chosen such a humble home to break into and rob. Surely the police were right that it was some sort of gang initiation ritual, with the idea that an old woman living alone would be easy to subdue if she happened to catch him. But Emir hadn't subdued her—or even harmed her in any way. He had instead jumped back out the window and ran toward home, sealing his fate with the watching gang members who knew they'd been betrayed. Though she still wished things had turned out differently, she was proud that Emir had risked his own life rather than injure someone else, particularly some-one as nice as Emily Thompson.

As Yusef Al Tamimi made his way back toward the limo to rejoin his family, Sara wondered if they would see Emily again. She was surprised to realize that she hoped they would.

The words were a whisper she
couldn't hear and yet felt at the
very center of her heart.

## Chapter 37

WHEN FAISEL RETURNED FROM WORK AND STEPPED INSIDE his home, he was struck by the quiet and the absence of the aromas of the evening meal that usually awaited him. Had he forgotten something? Had Sakeena and Nura made other plans?

Frowning, he went to the bedroom he shared with his wife, surprised to find the door shut. Was she lying down for some reason? His heart skipped a beat at the thought that she might be ill. In retrospect, she had acted a bit strangely before he left that morning.

Pushing open the door, he stepped into the semidarkness and squinted at the outline of the bed. It was empty. Then he saw her, sitting in the small, armless chair beside the window, her face away from him as she stared outside.

"Sakeena?" His voice seemed to echo in the still room, but his wife didn't respond. He quickly crossed the room to stand at her side and laid his hand on her shoulder, his heart racing at the implications that danced through his mind. "Sakeena, are you all right? Has something happened to Nura?"

At the mention of their daughter's name, Sakeena at last turned her head to look up into his face. Faisel was stunned at the puffiness of her eyes, but even more so by the fear he saw mirrored there.

"What is it?" he asked, falling to his knees and taking her hand in his. "What has happened, my love?"

Tears began to trickle from Sakeena's eyes, and he watched her struggle to speak. "Nura," she said, confirming his greatest fears. "She—"

Faisel gripped his wife's hand. "What is it?" he demanded, though his voice was hoarse and scarcely above a whisper. "What has happened to our daughter?"

He watched Sakeena swallow and take a deep breath before she spoke again. "She has been on the Internet, emailing and talking to people who..." Her chin trembled but she pulled herself together and completed her thought. "I tried to talk with her, reason with her, beg her, but..." She closed her eyes, not even trying to brush away the tears that dripped down her cheeks. "She has become an infidel," she whispered, nearly choking as she spoke. "One of those who believe that Isa is God."

At the final word, as if she had pronounced a horrible curse, Sakeena collapsed into her husband's arms. Faisel, stunned, held her wordlessly as her statement penetrated his heart, breaking it in the process. How could this be true? Nura? An infidel, joining in the beliefs of the people of the Book? No, it was impossible! It had to be.

But the look on his wife's face had told him otherwise. Sakeena would never make up something so awful, so life-changing and fearsome. If she said it, she certainly believed it was so. Now it was up to him to confirm it. If Nura could not convince him that she was still a faithful Muslim, it would be up to him to correct the matter—with whatever means necessary. It was a thought he refused to allow to dwell in his mind for even a moment.

❧❧❧ ❧❧❧ ❧❧❧

Nura hadn't been this frightened since she'd stood and watched the teenaged girl who'd betrayed her faith and her family, struggling against the very ones who claimed to love her as they held her head under the water. Though her family did not have a swimming pool in their backyard, she knew there were many other ways to deal with what was considered a rebellious child, particularly a daughter. If she were a bit younger, her parents might try to rehabilitate her. But at nearly seventeen, if she didn't readily denounce her beliefs about Isa being the Son of God and swear never again to read the words of the Bible or associate with those who did, her punishment would be swift and sure.

She had been so shocked during the night when she turned and saw her mother standing behind her that she hadn't reacted quickly enough to delete her messages to and from Farah or to exit the chat room page that was running in the background. Why wasn't her mother asleep? What was she doing in her room? But there she was, staring at her with eyes wide and mouth slack. For a fleeting second Nura hoped her mother wouldn't notice the words on the monitor, but that hope died quickly when Sakeena placed her hand over her mouth to suppress a cry of dismay.

Because her mother was relatively computer illiterate, she hadn't checked beyond the most recent email Nura was writing to Farah and what was currently posted on the chat room page. Still, it had obviously been enough to clarify to Sakeena just what it was her daughter did during her many hours on the computer.

Nura hadn't meant to hurt or upset her mother; it simply hadn't occurred to her that her email communications would ever be discovered. Now they had been, and Sakeena had taken the computer and phone with her so Nura couldn't delete any of the incriminating messages or even warn Farah. All she could do was wait in her room—and pray.

"Oh, Isa," she whispered, as she lay on her bed and squeezed her eyes tight in a vain attempt to hold back the tears, "what is going to happen to me now? I heard my father come home. He'll be coming for me any minute. I'm so scared. Please help me!"

*I will never leave or forsake you.*

The words were a whisper she couldn't hear and yet felt at the very center of her heart.

"Isa," she whispered back. "You are here!"

*Always. You have nothing to fear. I will carry you.*

The words still echoed in her ears when her door burst open and her father stepped in. It was the first time she could remember his entering her room without knocking first.

❧ ❧ ❧

Sara had been so exhausted by the time they returned from the cemetery and then visited and talked with the many people who had stopped by the house afterward that she thought sure she'd fall into bed and sleep uninterrupted. But she'd no sooner said good-bye to the last guest and escaped to her room than she'd heard a knock on her door. When Sara opened it, she'd found both of her parents standing there, waiting for the promised talk and prayer time.

Sara smiled now at the memory of it. The three of them had shared one of the best hours they'd had together in quite some time. Though tinged by their sadness that Emir wasn't there to join them, they came away knowing that God was healing their broken hearts.

Now, with the clock beside her bed reading 5:30, Sara wondered if she should get up and start getting ready for church, even though they didn't need to leave for several hours. She was surprised to realize she was anxious to be there, though she still wrestled with the question of whether or not Emir had somehow received Jesus as his Savior before he died. She'd heard stories of people hearing others talking to them while they were in a coma, so why couldn't Emir have had a similar experience? It was certainly possible, and Sara and her parents had agreed there was no reason not to believe it hadn't happened just that way. After all, God loved Emir even more than they did.

With that thought in mind, Sara rolled over on her side and decided to give sleep another try. Within minutes, she had drifted away, leaving the pain behind for just a little while longer.

Farah was nearly frantic. She'd considered trying to call Nura, but what would she say to Sakeena if she answered—which she usually did. Like Farah, Nura didn't have her own phone, just an extension of the family phone in her room, so Farah had resisted her impulse to call and concentrated instead on trying to reach her cousin through email. But despite countless messages flagged urgent, Nura had not responded. What could have happened? The possibilities were too frightening to contemplate.

As she helped her mother and Nadia prepare dinner and set the table, she did her best to carry on a normal conversation with them, but her mind wouldn't stay focused. And now she heard her father's and brother's voices as the two of them opened the front door and walked through the entryway toward the dining room.

"It smells wonderful in here," Ahmed observed, opening his arms to receive a hug and kiss from his wife. "I see my three favorite girls have prepared something special for us for dinner."

"It's your favorite chicken stew," Nadia said, beaming as she went to him and kissed his cheek. "Mom let me do most of the cooking."

Ahmed returned his daughter's smile. "Then I know it will be especially delicious." He turned his gaze to Farah. "And how are you today? No welcome for your father?"

Farah felt her face flame as she hurried to his side and planted a kiss on his cheek. "I'm fine, Dad. How about you? Did you have a good day?"

"I did," Ahmed said, as he began to tell them about it.

But Farah was distracted once again, this time by the suspicious glances cast her way by a sullen Kareem. Whatever was going on with Nura, Farah prayed it would never get back to her brother, for she sensed if it did, things would not go well for her.

*How could she warn her?*

## Chapter 38

FAISEL STOOD JUST INSIDE HIS DAUGHTER'S ROOM, THE DOOR firmly closed behind him. His heart ached even as his mind raged over the news Sakeena had delivered to him. Never in all his life had he imagined himself in this situation, confronting someone he loved so deeply with something so absolutely terrible. Oh, how he hoped she would somehow be able to convince him it wasn't true! Was it possible that Sakeena had misunderstood? It certainly didn't sound that way, but until he heard it from Nura's own lips, he would hold out the slimmest of hopes.

Nura's eyes were wide with what Faisel was certain was fear. Did she know how much he wished he didn't have to do this? *Please, Nura, tell me it isn't true!*

"Daddy?"

Her little-girl address for him nearly melted his heart, but he stood his ground. This was too serious to be overcome by sentimentality. He had to get to the truth—and then deal with it accordingly, whatever the cost.

He crossed the room to the side of her bed, resisting the urge to sit down beside her as he had done so many times over the years. Instead he maintained a stern countenance and allowed his gaze to challenge the child he loved.

"What is it?" he said. "Do you have something you wish to tell me, Nura?"

Tears pooled in her dark eyes. She opened her mouth, and Faisel waited. Then she closed it again and dropped her eyes. It was obvious he was going to have to be the one to open the conversation.

"I spoke with your mother," he said.

She nodded, her head still bowed.

"She told me what you've been doing on the computer. Is it true? Have you been emailing some infidel and studying the blasphemous faith of the people of the book?"

Nura's head jerked up, as a puzzled look crossed her face, causing Faisel to wonder if Sakeena truly had misunderstood after all. He grasped the slim hope as he waited.

The expression of surprise on Nura's face changed to acceptance, and she nodded, almost imperceptibly. "Yes," she whispered. "It is true."

Faisel's thread of hope quickly unraveled. "And what is your explanation for this?" he demanded. "May I assume that you are studying their despicable religion because you wish to be able to counter their beliefs with the obvious superiority of Islam?"

When Nura didn't answer and once again dropped her eyes, Faisel pressed harder. "If that isn't the reason, then what? I want to know, Nura, and I want to know now."

Nura's shoulders shook, and when she raised her head, her chin quivered as she spoke. "Because I believe in Isa, that He is the Son of God."

Faisel felt the air escape the room, sucked into the blackness of his thoughts and leaving him gasping for breath. He knew what he had to do, but he needed time to think. This was his daughter, his only child! How would Allah want him to handle such a disastrous situation?

Feeling as if his heart would burst, he spun on his heel and nearly ran from the room, stopping only long enough to secure Nura's door from the outside with a chair beneath the handle.

⤙⤚ ⤙⤚ ⤙⤚

Nura's heart raced as she jumped from her bed and tried the door handle. Just as she'd suspected, she was trapped. She should have escaped earlier, before her father returned from work, but she hadn't been able to bring herself to disobey her mother's orders to remain in her room.

What would happen to her now? She knew her father could not let such an act go unpunished, but would he show her mercy? They had always been so close. She knew without question that he loved her, as did her mother.

She tried to push aside the memory of the lifeless girl floating in the pool after her struggle against her captors had ended. Had she thought her father loved her too? Nura shivered at the thought of the cold water closing over her head, the feel of hands pushing her down, holding her—

No! She mustn't let herself think that way. Her father wasn't like that. He was kind and thoughtful. At times her mother even accused him of spoiling Nura. It was impossible to believe he would do anything so drastic or violent.

Her thoughts turned to Farah then, and the stunning reminder that her father hadn't seemed to realize who it was she'd been emailing when her mother caught her. Nura knew her mother wasn't at all experienced with computers, so perhaps she just read the messages without noticing who they were from. After all, Farah didn't sign her name, though it was incorporated into her email address.

Oh, if only she had her computer and could delete the incriminating evidence! Even if was too late for her, she might be able to protect Farah. But she didn't even have access to a phone. How could she warn her?

*Isa,* she thought. *You can warn her! You can protect her! You said You would be with me, that You would carry me. Carry Farah too, Isa, please! Warn her before it's too late.*

For suddenly she knew that even if her own father showed her mercy, if word of Farah's involvement ever reached the ears of her vengeful brother, Kareem, Farah wouldn't stand a chance.

അൈ അൈ അൈ

Sara sat between her parents, trying to focus on the sermon but unable to look at the pastor without staring straight at the back of Joni's blonde hair. The girl and her mother sat right in front of Sara, and she knew her friend was struggling nearly as much as she.

Joni's familiar face had been one of the first Sara had seen when they walked through the church doors into the foyer. Wordlessly, the two girls had embraced. Sara knew Joni had been at the funeral the previous day and had even come to the house afterward. Sara was also certain that they had spoken, but she couldn't remember one word that had passed between them.

Now she realized how pleased she was to see both Joni and her mother in church. Joni had always attended sporadically, and her mother even more so. Did this mean they truly had made a more complete commitment to Christ, or was Joni simply trying to cope with her grief over losing the object of her first crush? Either way, Sara prayed that God would use even Emir's death to bring them closer to Jesus.

*And please do the same for me, Lord,* she prayed silently. *You know I'm still hurting and confused, but after talking with Mom and Dad last night and praying about everything that happened, I do feel a little better. I just wish—*

She cut off the thought. Why wish for the impossible? There was no possible way to ever know for certain if Emir had received Christ as his Savior before he died. Would the agony of not knowing become the cross she would have to bear the rest of her life? She hoped not, but she saw no way out of it.

The pastor's words suddenly cut through her thoughts, and she sat up straighter as she listened.

"There are some things we will never know this side of heaven," he said, "but that doesn't mean we can't have peace about them. I learned that fact as a young boy when my grandfather died. We were very close, and the realization that he would never again take me fishing or let me ride on the back of his tractor was nearly more than my broken heart could stand."

Sara watched the man who had been at their side during the long hours at the hospital and then at the funeral home and cemetery as he looked out over the congregation and, she was certain, rested his eyes on her.

"Then," he said, "on the day of my grandfather's funeral, my dad picked me up and put me on his lap and said, 'Son, I'm going to tell you something that I don't ever want you to forget, no matter what happens. Life isn't easy, and it isn't fair, and so long as you expect it to be, you'll always be disappointed. But here's the truth that will see you through it all: God is always good, and He never makes mistakes.'

"That was all he said, and I never forgot his words. To this day I believe it was the wisest thing I ever heard. And my dad was right. That truth—that despite the fact that life isn't easy or fair, God is always good and never makes mistakes—has seen me through every tough time that's come my way. And there have been plenty of them, believe me—just like there have been for many of you."

As the pastor continued, Sara closed her eyes and considered his words. Life most certainly wasn't easy or fair, and never had she known it more surely than right now. But that God was always good and never made mistakes was something she was going to have to think and pray about long and hard. She knew in her mind it was true, but her heart was having a hard time accepting it.

Always remember that Allah is
merciful, he said, and then got up
and walked from the room.

## Chapter 39

I<small>T HAD BEEN THE LONGEST NIGHT OF</small> N<small>URA'S LIFE.</small> H<small>ER FATHER</small> had not returned to her room since leaving the previous evening, and her mother had stopped in only once to bring her some dinner. Sakeena had set the tray on Nura's desk and then turned and looked at her with such a haunting expression that Nura thought surely she was about to say something. Instead she blinked back tears and hurried out the door, securing it firmly behind her.

The food still sat untouched on the tray. The very thought of eating had nearly caused Nura to be sick. Rather than try to ingest food, she had concentrated on praying and talking to Isa, wishing she had the comfort of being able to read the Bible on her computer and trying to remember some of the verses she'd read the night before.

*I will never leave you or forsake you.*

The words of Isa had first come to her as she read, but also when she'd prayed. They were the words she had clung to throughout the long, black night. Now, as the first gray streaks of dawn pierced the dark skies outside her window, she heard the chair scraping the floor as it was moved away from her door.

She sat up against the pillows, trying to calm her breathing as she waited to see if it was her mother bringing her breakfast, or her father coming to tell her of her punishment.

The door opened, and Faisel stepped inside, carrying a tray with a glass of juice and a covered plate. Nura's eyes widened and her heart raced. Her father, bringing her food? Never in all her years had he done such a thing! Though he often came to visit her in her room if she was sick or unhappy, he always left the food preparation to his wife. Why would he do this today?

He smiled. "I brought you some breakfast." He glanced at the uneaten food on the desk, then back at his daughter. "Just as I thought. You haven't eaten. You must, you know." He stepped to the desk and set the new tray down beside the old one, retrieving the juice before walking to her bedside. Unlike the previous evening, this time he sat down beside her.

"Did you sleep well?" he asked.

Her heart rate just beginning to return to normal, she shook her head. "I couldn't," she confessed.

Faisel nodded. "I'm not surprised." He smiled again. "You have a lot on your mind, don't you?"

It was Nura's turn to nod.

"And what have you decided?" he asked. "I know what you've been thinking about, of course. Have you changed your mind?"

Nura raised her eyebrows. What exactly did he mean? "I'm not sure I understand," she said.

Her father laid his hand on her arm, as he continued to hold the juice in his other hand. "Do you still believe that Isa is the Son of God, and not merely a prophet as Islam teaches?"

It was the direct question she had dreaded all night, for she had known it would come, though she hadn't imagined it being expressed in such a kind or gentle way. And yet, wasn't that the type of man her father was—kind and gentle? No doubt he too had experienced a long and sleepless night and was now ready to talk to her in a reasonable manner. A stirring of hope flickered in her heart.

"Yes, Dad, I do." When his expression didn't change she added, "He's my Lord and Savior."

For a moment the air between them seemed to crackle, as time passed with agonizing slowness. At last Faisel smiled. "All right then," he said. "Then that's how it is, and I must accept that."

Nura thought she would explode with joy, that her heart would burst from her chest and soar around the room. Her father accepted her faith in Isa! What that meant at that point, she wasn't sure, but at least the immediate danger was past. If Nura hadn't already been lying in bed, she thought she would surely have fainted from the overwhelming relief.

"Oh, Daddy," she cried, leaning in to hug him while being careful not to knock the juice from his hand, "thank you! Thank you so much!"

Faisel stroked her hair and then pulled back to look down at her. "I must get ready to go to work," he said. "But first you must do something for me."

Nura smiled. "Anything! What is it?"

Returning her smile, he handed her the juice. "Drink this," he said. "I'm worried about you. Will you do this for me now so I can leave with a free heart?"

Gladly she received the glass from him and drank it down. The orange juice was slightly bitter, but she said nothing. It was so kind of him to be concerned and understanding, and she certainly didn't want to complain about anything so trivial.

When she'd finished, he took the glass from her and leaned down to kiss her forehead. "Always remember that Allah is merciful," he said, and then got up and walked from the room. This time she didn't hear him replace the chair under the door latch.

Sakeena watched Faisel as he prepared to leave for work. What had he decided about Nura? She had been so sure they would discuss the situation last night, but he had gone to see Nura and then said nothing about their conversation. When Sakeena could stand it no longer, she asked him what they had discussed and what he was going to do, but he assured her he had the situation under control. Yet throughout the night, as she stared into the darkness and watched the lit dial on the bedside clock creep from one hour to the next, she knew her husband wasn't sleeping either. Each time she considered bringing up the topic of Nura, she thought better of it and decided to wait until the next day. Surely by then Faisel would tell her of his plan of action.

Nura. How could her daughter have been so deceived? She'd always been such a compliant and obedient child, a delightful girl and the joy of Sakeena's heart. Who had gotten to her with such traitorous thoughts and turned her from her family and her faith?

And then her husband had left the bedroom and prepared something in the kitchen—strange behavior for one who seldom set foot in that room. When she got out of bed and peeked through the bedroom doorway just in time to see Faisel carrying a tray to Nura's room, her heart had melted. Her beloved husband had decided to deal with their daughter in mercy. Surely that would touch Nura's heart as well, and she would return to her senses.

Sakeena had gone back to the bedroom to wait, but now her husband was nearly ready to leave for work and yet had said nothing to her. As she straightened the sheets and smoothed the covers, she told herself it was best that she honor his wishes and wait until he left before she went in to talk to Nura. She would find out what had happened between the two of them, and then talk to her husband in more detail when he returned that evening.

"Sakeena."

Faisel's voice interrupted her thoughts. Looking up from her nearly completed job of making the bed, she tried to read her husband's expression as he stood in the doorway, watching her.

"It is time to say good-bye."

Sakeena nodded. "Yes, I know you must go to work now."

Faisel's eyes softened. "Not to me, my love. To Nura."

Fear pierced her heart and spiked in pinpricks across her face, though she told herself she was overreacting. "What do you mean?" she asked, her tone controlled but wary.

"Come with me," he answered, and then turned and walked from her sight, forcing her to comply with his demand as she hurried to catch up.

⚬⚬⚬ ⚬⚬⚬ ⚬⚬⚬

Nura's eyes were heavy. Even her arms and legs were growing leaden, and she wondered why she couldn't concentrate. Maybe she was just tired. After all, she hadn't slept all night, and her mind and body were no doubt exhausted.

The feeling of euphoria grew stronger, as she began to drift away, feeling as if she were wrapped in a very warm blanket. What was happening to her? This was more than simply drifting off into a pleasant dream.

"Isa," she whispered, though her lips wouldn't cooperate and the name came out as more of a hiss. The first feelings of alarm pricked her fading consciousness at the same time she realized her parents were standing over her.

"Nura?"

Why did her mother sound so far away? Nura had thought she was right there beside her, standing next to her father, who stared at her without speaking.

"Nura, what is it?" her mother demanded. "What's wrong?"

Wrong? Yes, something was wrong, but she couldn't imagine what it was. *Isa?* she called again, but this time without trying to speak aloud. *Isa, what's happening? Where are You?*

The answer carried over her mother's voice, which was now growing frantic, even as she leaned down and grabbed Nura's shoulders, shaking her as she called her name.

*I am right here, Nura. Don't be afraid. I'm taking you with Me.*

Nura felt herself slipping from her mother's grasp. *Where are we going?*

*Home*, came the answer. *I'll carry you.*

As the everlasting arms lifted her from the bed, she heard what she thought must surely be the heartbeat of God. And she smiled.

Yes. But we must not talk about it.
Sakeena was afraid even to tell me.

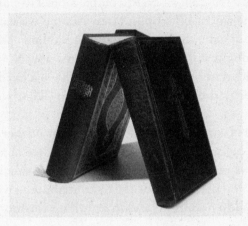

## Chapter 40

Once again Sara sat at the dining room table, picking at her food while her parents tried valiantly to keep a conversation going. But after a few moments, their efforts waned, and they joined their daughter in eating in silence.

Sara remembered little of the day, other than the pastor's words that seemed to have jumped out at her: "Life isn't easy or fair, but God is always good and never makes mistakes." She couldn't remember anything else the pastor had said or even what his sermon had been about. She could certainly attest to the fact that "life isn't easy or fair," but she continued to struggle with the "God is always good and never makes mistakes" part, though she felt a little closer to accepting it than she had been just a few days earlier.

She lifted a forkful of some sort of generic casserole to her lips but couldn't get herself to eat it. She set down her fork and looked up at her mom.

"May I be excused?" she said. "I'm really not hungry, and I'd like to go to my room."

Layla appeared confused, as if not sure how to respond to her daughter's request. She glanced questioningly at her husband. Sara did the same and found her father gazing at her with what she could only imagine as great compassion. He smiled.

"Sure," he said. "I'll stop in later. Maybe we can share some of that coconut cake that's sitting on the kitchen counter. I'm not sure who brought it, but it looks delicious, doesn't it?"

Sara nodded, though she knew she'd have a hard time getting it down if her dad brought it to her room. "That would be nice, Dad."

He nodded, and she stood up and carried her plate to the kitchen sink before heading for the stairs. Once in her room, she realized it wasn't any better there, but at least she didn't have to pretend to enjoy her dinner or try to contribute to a conversation when she couldn't concentrate on anything for more than a few seconds at a time.

Her first impulse was to flop down on her bed, but then she realized how close to the surface her tears were and decided against it. She simply wasn't ready to start her nightly crying jag quite yet. Maybe a slight detour on the Internet would keep her mind off the pain for at least a little while.

Skipping past her emails, which she knew would contain notes of condolence that she didn't want to read at the moment, she went straight to the chat room. *I haven't talked to Nura in a while,* she thought. *It would be good for me to think about someone else for a change, and to find out what's going on with her. I sure hope she's there.*

She wasn't, but Sara kept the connection open in case her friend dropped in. Sara figured it was morning in Riyadh, and Nura should already be awake and ready to start her day. Sara would just check a few other sites while she waited. Surely Nura would check in soon.

❧❧❧ ❧❧❧ ❧❧❧

Emily was more than ready to call it a day. She'd been up early for church and then visited with some friends afterward, enjoying a nice meal and conversation together. By the time she got home, Pepe was more than anxious to go out for a walk despite the fact that Emily would have preferred a nap. But dogs needed to be walked, and so she'd done her duty and taken her grateful pet around several blocks before finally getting home for some much needed rest.

After such a hearty after-church meal, Emily hadn't felt like eating any supper and had settled for a cup of chamomile tea. It had been too cool to sit out on the porch, so she and Pepe sat in the cozy living room in front of a darkened TV screen. The aging dog snored at her feet while Emily sipped her tea and thought of the Al Tamimi family.

*Father, You are amazing,* she prayed silently, smiling toward the ceiling. *Not only did You provide me with a ride to and from the cemetery, but You allowed me to get to know this precious family. It helps me pray for them more personally, and now they've even asked me to stay in touch and to call or drop by for a visit sometime. I just might do that. I really like those people, and I know they're in terrible pain right now, especially the young girl, Sara.*

Emily sighed as she thought of Sara's tears and her confession that she believed her brother's death had been her fault. Oh, how Emily had prayed during that exchange, and how glad she was that Sara's parents were such committed Christians. Emily knew they would help their daughter through this terribly difficult time. She also knew that she would like to assist in some way too.

"I'm open, Lord," she said. "Just direct me if You want me to help somehow."

And with that she roused her faithful companion and headed down the short hallway toward her bedroom.

❧ ❧ ❧

Farah's father and brother had already left for the day when she heard her mother's cries. Racing from her bedroom toward the bloodcurdling sound, Farah found her mother doubled over on the kitchen floor, crying and weeping. The phone lay on the floor beside her.

"Mom, what is it?" Farah fell to her knees and tried to scoop her mother into her arms, but the older woman was too distraught to be held. Visions of her father and Kareem danced in Farah's mind, torturing her with possibilities. "Please, Mom," she cried, "please tell me what happened!"

As if hearing her for the first time, Sultana lifted her head. Farah could tell she was trying to focus her thoughts as well as her fear-filled eyes, as she stared at her daughter. At last she whispered, "Nura. Nura is dead!"

Farah's heart felt as if it would lurch from her chest. Nura? Dead? Impossible! What was her mother telling her? Had she lost her mind?

She took her mom's shoulders in her hands and leaned in close. "Mom, what are you talking about? What are you saying? You're not making any sense. Nura can't be dead. She can't be!"

Sultana's lips quivered. "But she is," she said, her voice cracking. "I just heard it from Sakeena herself. Oh, my poor sister!"

Farah swallowed, the possibility that her mother was speaking the truth beginning to infiltrate her thought processes. "But how? What happened?"

Fear deepened in Sultana's eyes and flickered across her face. "We can't talk about it. It was merciful. She didn't suffer."

Farah gasped. The awful truth was taking shape in her mind. Merciful? This could mean only one thing.

She dropped her voice to a whisper. "Honor killing?"

Sultana's eyes widened, and she nodded. "Yes. But we must not talk about it. Sakeena was afraid even to tell me. But Faisel has gone to work now, as if nothing happened, leaving my poor sister to deal with this by herself. I want to go to her, but Faisel has forbidden it. He told Sakeena not to say or do anything, and to leave everything to him. He allowed her to say good-bye to Nura before she died, but now she is not even to go into her own daughter's room." She burst into tears again and shook her head. "How can it be? How can Sakeena survive such pain? I would never be able to. Never!"

268

The chill that had started in Farah's heart now spread like a horde of icy vipers to every extremity of her body. Nura was dead. An honor killing. And why? Farah knew without being told. The only thing she didn't know was if they would come for her next.

*Trembling, she turned the handle*
*and pushed open the door.*

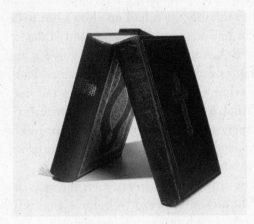

## Chapter 41

Sakeena had never known such pain. Losing her daughter was bad enough, though she had understood that possibility from the moment she discovered what Nura was doing. But she had trusted her husband completely, believing he loved their daughter as much as she did. She had been so sure he would find another way, or at least that he wouldn't have moved so quickly and without talking with her first.

Lying on her bed in the darkened room, the heavy damask drapes pulled to block out the daylight, Sakeena considered her options. There weren't many. She had talked with only one person, her trusted sister, and then only briefly. But at least Sultana and her family now knew of the honor killing. Sakeena couldn't help but wonder how many in Sultana's family approved of Faisel's actions. It was one thing to be a faithful Muslim and to know the punishment for betraying faith and family; it was quite another to see that punishment meted out to one who owned such a large portion of your heart.

*My only child*, Sakeena lamented, wishing she could vocally and loudly proclaim her grief and loss. But her husband had instructed her to grieve silently and privately, as he would do. Nura had brought it on herself, Faisel explained, and though they would miss her terribly, he'd had no choice but to do exactly what he'd done. He had assured her he would "take care of things," meaning that Sakeena should not be involved, and then he had left for the day as if nothing tragic or unusual had happened.

Before leaving, however, he had reminded her that in accordance with Allah's mercy, Faisel had administered justice in a merciful manner, without pain or suffering or public humiliation. Sakeena supposed she should be thankful for that, but it was of little comfort to her at the moment.

Would it be any better tomorrow, or the next day, or ten years from now? She saw no reason to believe so, and that made the burden of her heartache so much heavier.

She rose from her bed. The emptiness in the house seemed to suck the air from her lungs, and she struggled to breathe as she walked to the kitchen and sat down at the table where she could stare at the cupboard that held the last of her daughter's secret. She supposed she should give the computer to Faisel, but he would find it eventually. Why rush the process? What was the point, now that Nura was dead? Sakeena hated the very thought of the computer that had revealed her daughter's treachery and sealed her fate. She would leave it where it was for now. Sooner or later Faisel would hear the ringing phone in the cupboard, track it down, and find the computer. For now, there was something else much more important that Sakeena needed to retrieve, and she suspected she knew exactly where to find it.

Rising from her chair she walked to her husband's study. It wasn't locked. There was no need, as he had strictly forbidden anyone from entering there unless he invited or escorted them in. But Faisel wasn't home, and Sakeena needed what she was certain was in one of the drawers of her husband's desk.

Trembling, she turned the handle and pushed open the door. She'd been in the room countless times over the years, but never without Faisel. What would he say if he knew what she was doing?

She shook her head. It didn't matter what he would say. By the time he found out, it would be too late.

Crossing the room to the desk, she pulled open the drawers one by one. In the bottom drawer on the left, she found the poison Faisel had added to Nura's juice. Slipping the bottle into her pocket, she walked from the room, closing the door behind her, and returned to the kitchen.

∽∾ ∽∾ ∽∾

Farah alternated between terror and grief. One moment she threw herself on her bed and wept over the loss of her cousin; the next she paced the floor, listening for the sounds of her father and brother returning home. Did they know about Nura yet? If so, did they know the rest?

Farah could only wonder how much her aunt actually knew, though apparently she hadn't said much to Sultana. No doubt Sakeena was too distraught to get into details, but Farah was certain those details would soon come to light—and her name would be right in the middle of them. How could it not be? Nura's computer had no doubt been the primary witness against her, and its messages would incriminate and convict Farah as well.

Halting her pacing, Farah spun on her heel and focused on her own computer. True, the damage had already been done when the messages on Nura's computer were discovered, but there was no sense making it worse by leaving them on her own.

Quickly she sat down and booted up, determined to delete every message that even remotely referred to Isa or the new-found faith Farah had so briefly shared with Nura. The thought brought fresh tears to her eyes, but she refused to give in to them. Brushing them away with her hand, she continued to go through her email files and delete all messages to and from Nura. She hadn't realized there were so many of them! Her heart called her to reread them before erasing them, but fear drove her onward.

When she was certain there was nothing left, she heaved a huge sigh of relief and allowed her shoulders to relax a little. She knew enough to realize that someone who was computer savvy could still retrieve the messages, but she was relatively sure that not even Kareem would go to the trouble to do that.

*Not that he needs to,* she reminded herself. *Once my family learns of the messages on Nura's computer, I will have no defense left. And if Uncle Faisel, who doted on his only child, didn't even hesitate to kill her, what chance do I have—especially with Kareem to turn my parents against me?*

The tears were back, and this time she didn't fight them, even as her cousin's face took shape in her mind. *Oh, Nura,* she thought, afraid to speak the words aloud, *I thought we would take this dangerous but wonderful journey together—you, me, and Isa! Now you're gone. I have no one left to talk to! What am I going to do?*

Nura's face faded, and in its place she saw Isa, standing in the garden, His arms outstretched so she could see the wounds in His hands. "Come," He said. "I came to call you to My heart, remember? You will be safe there."

Farah nodded. Isa would keep her safe. She shoved aside the thought that He hadn't protected Nura, instead closing her eyes and focusing on His outstretched hands. "Yes, I will come to Your heart. Keep me safe, Isa. Please, protect me!"

❧❧❧ ❧❧❧ ❧❧❧

Dinner was a quiet affair, as Farah and her family sat around the dining table that evening. Farah had remained in her room even after she heard the voices of her father and brother, speaking in hushed tones with her mother. When Nadia's voice joined in, the others quickly ended the conversation.

"Your father does not wish to discuss the situation," Sultana had informed Farah when she came to her room to tell her to come and help with dinner preparations. "It is best that way."

Farah wasn't about to argue, as "the situation" was the last thing she wanted to talk about. She would gladly avoid the subject, though the gloom that weighed over the entire household was impossible to ignore.

*The worst part,* she thought as she kept her eyes on her plate and forced herself to eat, *is the way Kareem keeps glaring at me. Does he know something? If he does, he hasn't told Mom.*

For a moment only, she dared to raise her eyes, only to confirm her suspicions that Kareem still watched her. Quickly she averted her gaze and glanced at the others. Her parents were eating, speaking only occasionally, but Nadia's head was bowed and she didn't even make a pretense of trying to eat. Farah realized for the first time that her younger sister must be devastated at the news of her cousin. Was she more upset over Nura's death or over the reason for it? Both Nadia and Farah were aware of honor killings, but they'd never personally known anyone who actually died that way.

It was ironic, Farah thought, that the only person they knew who did have such personal knowledge and had actually witnessed such an event was Nura herself, as she had told them about the swimming pool incident on more than one occasion. And now she too was dead.

Would Farah be next? Though she tried to cling to the hope that somehow Isa would protect her, she couldn't imagine how that could happen once her uncle told her father about the messages on Nura's computer.

The chimes interrupted their meal, and Ahmed rose to go to the door. When Farah heard her uncle's voice, she thought her heart would stop. She couldn't distinguish his words from that distance, but it was obvious he was distressed.

Kareem glanced around the table and then quickly rose and headed toward his father and uncle, leaving the three women to stare wordlessly at one another. Wide-eyed with fear, they waited, but Farah was certain she was the only one who knew why her uncle had come.

But Zarah appeared stunned, more
shocked than grieved. On top of
that, she looked terrified.

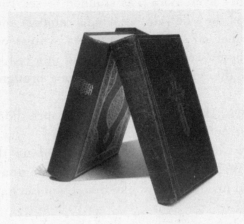

## Chapter 42

THE WEEKEND WAS BEHIND THEM, AND SARA KNEW SHE
should probably go back to school, but she just wasn't ready
yet. Her parents had understood and readily agreed when she'd
asked for a couple more days, but now she wondered if she'd
made a mistake. Would it have been easier to fall into the old
patterns, walking down the sidewalk with Joni and trying not to
cry as each step reminded them of Emir?

No, she hadn't made a mistake. She was definitely not ready
to return to school. Apparently Joni wasn't either. Sara had
called her earlier to tell her, and Joni said she was staying home
for another day or two also.

Sitting out on the front porch, wrapped in a quilted jacket
and sipping warm tea, Sara closed her eyes and tried to ignore
the fine mist that fell from the morning skies, soaking the lawn in
front of her. Summer was definitely over, and though they might
get a pleasant day or two before winter set in for good, Sara
knew they would be few and far between. And spring seemed so
very far away.

"Hello, young lady."

The voice snapped her to attention. Where had it come from? And why did it sound familiar?

Opening her eyes, Sara was stunned to see Emily Thompson standing on the sidewalk, wearing a raincoat and holding an umbrella over herself and her Chihuahua, who stood obediently at her feet. The overweight dog was clad in a red knit sweater, and somehow the whole unexpected scene brought a smile to Sara's face.

"Hello, Mrs. Thompson," she said. "I sure didn't expect to see you outside on a day like this."

The elderly woman grinned and started up the walkway toward her. "Well, now, we do live in Washington, you know. And if I stayed inside on days like this, I wouldn't get out much at all, would I?"

Sara smiled again. "You're right," she said, glancing down at the woman's companion. "And who is this? I've seen you walking him before but don't know his name."

"This is Pepe," Emily answered, glancing down at the dog who quickly wagged his tail in return. "Next to Jesus, my best friend."

Sara laughed. "I think he feels the same way."

"That's a nice sound," Emily said. "I've never heard you laugh. In fact, I don't think I've even seen you smile." She sobered and then continued. "Not that I blame you. We didn't exactly meet under the most pleasant of circumstances, did we?"

She took a step up before Sara could answer. "Do you mind if I join you?"

Sara was still recovering from Emily's comments and feeling somewhat guilty that she could have laughed so soon after Emir's death, but she nodded. "Please do," she said. "I'd like that."

Emily leaned her umbrella against the wall and let it drip onto the porch before settling into the rocker beside Sara's lounge chair. Pepe quickly made himself at home by curling up at the foot of the rocker and closing his eyes.

"So," Emily said, laying her hand on Sara's arm, "how are you doing? Really?"

Sara was surprised that the woman's familiarity seemed so natural and right. They scarcely knew one another, and yet it felt as if a longtime friend or even a family member had dropped by for a visit.

"Not too good," she said, deciding there was no sense putting on a front with the person who was the last to see her brother before he was shot and who had later accompanied his family to the cemetery to say a final good-bye. The woman had heard Sara's confession of guilt over Emir's death, so there really wasn't much left to hide.

"I'm sorry, my dear," Emily said, "but I wouldn't expect anything else from you. It's only been a few days since you lost your brother. Even as Christians who know we will see our loved ones again, we feel the loss, and it hurts."

Tears stung Sara's eyes, and she bit her lip before she spoke. "That's just it," she said. "I think I could stand it if I just knew for sure—"

She stopped, unable to say another word, as tears slid down her cheeks.

Emily fished in her purse and pulled out a handkerchief. Handing it to her she said, "If you knew for sure your brother was with the Lord."

Sara nodded, grateful for the handkerchief and for the woman's understanding.

"That's what we all want, isn't it?" Emily asked. "To know that when our loved ones die, they will go to be with Jesus. What else matters, really? All the success in the world means nothing when we breathe our last and stand before God. Either we've received Jesus as our Savior or we haven't. Eternity itself hangs on that decision—for each of us."

Sara nodded again. She knew every word the woman spoke was true, but how did that help her to know where Emir was right now?

"I told you about my car accident," Emily said, "and how I could hear Hank talking to me, even when he had no idea I could. Besides hearing him agonize over what he considered his fault in the causing the accident, I also heard his prayers—and they gave me the will to pull through."

Sara studied the wrinkles in the woman's face. Somehow they seemed to emphasize her wisdom, and she smiled. "I talked to Emir before he died," she said. "So did my parents and our friend Joni."

Emily nodded. "I'm sure you did. And I'm sure you prayed with him and for him, and that you talked to him of his need to receive Jesus as his Savior."

Sara waited, afraid to speak.

"If you want me to assure you that he did," Emily said, "I can't do that. But I can assure you that God enabled Emir to hear what was necessary for him to be able to make the choice to say yes to Jesus. And ultimately, my dear, that's all any of us can do for our loved ones. We pray for them, we do everything we can to tell them about their need for Jesus and how to receive Him as Savior, and then we trust God to draw them to His heart. For only He can do that, you know."

"I know," Sara whispered, surprising herself that she really did know, that she truly did understand that God had not abandoned them or taken Emir too soon.

"One more thing," Emily said, patting Sara's arm. "God doesn't make mistakes. We don't always understand why He does things how or when He does, but whatever He does is always right. We can trust Him in that."

*God doesn't make mistakes.* The pastor's words drifted back to her, reminding her that she'd now received the same message twice in the last two days. Now, at last, the truth of those words had settled into her heart.

∽∾ ∽∾ ∽∾

Kareem had listened to every word and watched every reaction of everyone in the living room where they had ultimately gathered, and it was clear there was more to the story. He would be willing to bet that it had to do with Farah. If only he could prove it.

True, she wasn't the only one who was upset. Understandably their mother was near hysteria, first from the news of Nura's honor killing and now Sultana's suicide. Nadia was inconsolable over this double tragedy, and even his father and uncle seemed grief-stricken. But Farah appeared stunned, more shocked than grieved. On top of that, she looked terrified. Why? What reason would she have to be scared, unless Kareem's suspicions were true and Farah was somehow involved in Nura's emails to and from some infidel?

Wait a minute. The picture was starting to come together. Was it possible? Could Farah be the one Nura was corresponding with? Even if she weren't, Kareem was certain now that she knew more than she was telling. And he had a good idea of how to expose her once and for all.

Slipping away from the emotional group, he sneaked down the hall to Farah's room and let himself in, smiling at the blank computer screen that greeted him.

❧ ❧ ❧

At first Farah was relieved when Kareem left the room, but the more she thought about it, the more uneasy she was about his absence. Certainly he wasn't that distraught over his cousin or aunt's death that he'd gone to his room to vent his emotions. That simply didn't make sense. So where was he, and what was he doing?

Shards of icicles pricked her heart at the sudden realization that he was in her room, looking for something. But even if he were, what could he find? She'd deleted all her emails to and from Nura, and there wasn't anything else... was there?

A quick glance around told her that no one would be alarmed if she left, so she made a silent but hasty exit and headed straight for her room. Noiselessly she opened the door and peered inside. Sure enough, there was Kareem, sitting in front of her computer, scrolling through her inbox. Quite obviously he'd had no trouble figuring out her overly simple password. Thank God she'd gotten rid of all the emails in time!

Not wanting to antagonize her brother further, she considered backing out of the room and closing the door so he wouldn't even know she was there, but Kareem turned to look at her before she could.

"I knew you'd come looking for me," he said. "Now that you're here, why don't you just tell me what you know? You were in on this with Nura, weren't you?"

Farah swallowed, trying to control her breathing. "What are you talking about? And why are you in my room, using my computer?"

Kareem's face darkened, and he stood to his feet. Farah felt as if she'd shrunk in comparison, and she wished she hadn't come in at all.

"You don't fool me," Kareem snarled, his lips curled in disdain. "You might have gotten rid of the evidence before I got here, but I'll find out somehow. You and Nura were involved in this blasphemy together, I know it. And I promise you, dear sister, that I will find a way to prove it. And when I do, you will pay."

*I will definitely pray for you,*
*I promise, she wrote.*

## Chapter 43

Emily Thompson's words, along with the pastor's, echoed in Sara's heart as she climbed the stairs to her room.

*God doesn't make mistakes.*

Though her mind still had problems wrapping around that statement, her heart was beginning to find peace in its expansive truth. Its very simplicity put everything else into proper perspective.

Flipping on her computer, she realized she desperately wanted to share that statement with her Saudi friend. Would she finally be back online? Sara had missed her and hoped they would connect again at last.

She entered the chat room, but Nura wasn't there. Another name caught her eyes, though, one she hadn't noticed before: Farah. A fairly common name among Muslims, yes, but hadn't Nura mentioned that she had a cousin with that name? Sara's heartbeat escalated at the possibility, and she quickly made the connection.

*Yes,* came the response, *I am Nura's cousin. I was praying to find you here. Nura told me about you and about this site before…*

The message stopped abruptly, and Sara frowned. Before what? She fired the question back. After a momentary pause, she got the reply.

*Nura is dead. She has gone to be with Isa. I am heartbroken, but I'm so glad to know where she is. That's why I took a chance to get online and try to connect with you, so I could tell you what happened.*

Sara gasped, feeling as if the words had come as a dagger, slicing through her gut and piercing her heart. Dead? How could Nura be dead? They were the same age—not quite seventeen! How was that possible? What had happened?

Sara's fingers flew as she poured out her questions, praying as she typed and waited.

Again, after a brief pause, she received the response.

*I shouldn't be telling you this, but it may be my last and only chance to tell anyone. It was an honor killing, and I fear I may be next. Please pray for me! I'm really scared.*

Sara's eyes filled with tears. Honor killing? She'd heard of them, of course, and even knew they were still practiced in some Muslim communities. But Nura? Someone she knew, even if just online? Was it because she had become a Christian, a believer in Jesus?

Trying to focus through her blurred vision, she asked those questions and waited.

*Yes,* came the reply, *that's the reason. And it's also the reason I believe they will come for me soon. After this, you probably won't hear from me again. My brother suspects that I was involved in what he considers Nura's blasphemy, and he is trying to prove it. If he does, I'm finished.*

"Oh!" Sara cried aloud, covering her mouth with her hand as if she could hold back the pain. *I didn't realize you too were a believer in Isa,* she wrote after a moment of trying to calm herself. *I'm sorry your life is in danger because of it, but I'm thankful that your eternal future is secure, regardless of what happens.*

Farah's answer was quick and to the point. *Exactly. Please don't forget to pray for me. I don't think I have long before I join Nura.*

Sara struggled to absorb her new friend's pronouncement, even as her memory of the words she'd heard from

Emily and also from her pastor came to the forefront of her thoughts.

*I will definitely pray for you, I promise,* she wrote. *And please remember these wise words that a couple of people spoke to me recently: God doesn't make mistakes. Forgive me if that sounds trite, as I know it's a lot easier for me to say in my situation than for you in yours. But the God who loves and guides me each step of the way does the same for you.*

The reply was a few moments in coming, as if Farah were considering the words before responding. *Thank you, Sara. I will remember those words, whatever comes. And thank you for praying. I must sign off now. Good-bye, my friend and sister.*

Tears spilled over onto Sara's cheeks as she spoke aloud to the silent monitor: "Good-bye, Farah. I'll pray for you, and I know we'll meet one day, either in this life...or the next." She sobbed then and lowered her head into her hands. "Oh, Father, keep her safe!"

అఁ৶ అఁ৶ అఁ৶

Farah knew she'd taken a big chance going to the chat room, but she had so wanted to connect with the American Nura had told her about. Now it was done, and she turned off her computer and went to rejoin her family, glad she had decided not to mention her aunt's suicide to the American. With the poor girl just losing her brother, news of Nura's death was undoubtedly more than enough tragedy to heap on her at one time.

Farah also didn't want to seem uncaring by ignoring her family, nor did she wish to compound the suspicions Kareem would no doubt be happy to share with everyone else. But when she returned to the living room, Kareem wasn't there. Had he gone to his room after leaving hers? And then she saw that her uncle was gone as well. Only her parents and Nadia remained, huddled together on the couch, as the parents tried to comfort the weeping girl.

"There you are," Sultana observed, glancing up at Farah, who stood in the doorway. "We wondered where you'd gone."

Farah felt her cheeks flush. "I'm sorry, Mom," she mumbled. "I just needed to go to my room for a few minutes to collect my thoughts."

Sultana nodded. "Of course. So much to absorb all at once." Tears pooled in her already puffy eyes as her voice cracked. "First Nura and now my sister." She sobbed then, and the tears spilled over onto her cheeks. "Suicide! I still can't believe it, though I can certainly understand."

Farah's heart constricted as she realized how she had allowed her own fears and uncertainties to overshadow her concern for everyone else's pain. Aunt Sakeena, committing suicide! It was nearly unthinkable. But then, Nura had been her only child, and they were so close. Now her uncle, who had done what he believed he was honor-bound to do, would be alone.

"Where is Uncle Faisel?" she asked. "Did he go home already? I thought he would stay here with us for a while."

Her father's expression was grim as he answered, his arm still around the shoulders of his youngest daughter. "He said he was still confused about the details of what Nura had done. He had expected to talk to Sakeena about it tonight, but..." His voice trailed off, and Farah saw his Adam's apple bob before he continued. "Sakeena had told him that Nura had been involved with people on the Internet, people of the Book who believe the prophet Isa is God, and that Nura had adopted their beliefs and was communicating with them regularly and studying their Bible online. Faisel wanted to check the computer to try to discover who it was that had enticed his daughter into such blasphemous behavior, but he hasn't been able to find it. Sakeena must have hidden it when she took it away from Nura, so Faisel went home to try to find it."

An icy finger of fear trailed its way up Farah's spine as she asked, her voice shaking, "And where is Kareem?"

"He went with your uncle to help," Ahmed explained. "He didn't want him to have to be alone in his search for answers to this tragedy."

The icy finger reached the top of Farah's spine and slowly wound its way around her throat. She had no way of knowing where Sakeena might have put Nura's computer, but if it was anywhere in that house, the two men would surely find it. And then they would come for her.

∽❀∾ ∽❀∾ ∽❀∾

Kareem's heart beat with anticipation. Surely he would find something before his search was over! If Nura and Farah had been communicating through email—and there was little doubt in his mind that they were—he would find that computer and at last obtain the proof he needed to convict his sister.

Faisel had gone to the bedroom he had shared with Sakeena, avoiding Nura's room, where he had found his wife's lifeless body sprawled across her daughter's bed, next to Nura's. He had told Kareem that he was sure his wife would have hidden Nura's computer in their room, but Kareem suspected she might have stashed it somewhere in the kitchen. She was a woman, wasn't she? And isn't that where women spent much of their time? If Faisel didn't locate it in his search, Kareem was confident that he would in his.

Resisting the impulse to empty cupboards and drawers onto the floor, Kareem took his time peering into every crevice large enough to hold his cousin's laptop. He was quickly growing discouraged when the cold touch of metal against his fingers as he rummaged through the back of an obscure cupboard made his heart leap. Surely this was it!

Leaning closer and peering into the cupboard, he smiled. His diligence had been rewarded. He had indeed located Nura's computer, lying right next to a cordless phone. All Kareem had to do now was turn the laptop on, figure out how to get into Nura's email, and scroll through the inbox. There was little doubt that Farah's fate was already sealed.

"No matter what you hear,"
she said, "do not come out!
Do you hear me?"

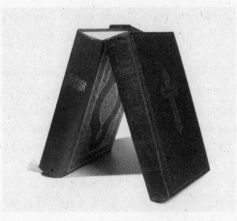

## Chapter 44

FARAH HAD CRAWLED INTO BED AND PULLED THE COVERS UP around her neck, as if they could somehow protect her. But sleep had eluded her. Though her parents had turned in for the night, Kareem had not yet returned from Faisel's house. Farah listened for him in the darkness, her stomach churning as she tried to focus on Isa and the great compassion in His eyes when He told her He had come to call her to His heart.

Should she run, try to escape before her brother returned? But where would she go? She couldn't drive, and she had no money. If word got out that she was an infidel and her family was looking for her, no one would hide her. She was trapped.

At last the sounds of the front door opening and someone stomping through the house invaded the room where she lay. The noise of heavy, determined footsteps approached her room but kept right on going, stopping outside her parents' bedroom instead. Then she heard pounding on their door, followed by Kareem's voice.

"Father," he called, and Farah froze. Kareem never used the more formal term for their dad unless he was extremely upset.

"Open the door," Kareem continued. "I need to talk to you right away."

Tears began to drip from Farah's eyes, as the shaking in her stomach spread to her limbs. "Isa," she whispered. "Isa, help me!"

She heard the door to her parents' room open, as voices became hushed and she had trouble making out details. But she was able to distinguish enough to know that she was the topic of the men's conversation. When her mother tried to join the discussion that now took place in the hallway, she was ordered back to her room.

At last the dreaded sound of footsteps at her door alerted her to the fact that her waiting was over. Very soon she would join Nura—and Isa. It was the only thought that kept her from screaming as the door opened and the two men stepped inside.

ॐॐ ॐॐ ॐॐ

Sultana paced beside her bed, frantic at the thought of what was going on in her daughter's room. What had happened while Kareem was at Faisel's house? What had they discovered that had caused such a reaction directed toward Farah?

Sakeena's last words to her echoed in her ears: "He has killed Nura! He murdered my daughter! I should never have told him—and I wouldn't have if I'd known what he would do. I should have protected her!"

And now it seemed that Farah was somehow involved in Nura's tragedy. What could she have done? Surely it wasn't anything so serious that Ahmed would react as Faisel had done with Nura! No, he would never do such a thing. But hadn't Sakeena thought the same about Faisel? And now their daughter was dead.

*Kareem!*

The realization that her son was the instigator of this situation struck her in the chest, nearly knocking her to the floor. Even if Ahmed wouldn't hurt Farah, would Kareem? The answer drove her to the door, and she raced to Farah's room. Seeing Nadia peeking from her own room, Sultana ordered her back inside. "No matter what you hear," she said, "do not come out! Do you hear me?"

Nadia, wide-eyed with obvious fright, nodded and retreated behind her door, as Sultana discarded all sense of caution and burst into Farah's room. The sight that greeted her forced a scream from her heart that she thought surely would cause her chest to explode.

Farah lay on the floor, bleeding and moaning, as Ahmed and Kareem stood over her. They turned at the sound of Sultana's scream, the anger on their faces redirected toward the one who had interrupted their efforts.

"Get out!" Ahmed roared. "I told you to stay in your room!"

Sultana struggled to breathe, her husband's words scarcely registering as she stared in disbelief at the battered body of her beloved daughter. What had she done to deserve such a beating? And would they stop before they killed her?

She threw herself at her husband, falling to her knees and lifting her head to beg for mercy. Ahmed's slap knocked her to the floor, as lights flashed in her head and the sound of angry voices faded to a dull buzz. Determined to save her daughter, she dragged herself back to her knees and struggled to rise to her feet, but another blow knocked her down again. The rusty taste of blood filled her mouth, and she felt what she imagined were dislodged teeth grating against her tongue. When she tried to rise one last time, the effort was too much, and blackness closed in.

✥✥ ✥✥ ✥✥

Kareem was furious. He had proved to his father that Farah had been as involved as Nura in the online treachery and betrayal of their faith. He had been sure that at last his father would turn against Farah and act as honorably and nobly as Faisel had done in killing his own daughter. And Kareem had been more than pleased at the opportunity to help carry out the sentence against Farah.

But then his mother had intervened. For a moment Kareem thought that perhaps his father would kill her as well, but when

293

she passed out, something seemed to snap in Ahmed, and he stopped beating both the women. Instead he looked at Kareem, his eyes wide as if he'd just realized what they were doing. That look of realization told Kareem that his father had no intention of continuing, though Shariah law afforded him every right to do so.

"It is enough," he'd said, holding out his hand to indicate that Kareem too should cease from pummeling and kicking his sister. "They have been punished enough."

Kareem had scarcely restrained himself from punching his own father. "Why?" he had protested. "Why should we stop? Maybe Mom has been punished enough for interfering, but Farah? She must die for what she has done."

Ahmed's eyes had filled with tears, and Kareem felt sickened by his father's weakness. At that moment Kareem knew that if justice was to be done, he would have to find a way to mete it out himself.

"No more," Ahmed said. "I will take your mother to our room so she can recover there, but we will leave Farah here to suffer for a while and to consider what she has done. Maybe her punishment will enable her to see the evil of her actions and return to the true faith."

Kareem bit back his words, turning from his father and leaving the room before he said something he knew he would regret. In his heart he knew Farah would never return to Islam, for he would personally see that she didn't live long enough to do so.

❧ ❧ ❧

Farah managed to open one eye just long enough to see her father lift her mother from the floor and half-carry, half-drag her limping form from the room. But in that split second, seeing the damage to Sultana's once-beautiful face had hurt Farah more than anything her father or brother had done to her before her mother tried to intervene.

What Farah couldn't understand was why she was still alive. Why hadn't they finished what they started? When they first entered her room, they had dragged her from her bed and told her they knew what she had done—that she had conspired with Nura to betray Islam and to humiliate her family. A dozen retorts had risen up in her mind, but she knew they wouldn't believe any of them. And so in the beginning she had said nothing in her own defense, for she knew there was nothing she could say that would make a difference at that point. Later she had said nothing because she was in too much pain to speak.

And then she had heard her mother's voice, begging for mercy—not for herself, but for her daughter. Farah's heart had nearly imploded when she heard the slap, followed by her mother's cry. From that moment on she had forgotten about herself and prayed only for her mother—until she opened her eye and saw her father helping his wife from the room. The battered look of her mother's face had made Farah wish for death.

*Oh, Isa,* she prayed silently as she lay there on the floor, *You said You came to call me to Your heart. Please take me there now—to Your heart and to Your home. I cannot bear to stay here another minute.*

The answer soothed her aching heart like a warm, gentle breeze. *Not yet, beloved. Soon. First I have something for you to do.*

Regardless of how strong their
family ties might seem, the strict
customs of the Saudi Kingdom
were stronger.

## Chapter 45

SARA WONDERED IF THE SOGGY PACIFIC NORTHWEST CLIMATE was getting to her brain. There had to be something to explain why she would stay home from school for the day, planning to hibernate, and then deliberately head out into the steady drizzle on foot. True, she had an umbrella, but it was hardly a day for a stroll.

She couldn't decide if she was surprised or not when she showed up in front of Emily Thompson's modest home. It had been only a couple of hours since the elderly woman and her dog had stopped to visit her on the porch, and now here she was, seeking out another conversation with the wise senior saint. But whether it made sense or not, she knew that her heart was drawn to this house and the woman who lived here.

No sooner had she knocked on the front door than a persistent yapping announced her arrival. Sara smiled. Pepe. He might be getting old and snoozed a lot, but he was still a good watchdog.

Her smile faded as she remembered that Emily had told her how it was Pepe's barking that had alerted her to the fact that someone had broken into her home. That someone was Emir, Sara's now dead brother. Had that really been less than a week ago? How could so many life-altering events have taken place in such a short time?

And now it wasn't just Emir who had died, but Nura as well. For all she knew, Farah had joined them. It was almost more than her mind could fathom. Before she could wonder another moment at the complexity of it all, the door opened and there stood Emily Thompson, beaming at her.

"Come in, my dear," she exclaimed. "I had so hoped you would come and visit me one day, but I certainly didn't expect it so soon."

Sara stepped into the tiny living room and was immediately greeted by an excited Chihuahua, who refused to stop barking until she bent down to pet him.

"I'll put the kettle on for tea," Emily announced, "while you and Pepe get better acquainted." Then she hustled into the kitchen and left Sara squatting beside the dog, wondering just how much of her heart she was about to unburden on this sweet but unsuspecting old woman.

⤜⤜⤜

Sultana thought her heart would break—literally. That it would simply stop working and she would die. It was a welcome possibility as she lay there on the bed throughout the long hours of the day, reliving that horrible scene where she beheld the nearly unrecognizable body of her daughter, lying at the feet of her closest male relatives—who were also her attackers.

*Ahmed*, Sultana thought. *How could you? Kareem, yes. I always suspected he was capable of such anger and violence, even against one of our own family members. But you, my husband? I thought you loved our children as much as I.*

She paused, readjusting the cool cloth Ahmed had laid across her forehead before leaving the room. Hadn't Sakeena believed the very same thing about Faisel? How wrong she had been!

And now Sultana knew the ugly truth as well. Regardless of how strong their family ties might seem, the strict customs of the Saudi Kingdom were stronger.

And yet Ahmed had told her that Farah still lived. Perhaps he did care for their daughter after all. Could Sultana trust him? She could no longer be sure, but she was certain that she could not trust her son. If Kareem had the chance, he would kill Farah without a second thought and without mercy. What could she do to ensure her daughter's safety? How could she protect her?

She couldn't, and the weight of that realization nearly crushed her. Not only could she not ensure Farah's safety, she couldn't ensure Nadia's or even her own. They were women, chattel belonging to the men in their lives. They were more fortunate than some, and would be loved and cared for so long as they obeyed and stayed within the boundaries drawn for them. The moment they stepped outside those lines, they would find themselves at the mercy of the merciless.

*Farah*, Sultana thought, as tears burned her eyes. *Oh, how I long to go to you and help you! But your father has forbidden me. He threatened me that if I tried to interfere again, he would allow Kareem to punish you as he sees fit. You would have no chance at all then, my beloved daughter. Oh, forgive me for not coming to you! I would if I could. But I can't. Your only hope is for me to leave you to suffer alone, though I don't know how long my heart can bear it.*

⁕⁕⁕ ⁕⁕⁕ ⁕⁕⁕

Sara sipped her tea and wondered how she could so quickly feel at home in this humble but cozy little bungalow. Pepe once again slept at his mistress's feet, as Emily too sipped from her teacup and offered some homemade butter cookies to her guest. Sara started to decline but thought better of it, taking two and placing them on a napkin on the lace-covered end table beside her chair.

"This is so pleasant," Emily said. "I don't have much company, and it's nice to have someone to share a cup of tea with now and then. I hope you'll consider dropping by regularly."

Sara smiled. "I'd like that," she said, meaning every word, even as she wondered how to broach the subject that weighed on her heart.

Emily set her cup down on the coffee table in front of her and fixed her eyes on Sara. "What is it?" she asked. "I sense you came here for a reason. Is there something you'd like to talk about? Emir, perhaps?"

Sara shook her head. "No, not really. I mean, I do have something I'd like to talk to you about, but it's not Emir. To be honest, you've made me feel a lot better about the way things happened with my brother, and I really appreciate that."

Emily nodded and waited.

"Actually..." Sara paused, took a deep breath, and plunged ahead. "I'm curious about your life. You and your husband did some missionsary work, didn't you?"

Emily beamed. "Oh, we certainly did! Dedicated nearly our entire married life to it, as a matter of fact. And I wouldn't have traded it for the world. We had no children of our own, but we have more spiritual children and grandchildren than I can count. Every year I get Christmas and birthday cards from around the world, thanking me and Hank for the work we did in a specific country. I can't begin to tell you the level of satisfaction I get from knowing that because of God's work in and through us, others came to know and serve Christ as well."

Sara nodded. It was exactly as she had thought. And yet....

"Did you... were you ever scared?" she asked. "I mean, did you go to places that were dangerous?"

Emily chuckled. "If we allow ourselves to think that our physical lives are what this is all about, then everywhere is dangerous. We could walk out the front door and get hit by a bus. Or a plane could fall out of the sky and plunge through the ceiling and kill us both where we sit. There's nowhere really 'safe' in this world if our concern is to protect our temporal, physical beings. But if we place our faith and hope in Jesus Christ and allow Him to keep and protect our eternal, spiritual beings, then nothing can harm us. So long as we walk with Him and go where He sends us, we needn't worry."

She leaned over and reached out to place her hand on Sara's. "The Scriptures are clear that nothing can separate us from Christ's love. Do you believe that, my dear?"

Sara nodded. She did, truly—more so at this moment than ever before.

"Then you're safe. Nothing or no one can harm you. The missionsaries who go into the most dangerous and remote places in the world know that great truth. They know too that even if they give up their physical lives in the process, their death only serves to further the cause of Christ."

"I heard a missionsary in our church say something like that once," Sara said, as the memory came floating back. "He said something like the blood of the martyrs is the seed of the church. Is that what he meant?"

"Exactly," Emily said, nodding emphatically. "If God sees every teardrop that falls—and the Scriptures assure us that He does—then He certainly makes note of every drop of blood shed by His beloved servants, whether the missionsaries or the nationals in hostile countries. And those who witness that bloodshed here on earth are often impacted by the strength of the martyrs' faith and turn to God as a result. That's how the Church has grown through the centuries—through the blood of the martyrs who followed the example of their Lord and Savior Himself."

"But..." Sara had one last question, and she knew it would nag her until she asked it. "What do you do about the fear? I know the truth of what you say, that God will never leave us and that even if we die because of our faith, we don't have to worry because we will go straight into His presence forever. But knowing it doesn't get rid of the fear."

Emily squeezed Sara's hand. "Of course it doesn't. Nowhere in the Bible does it say that knowledge overrides fear. But it does say that perfect love casts it out. In other words, the more deeply you fall in love with Christ and the closer you draw to Him, the more His perfect love will flood your heart and drive out any fear that remains. There is no other way to lead a fearless life but to be madly, passionately, wildly in love with Jesus Christ."

Emily chuckled. "And that, my dear, is what has gotten me through nearly eight decades of life—the good times, and certainly the bad. I love Jesus more than I love my own life, and that's why I'm free and full of joy, whatever each day may bring."

Sara nodded again. At last the pieces of the puzzle seemed to be coming together. She only wondered what God's purpose might be in allowing that to happen to her at this particular time in her life.

Tears of fear began to fall from Nadia's eyes as she stood now in front of Zarah's door.

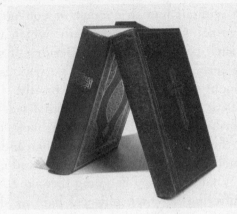

## Chapter 46

F ARAH MOANED, WAKING HERSELF AS SHE TRIED TO TURN TO HER side. What was that horrible smell? And why was she in so much pain? Why did seemingly every inch of her body ache? It even hurt to open her eyes, but she forced one open slightly and could tell, even in the darkness, that she was on the floor in her room.

Then she remembered. Her father and brother, trying to kill her—and then her mother, trying to rescue her. But had her father truly been trying to kill her? She didn't doubt that her brother fully intended to do so, but her father had stopped the beating before it came to that. Why? Was it because of her mother's intervention? Farah could only imagine so, though she knew her poor mother had paid a terrible price for it.

Farah would never forget the mangled look of her mother's face as her father helped her from the room. If her mother looked that bad, how must she herself look?

Not that it mattered. Her life was over, whatever happened. If her father decided to let her live, it would be without any of the freedoms or privileges she'd enjoyed before. She'd even heard of women in the kingdom who had been banned to "silent rooms," where they spent the remainder of their lives in solitude, never speaking to or seeing anyone ever again. Their food was delivered daily but without human contact or conversation. Could anything be worse? Certainly not death, which would be far preferable to such prolonged torture. Besides, if she died, she now knew for certain she would go to be with Isa—and with Nura. The thought comforted her, even if briefly.

She decided it was the not knowing that was the hardest. Would her father and Kareem come back to beat her again? Would they kill her or just torture her and leave her to die alone? Would she ever get to see her beloved mother again, or her sister? What must they be going through? No doubt her mother was suffering her own physical pain as she recovered from her beating, while Nadia must be tortured mentally and emotionally as she agonized over her sister's fate.

Such thoughts added guilt to Farah's existing pain and anguish, though she used them to help her pray more fervently for Isa to reveal Himself to her mother and sister—and yes, to her father and brother as well.

Oh, how she longed to escape to the garden and see Isa's loving face again! Somehow she knew if she could just look into His eyes, she could endure anything.

⋙⋘ ⋙⋘ ⋙⋘

By the time he had returned home at the end of the day, having been ordered by his father to leave Farah alone, Kareem was determined to take matters into his own hands, and he knew just the people who could help him do it. A few of his friends had already joined the Muslim Brotherhood and had been trying to enlist him to do the same. So far he had resisted, but now he decided it was time. This was a group of true Muslims, men who weren't afraid to exert their power and authority over women, as well as fight against the infidels and any who threatened their way of life. They were a violent bunch, willing to stop at nothing to preserve and promote their cause.

Mustafa was his closest connection in the group, so he would go to him first.

*My father will be furious, but what does it matter? If he weren't so soft on the women in our family, I wouldn't have to resort to such extreme measures. That my father allowed Farah to live after such a blatant defiance of Muslim authority just proves he's not strong enough to deal with the matter properly. I must do what is necessary myself.*

He smiled at the thought. He would take care of the matter before Farah had a chance to regain her health or her strength.

✤✤✤ ✤✤✤ ✤✤✤

Nadia waited until the next morning, after she'd heard her father and brother leave the house, to finally creep from her room. She checked first on her mother, who still slept, and then turned toward Farah's room. What would she find when she got there? The thought terrified her, but she could no longer keep herself from checking on her sister. Was she dead? And if not, how badly was she hurt?

The second question brought yet another one that nearly stopped Nadia in her tracks. If Farah was injured and not dead, who would care for her? Their mother was in her room recovering from her own injuries, so that left only Nadia. Yet her father had forbidden her to go to her sister's room.

Tears of fear began to fall from Nadia's eyes as she stood now in front of Farah's door. Never before had she disobeyed her father, but never had she been in fear for her sister's life. What would happen when she opened the door? Would she find Farah's dead body? Would the room be empty? Or would Farah be wounded and in need of help? Though she hoped the latter would be the case, the implications terrified her.

Slowly she turned the knob and opened the door, peering inside. The room reeked of blood and human waste. She recoiled at the offensive odors but forced herself to stand her ground. Why was the room so dark when it was already daylight? Then she made out the heavy blankets covering the windows and she understood that her father and brother had put them there to

307

darken the room. Why? To hide the body, or to prevent Farah from knowing whether it was day or night?

Either way, Nadia knew she would have to turn on the light to find out the truth. Trembling, she flipped the switch and gasped. The sight of Farah's bloody, battered body nearly caused her to pass out, but she grabbed the wall and breathed deeply, forcing herself to remain standing. Was her sister dead? She certainly appeared to be, but Nadia couldn't be sure.

Daring to step closer, she whispered, "Farah? Farah, can you hear me?"

A groan and a slight movement of Farah's head assured Nadia that her sister was still alive, though Nadia wondered for how long. She crept closer and knelt at Farah's side, too frightened to touch her.

"Farah, it's me, Nadia," she whispered, holding back a sob that longed to escape. "Can you hear me?"

Farah's lips were swollen and caked in blood, but it was obvious she was trying to move them to speak. "Yes," she said at last. "I hear you."

"Are you all right?" Nadia asked, and then quickly reprimanded herself for the ridiculous question.

"I'm OK," Farah answered. "Thank you for coming. But you must leave, quickly. If they find you here . . . "

"Shh," Nadia whispered. "Dad and Kareem are gone. They won't be back for hours. Can I help you somehow? Get you something to eat, or . . . ?"

"Water," Farah croaked. "That's all. Just some water."

Nadia nodded. "I'll be right back," she said, and then hurried into Farah's bathroom. Returning with a small cup of cool water, Nadia again knelt at Farah's side and tried to lift her head enough to sip the liquid. The effort ended in only a few drops trickling into Farah's mouth, while the rest dribbled down her chin and cheeks.

"Thank you," Farah said. "But you'd better go now. Please, Nadia. Don't take any chances. Please."

Nadia was weeping openly by then, but she nodded. "OK," she agreed. "I'll go, but I'll be back. I'll do whatever I can to help you."

The tortured movements of Farah's lips told Nadia her sister was trying to smile, and the effort only made Nadia cry harder. How was it possible that her father and brother had caused such pain to their own flesh and blood? She had always believed they had a loving family, but how could she ever believe such a thing again?

As she tiptoed from the room, Nadia's tears continued to flow, and she wondered if she would ever be able to stop crying. She wondered too what could possibly have driven Farah to do something that would cause their father and brother to turn against her this way. Through her cracked bedroom door she'd overheard the men talking the day before about Farah becoming an infidel, saying that she now believed Isa was God. The very thought struck terror into Nadia's heart, even as she wondered briefly if such a thing could possibly be true.

⁓⊱⊰⁓ ⁓⊱⊰⁓ ⁓⊱⊰⁓

Mustafa grinned. He loved such assignments. How dare a woman defy Allah and the Muslim faith? He was glad Kareem had come to him, pleased that his friend would now join their ranks in defending their honor and preserving their customs. Though Mustafa didn't personally know this young woman named Farah, it was obvious she deserved to die. Too bad her own father wasn't willing to do what was necessary for the family's honor.

But at least Kareem was more than willing. And now he had enlisted Mustafa, who was happy to help. There was nothing he liked more than carrying out an honor killing. Before the day was over and Kareem's father returned home, the duty would be done.

Daring to peek around the door,
she felt her eyes go wide at the
scene that greeted her.

## Chapter 47

SARA HADN'T BEEN ABLE TO STOP THINKING ABOUT HER VISIT with Emily Thompson. It was more than just a visit, she decided as she sat at her computer the next evening. It was as if God had been talking to her, helping her to get her bearings, clear direction for her future. The thought stirred up butterflies of excitement and apprehension at the same time, leaving her stomach churning with anticipation.

But as she checked into the chat room and again found no sign of Farah, the excitement left her, replaced with a sense of urgency to pray. What was happening to her new friend? Would she meet the same fate as Nura?

Slipping from her chair to her knees, she began to talk to God with a level of passion she had never before experienced.

❧ ❧ ❧

Mustafa, Kareem, and Samir, another member of the brotherhood, had slipped in the back door of Kareem's house, unnoticed and undetected by the three women who lived there. Mustafa would have preferred to do this under cover of night, but Kareem had insisted they do it when his father was gone to work. He had also insisted that they not kill Farah in the house but take her away to do it somewhere else. Kareem had said he wanted her to have a chance to ask forgiveness before she died, but Mustafa suspected it was just an excuse to torture her first. Either way, Mustafa didn't care. The girl must die, and if they prolonged her death with a bit of additional pain first, so much the better.

Once inside, Kareem hurried down the hallway to his parents' room. His assignment was to keep his mother from coming to investigate if she heard any noise from her daughter's room, and Kareem had assured them that Nadia would be too frightened to do anything but hide behind her closed door. With Sultana and Nadia out of the picture, Mustafa and Samir would quickly gain entrance to Farah's room and spirit her out of the house to their waiting car.

❧ ❧ ❧

Farah was so grateful to her sister. Who would have thought the young girl would be so brave as to come to her, bringing her water, and now helping her to the bathroom? But that's exactly what she'd done. In the process, Farah had even had an opportunity to talk to Nadia about Isa. She was thrilled when the younger girl had promised to consider her words, and Farah prayed that she would one day understand. After all, Isa had reached her through dreams. Why not her sister? If it was true what Sara had told Nura about there being other believers in Isa within the Saudi Kingdom, then surely there was hope for the rest of her family as well.

Now, moving ever so carefully so as to avoid any more pain than necessary, Farah was about to turn on the faucet to rinse her aching face with cool water when a slight noise caught the girls' attention.

Farah swallowed a gasp. Had her mother come to check on her at last? Until now Sultana had obeyed her husband and stayed away, but perhaps she had changed her mind. Oh, how

Farah prayed it was her mother and not her father or brother coming home early! She couldn't bear to think what would happen to Nadia if they caught her here.

Nadia put a finger to her lips. "I'm sure it's Mom," she whispered. "I'll check."

Before Farah could protest, Nadia opened the bathroom door and stepped into Farah's room. The ensuing yelp of surprise and scuffle nearly stopped Farah's heart in her chest. What had happened? Obviously there was a struggle of some sort going on in her room, which ruled out Farah's mother. And if it were her father or brother, she would hear their voices, wouldn't she?

Daring to peek around the door, she felt her eyes go wide at the scene that greeted her. Two men with their heads and faces covered were in the process of subduing Nadia and trying to carry her from the room. One held Nadia from behind and had his hand over her mouth, while the other tried to hold her flailing legs.

*They've come for me,* Farah realized. *Kareem must have sent them to kidnap me, and they've taken Nadia by mistake.*

Terror froze her where she stood. She knew that if the two men succeeded in carrying Nadia from the house, she would never return alive. She knew too that if she was going to save her sister, she'd have to move fast. If only her feet would respond!

The image of Isa in the garden rose up before her, and in that moment she saw His eyes. And just as she'd suspected all along, she knew that she could endure anything. She also realized in that split second that Isa had promised to call Nadia and the rest of her family to His heart, even as He had done for her.

Stepping from the bathroom into her bedroom, she opened her mouth and called as loudly as she was able, "Let her go! You have the wrong girl. She is Nadia. I am Farah." She swallowed, dizzy from the exertion. "I'm the one you want."

The struggle in front of her stopped, and the men put Nadia down, though they stood hesitantly as if undecided what to do next.

"Run, Nadia!" Farah ordered. "Go to Mom's room, and don't come out. Now!"

At that moment Kareem appeared in the doorway, scanning the scene as he entered. "Nadia," he said. "What are you doing here? Get out!"

With a final pleading look at Farah, Nadia obeyed and scampered from the room, as the two men reached for Farah. Her pain intensified as they grabbed her roughly and rushed with her toward the door. But she was able to catch one last glimpse of her mother and sister, clinging to one another as they stood in her parents' bedroom doorway, sobbing. Farah knew it was the last time she would see them in this world, but she was grateful that God had spared her long enough to talk to Nadia about Isa's love for her. She would pray until her last breath that her entire family, Kareem included, would come to know Isa as she did.

∽≈∾ ∽≈∾ ∽≈∾

Somehow Sara knew there was no need to continue interceding for Farah. Both of her Saudi friends were now with Jesus—Isa, she reminded herself. And she would just have to wait until she too had left this life behind before she could speak with them again.

And yet, during her most recent hours of prayer, she had come to understand what God had purposed for her life. The joy of that knowledge somehow overshadowed her sorrow at having lost her brother and her two Internet friends. It was time to tell her parents about it.

They were already in bed, of course, as it was nearing midnight. But she just couldn't wait until morning to share her news with them, and somehow she knew they wouldn't mind.

She knocked on their door twice before they called to her to come in. As she opened the door, her mother was already reaching for the lamp beside the bed.

"What's wrong?" Layla asked. "Did something happen? Are you all right?"

Sara sat down on the edge of the bed beside her mother. Both of her parents were now awake and alert, sitting up and watching her expectantly.

"I'm fine," she said. "Nothing's wrong, so don't worry. I just... I had to share something with you. I know I should have waited until morning, but—"

"It's all right," her father interrupted. "We're glad you didn't wait. If it's that important to you, we want to know about it now. Please, tell us. We're listening."

Sara smiled. "I know you are. You're the best parents in the world. You're always available and always listening. I know how blessed I am, believe me."

Her parents returned her smile as she continued.

"I... I've been praying lately. A lot. And I've been talking to Emily Thompson too, and thinking about things the pastor said, and a missionary who was at our church once."

She took a deep breath and launched into her story about Nura and Farah, and about how meeting them had so deeply influenced her own life. "I believe God has called me into missions, probably overseas somewhere, though I don't really know exactly what that means yet. And I know I have to finish high school first and then college, but at least I know what God wants me to do with my life." She sighed, relieved to have shared her thoughts with her parents. "It's a good feeling."

Tears formed in her mother's eyes as she spoke. "Are you sure? You know there's nothing we'd like better than to see you in full-time ministry. But, Sara, the overseas missions... That can be dangerous, you know."

Sara swallowed. "I know. But we've all learned that life can be dangerous here too."

She dropped her eyes for a moment, as the silence hung heavy upon them. Then she raised her eyes and continued. "I talked to Emily about the dangers of foreign missionary service, and she reminded me that only perfect love can cast out fear—wherever we are."

She saw the pride spread across her father's face as he nodded, though his chin quivered and she knew he wasn't able to speak quite yet.

Layla took Sara's hand in both of hers and held it tightly. "There are some who go to the missions field and never return," she said.

Sara nodded, knowing that her mother was making one last effort at changing her mind. Gently she answered, "The missionary at church said the blood of the martyrs is the seed of the Church."

Tears slipped from her mother's eyes to her cheeks then, but she nodded and said, "Yes. That's true. And there is no greater calling."

Sara looked from her mother to her father, and back again. "Do I have your blessing?" she asked.

For a moment the only sound she heard was the ticking of the old grandfather clock that had stood in the corner of her parents' room for as long as she could remember. At last her father said, "Of course you do, sweetheart."

Teary-eyed, Layla nodded her agreement.

# Deliver Me from Evil

## Prologue

MARA FOUGHT TO RAISE HER HEAD AGAINST THE THICK darkness that pressed her down, making it difficult to inhale a full breath. The closet was so small... so dark and cramped. Impossible to stretch out unless she was lying flat, as she'd been doing most of the time since she'd been here. How long had it been now? Hours? Days? The blackness was too complete, the confines too cramped even to venture a guess.

She'd been in what they all termed "the hole" before, but not for a while now. In the beginning, before she'd learned to obey the rules without question or hesitation, she had often found herself lying flat on her back in what seemed like an oblong tomb, wondering how long it would take before she crossed so far into insanity that there was no way back. And though the times in the hole were the worst, life outside the silent box wasn't much better. To survive, Mara had quickly learned to remove herself from the horrifying reality that had become her life, to travel far away in her mind where the torture was only a distant terror, one she could endure if she disciplined herself to think of something else. Eventually she had become one of the most compliant of the twenty or more wretched creatures that dwelled in this nameless location, which she had come to understand was somewhere in the San Diego area of Southern California, not far from the Mexican border. As a result, her trips to the hole became only a vague yet obedience-motivating memory.

But this time she had dared to break a rule, not openly but secretly, praying to a god she didn't really believe in to protect her. Unfortunately, the nonexistent god had apparently chosen not to answer her prayer, and she had been caught and severely punished—beaten mercilessly and thrown into the hole without food or water—because she had allowed the face of a young child to entice her to venture beyond the tentative bounds of safety.

And for what? Not only had she failed to help the girl escape, but she had probably caused her to be thrown into the hole as well, for there were several such confines within the compound. Nearly as bad as being in the claustrophobic enclosure herself was knowing that a captive no older than six or seven was undoubtedly being held in a similar prison nearby, terrified beyond imagining.

When would Mara learn? She herself hadn't been much older than the tiny child when she was spirited away from her previous life, never again to see her home or family or anything else familiar. Thrust into a world of violence and perversion, Mara had learned to endure the most nightmarish and degrading of conditions. Though at first she had cried and begged to go home to her parents, even though they too had beaten and abused her, she finally came to understand that it was her father who had sold her into this new life from which there was no escape—and her very own uncle, her "tio," who had arranged the sale and was now her owner. And that was the worst part of it all—realizing that no one would ever come to rescue her, for those who should care enough to try were the ones who put her there—all for the price of a few weeks' worth of drugs or alcohol, possibly even some food.

With that realization, Mara had chosen to harden her heart and do whatever she must to get through, one day at a time—sometimes one moment at a time. That was how she had gained the tiniest amount of freedom and privileges, being fed more regularly and even allowed to walk unchained around the small compound that had become her world—so long as she continued to obey her tio and his two henchmen without question. But then the little girl with the terrified eyes had arrived, bound and gagged, bloody and bruised...and everything had changed.

Use the QR reader on your
smartphone to visit us online at
**www.newhopepublishers.com**

If you've been blessed by this book, we would like to hear your story. The publisher and author welcome your comments and suggestions at: newhopereader@wmu.org.

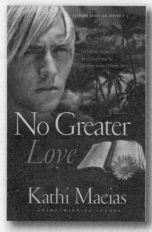 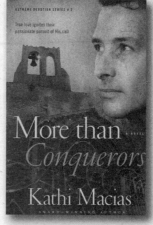
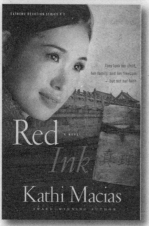 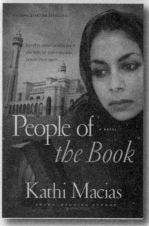